DEAD ZONE

ALSO BY ROBISON WELLS

Variant
Feedback

Blackout
Going Dark: A Blackout Novella (available as an ebook)

ROBISON WELLS

DEAD ZONE

HARPER TEEN
An Imprint of HarperCollins Publishers

HarperTeen is an imprint of HarperCollins Publishers.

Dead Zone
Copyright © 2014 by Robison Wells
Library of Congress Cataloging-in-Publication Data
Wells, Robison E.
Dead zone / Robison Wells. — First edition.
     pages cm
Sequel to: Blackout.
Summary: "America faces invasion by a hostile nation, and Aubrey, Jack, and a group
of other superpowered teenagers are its only defense"— Provided by publisher.
ISBN 978-0-06-227502-8 (hardback) — ISBN 978-0-06-236252-0 (int. ed.)
[1. Supernatural—Fiction. 2. Ability—Fiction. 3. Terrorism—Fiction. 4. Science
fiction.] I. Title.
PZ7.W468413De 2014   2014001889
[Fic]—dc23   CIP
                                                                                AC

Typography by Erin Fitzsimmons
14 15 16 17 18   LP/RRDH   10 9 8 7 6 5 4 3 2 1
❖
First Edition

For my dad,
who got me reading about both superpowers and the military

PROLOGUE

SEATTLE SEEMED COMPLETELY DESERTED. ALEC sat in an over-stuffed chair in the Columbia Center, one of a dozen empty skyscrapers in the center of the city. He was on the twenty-fourth floor—it was the highest he felt like climbing; the electricity to run the elevators was out. Between him and the window, there was a PlayStation, its wires trailing behind it like a jellyfish. Alec could just imagine the conversation. Some kid wanted to take it along when his family evacuated, and a parent had said it was too much unnecessary weight to carry.

Alec smiled and looked off into the bay, wondering how much longer it would be before his people got here.

ONE

ZASHA LITVYAK FLEW ACROSS THE northern Pacific, low enough that she could feel the salty spray as the ocean surged. This was the culmination of years of preparation; everything had led to this moment, and the work that would follow.

The Russian Federation had invaded Alaska.

It sounded worse than it was. It was a tiny landing force at the northernmost part of the state, just enough to startle the residents and seize the oil reserves. The real invading force was coming now.

Fyodor Sidorenko groaned as he dangled in a harness underneath her.

"Shh," Zasha said. "It's about to start."

"We've been waiting long forever," he replied, pain apparent in his voice. "Let's get it over with."

He'd do his part soon enough. He was the real weapon. She was just the transportation.

"They're here," she said as she spotted the lights of the American task force in the distance. She saw the first carrier, 70 painted on its superstructure. "The USS *Carl Vinson*. And behind it is the *Ronald Reagan*." In addition to the carriers, Zasha could name most of the destroyers and frigates in the group. But there were a dozen support craft that she couldn't identify. They were auxiliaries that had fled the terrorist attacks at Bremerton: research vessels and hospital ships and cargo carriers. This group was a cluster of unprepared misfits, not a war-bound task force.

"I wish I could see," he said.

"You'll see the fireworks."

He laughed at that—a wet, raspy laugh in which she could hear the damage to his body. Too many drugs.

No, that wasn't right. It was the perfect amount of drugs—a formula that had been tested on him time and again until they'd gotten the results they wanted. Fyodor meant *gift from God*. It was his new name, given by their overseers at the training facility. And if this plan worked, he would be.

Zasha liked her new name, too. No longer was she Inna Fedorov, a name that meant little. Zasha meant *defender of the people*, and her surname came from Lydia Litvyak, the world's top female flying ace. At training school Zasha had put on a dour expression and pretended the title was a solemn honor, but out here—soaring over the ocean—she adored it. Soon she would be an ace, a flyer who aimed her weapon with such precision and grace that the enemy wouldn't even know how they'd been hit.

Zasha moved slower now, so she could fly closer to the rolling ocean. Two teenagers wouldn't show up on the fleet's radars; even if someone did track them, they'd give off signatures no different from birds. And should anyone catch sight of them from the deck, their black-and-white camouflage would blend in with the dark sea and breaking waves.

As Zasha neared the fleet she felt her heart leap, knowing that the plan was going better than they had hoped. The flagship was the legendary USS *Nimitz*. Two carriers was a feat. Three carriers was a miracle. Of course, the carriers were surrounded by a host of defensive ships and air cover, but that was what Zasha and Fyodor were for.

Zasha checked the GPS on her wrist. Everything hinged on being in just the right place. She glided around a tall, blocky cruiser—the USS *Princeton*, she noted, the names drilled into her by her trainer—and moved farther back into the group.

She checked the GPS again. Just about right. She made an adjustment, flying two hundred yards to her right. Fyodor had a range—a diameter—of just under twenty-six kilometers. Zasha hovered in place and pulled a syringe from her hip pouch. It was already filled, and she checked it for air.

"I'm ready," Fyodor said through a tense jaw. They both knew the pain he'd feel. Maybe she knew it better than him—her mind was clearer while it was happening.

"You're going to be a hero." She jabbed the needle into Fyodor's shoulder and depressed the plunger.

He strained, his whole body going rigid. She gazed up at the stars, waiting for the inevitable, and then she saw it. First one, then two, then four fighter jets fell from the sky, careening uncontrollably. Soon all the aircraft that had been flying above the carrier group were falling, followed by their parachuting pilots.

One plane was in the distance—outside of Fyodor's range. It was foolishly moving back toward the group. A moment later it began a sharp descent into the inky black sea. No parachutes emerged from that one.

Every ship was dark. Every door light, every cabin window, every beacon. Everything. It was just like Zasha had imagined, and it thrilled her.

She checked her watch—an old wind-up one that didn't rely on batteries; Fyodor's abilities shut down anything with an electric current. She was right on schedule, which meant her backup wouldn't be far behind.

Thirty-two Backfire bombers were coming at the carrier group, flying low over the ocean, using strategies not seen since the Second World War.

It was an old admiral who had come up with the plan, or

so the story around training camp went. In World War II, torpedo planes would fly low to the water—hoping to dodge the incoming anti-aircraft fire—and then drop their torpedoes.

The problem now was Fyodor's dead zone. The Backfires needed to get their projectiles through the bubble without entering the dead zone themselves; Fyodor's abilities did not distinguish between friend and foe. The Backfires had been equipped with special torpedoes, created just for this mission. Long range, accurate, and with an impact detonator. Each plane would drop two torpedoes without having to watch out for anti-aircraft fire. The only challenge was to aim.

Zasha wondered what was happening on the American submarines caught inside the bubble. They'd be nothing more than steel pipes in the water, completely dark and powerless, drifting aimlessly. Their crews would have no idea what was happening on the surface—no sonar, nothing.

And then Zasha saw the first of the Russian Backfires, screaming up and away, its torpedoes dropped.

She checked her watch. The torpedoes had a range of eleven kilometers.

"Four minutes," she said to Fyodor, even though she knew he couldn't understand. Or maybe he could understand—maybe he just wouldn't remember any of this.

The sky was filled with Backfires now, pulling back and turning away from the dead zone. One didn't make it—it pushed too far and came to a stop in midair, then began to spin down into the ocean. The first Russian casualty of the American War.

Fyodor was writhing in his harness, the powerful drugs amplifying his abilities and wreaking havoc on his mind. Zasha had sympathy for him, but his name was accurate: he was a gift from God, and a gift to be used.

Two minutes to go. She hoped the torpedoes would get past the ring of ships at the outside of the carrier group. For that matter, she hoped that the torpedoes would be on target at all. She knew the Backfire pilots had been practicing for months, but it was a tricky maneuver, and trickier still under pressure.

Somewhere in the distance, the Backfires were reforming, opening their bomb-bay doors and getting ready to drop heavy missiles.

For just a moment—an instant—Zasha had a flicker of remorse. Or was it pity? More than thirty American ships, including three Nimitz-class carriers—three of the largest ships ever to sail the oceans—were about to be destroyed. It was easy for a Backfire pilot to fire an anonymous torpedo and watch it sail away into the dark. It was harder to be among the ships—to hear their crews' calls as the sailors scrambled for some kind of defense.

The first torpedo hit, a geyser of flame bursting upward from the side of a frigate. Zasha was thrown backward a dozen yards by the impact blast. Before she could get her bearings there was another impact, and then another. The sky was blazing with orange-white fire.

Three ships were engulfed; soon it was four, then six, then eight. Finally, the first carrier was destroyed—the *Ronald Reagan*. Then it seemed as though the entire *Carl Vinson* rolled, hit by half a dozen torpedoes in a single moment. Zasha could see sailors falling overboard as the massive steel beast shuddered and swung back to right itself.

"Look at it, Fyodor," she said in awe. "Look at the fires."

Smoke was pouring from a dozen ships now, billowing in the Pacific winds and obscuring her view. Zasha watched the raging inferno, pride swelling in her chest. The American fleet was in ruins.

She checked her watch and marked the time, then flew east, away from the burning ships. Now she would set the trap.

It had to be done by sight. She couldn't administer the drugs to Fyodor to calm him down; she wasn't done with him yet. So she couldn't use her GPS to track the thirteen kilometers she would need to fly to move the bubble off the carrier group—she'd have to do it by sight. But she'd trained for this, long and hard. She could judge thirteen kilometers on land, or on sea, in the light or the dark.

At thirteen kilometers out she stopped, hovering over the waves. She watched the undamaged ships' lights come back on.

She checked her watch again. It had been two minutes. By now any carriers that were still operational would have launched their first wave of waiting aircraft. Zasha knew the fighter jets wouldn't pursue the Backfires, not yet. Not until they had a substantial force in the air, and not until their radars saw the Russian planes returning.

Fyodor groaned and mumbled something that she couldn't hear over the rush of the ocean. She wished he could see this. He was her partner. She was the gun and he was the bullet.

"It's okay, Fyodor," she told him. "Everything is okay."

The burning ships were oddly beautiful, like a distant row of campfires billowing in the night sky. She wondered what the sailors on board were doing—what procedures they had in place to deal with this kind of unexpected attack. Firefighters would be out in force, and the captains and admirals would be scrambling to save their vessels. They'd be waiting for another attack, watching their radar, anticipating a return of the Backfires.

But they wouldn't be anticipating a return of Zasha. She flew back toward the fleet, watching as lights began to disappear on the nearest boats, and made her way to the center of the fleet. She arrived just in time to see one of the Nimitzes' catapults—running on steam power, not electronics—launch a powerless fighter jet over the edge and into the water. She knew that the rest of the air patrol would be falling now, and she strained to see them, but there was no sign of the planes against the darkened sky.

And again she would wait, her bubble directly over the carrier group once more, disabling all their sensors and radar. The Backfires would return, their bays open and their missiles ready for a killing blow. They'd be followed by Mainstays with radar arrays to guide them in, and Fullbacks to provide fighter support. Not that they needed it. Fyodor was stopping every American aircraft that was trying to move.

It was a longer wait this time, but Zasha didn't care. How many years had they planned this? Decades? It was ever since they learned of Fyodor's abilities, and then they'd sought out a flyer with Zasha's strength and intelligence. Not many could make the distance, or hold so steady over the water. Not many could follow the exactness of the plan.

The thought struck her: How many men would be killed in this glorious battle? Carriers had nearly five thousand each. A frigate had about two hundred, and a destroyer had as many as two fifty. And who knew how many all these extra ships had.

More than fifteen thousand. Maybe twenty?

She checked her watch one last time. The missiles would be nearing her bubble now, and it was time to get out of there. She only needed to stay long enough to keep the missiles off the radar. Zasha turned and headed east again. As she flew she withdrew another syringe from her pouch, flicked away the air pockets, and stabbed it into Fyodor's arm. He'd drift to sleep, and the electronic interference would melt away. She could return to the Varyag to debrief and celebrate. And then the preparations for landing the ships in Seattle would begin.

TWO

AUBREY DISAPPEARED, TURNING INVISIBLE AS she climbed out of the swampy wetland and onto the bank. She was breathing heavily, carrying full gear and her M16A4 over her mud-soaked ACU—her Army Combat Uniform. This wasn't regular boot camp, and she couldn't imagine what that was really like. Was it harder than lambda training, or was it easier? Granted, most lambdas here were younger than the average recruit—though, at seventeen, Aubrey wasn't—but she didn't think the trainers were cutting them any slack.

Which was why she was walking on the solid shoreline instead of the muddy ditch. Aubrey didn't technically turn invisible; her brain talked to someone else's brain—anyone nearby—and convinced them that she wasn't there. As long as she was close enough for her brain to interact—they'd measured her range at a little less than a hundred and forty yards—she was effectively invisible.

And it was more than just being invisible. People simply didn't notice her. So she could sneak out of the line of lambdas trudging through the muddy swamp. No one would notice a gap, or an Aubrey-shaped hole in the water. Their brains filled in the cracks.

She wasn't supposed to sneak out of the line, of course. She was supposed to be in the water with Tabitha and Matt and all the rest of them. But she could, so she did.

"Jack, are you listening?" she asked, trying to catch her breath.

She didn't know where Jack was on the small makeshift army base, but he was training somewhere. She always talked to him. He could hear her most of the time, if he was paying attention. He could hear anything.

"I don't know if I'm ready for this to be over," she said. "We already did our duty. We fought the bad guys and won. Shouldn't that be enough?"

Aubrey plodded alongside the river, dripping on the dry leaves. The sergeant was fifty feet ahead of her, watching the line of soldiers plow through the final days of basic training. She took a drink from her canteen and wished, not for the first time, that Jack could talk back to her.

"No," she said. "I *am* ready to be done. You and I saw what the battlefield was like, and there weren't any ditches we had to wade through. Well, there was that flooded basement in Salt Lake City. But that was still technically part of training."

The sergeant started walking toward her, and she replaced her canteen and then lowered herself back down into the ditch. She reappeared when he was fifteen feet away.

"Keep that gun up, Parsons," the trainer barked, and she held her M16 higher above the water. It made her shoulders sting and her triceps ache. She couldn't remember the last time she hadn't felt tired, or the last time her feet were dry for more than half a day. She felt like her time would be better spent working on her ability, not re-creating Vietnam. The Russians had invaded Alaska, not the Louisiana bayou.

Granted, she still had plenty of lambda training. When she wasn't doing field exercises or physical training or weapons training or first-aid training or any other number of trainings, they had her practicing her invisibility. Most of it was simply trying to build endurance. Disappearing made Aubrey tired, so they practiced all of these same physical exercises while she was invisible, making her run farther, stay hidden longer. It was brutal.

She had glasses now, too. Every ability had negative side effects—Aubrey's friend Nicole had kidney failure; Jack got migraines. Aubrey was going blind. Doctors had examined her to see if surgery could help, but they weren't hopeful. So she wore glasses. She loved the individuality of them in a sea of identical soldiers. She loved unpinning her long brown hair at night and putting on her glasses and feeling like she was a different person than who she'd been back home. But right now the lenses were spotted with drops of muddy water, and she had to keep pushing them up on her nose.

The ditch was coming to an end, and the lambdas were climbing out onto the shore, then continuing in a line into the trees. Aubrey followed, grunting as she scrambled up.

Everyone's ACUs were brown and soaked from the chest down, and their tan boots were thick with mud. But they jogged, and Aubrey jogged with them—the half-defeated jog of soldiers who were too tired to disobey. At least she didn't have to hold her rifle up anymore, and the muscles in her arms felt light when she let them down.

Someone in front of her groaned, and Aubrey saw a wooden wall ahead. She had climbed one of these walls every single day for the last three weeks. She knew how to go at it, how to sling her weight over the top, even how to get a grip when the boards were wet—she'd done it in rain more than once.

But not today. She couldn't face it today.

She disappeared and worked her way through the crowd to the other side. There was no trainer here watching. And even if there was, he wouldn't notice her reappear—he'd just realize she was there, and his mind would assume that she had climbed.

"Jack, forgive me," she said with a halfhearted smile.

She pushed her glasses up on her nose and reappeared in front of the wall as another lambda—Tabitha—landed next to her. Tabitha wasn't Aubrey's favorite person in the camp, but they had cots next to each other, so they had spent their fair share of time talking.

"When is this going to end?" Tabitha said with a grimace.

"Not soon enough."

As they jogged down the trail, Aubrey wondered again where Jack was. A few of the lambdas had been sent to specialized training, and even though she'd spent a few nights invisible, trying to find him in the dark, she hadn't discovered anything more than his locked barracks. She talked to him incessantly, assuming he had to be listening at least some of the time, but she hadn't seen him face-to-face in at least a week. She wondered if he'd graduate early, or get called away on a mission and not graduate at all.

But that didn't make sense. They were a perfect pair. Their powers complimented each other's. The army had to keep the two of them together.

"I don't know where you are, Jack," she said. "But stick around. I don't want to be assigned somewhere without you. I'm serious. I want you with me."

The forest opened up into the base's shooting range, and Aubrey breathed a sigh of relief. She could shoot. She could outshoot half the trainers. Even without her glasses.

"Okay, team," the trainer shouted. "Take a position."

Aubrey moved into one of the plywood frames that she was supposed to treat like cover—hiding behind the wall, peeking out only to take her shots. Targets would appear downrange at intervals between fifty and three hundred yards. Aubrey took a deep breath and raised her gun. She was still getting used to the M16A4. It was different from the guns she'd fired at home, and even different from the standard-issue rifles of the army—it was used more for special ops.

A target—a plastic, human-shaped silhouette, painted with the outline of a man—flipped up at one hundred fifty yards. Through the scope she could see a couple dozen holes from previous bullet impacts. She let out her breath slowly, and squeezed the trigger. The board disappeared from sight.

She'd been shooting deer every year since she was eight. Jack's family had always invited her on their hunts. Venison had been an important part of her diet, since her dad never seemed to hold on to a job for more than a few days at a time. She'd taken to rabbit and pheasant hunting, too—anything she could legally go after, and sometimes not even legal stuff.

That life seemed so far away. It didn't even feel real anymore.

Another silhouette appeared at three hundred yards and she knocked it back down.

THREE

"JACK, FORGIVE ME," WAS THE last thing he heard from her. Jack guessed Aubrey was skipping the wall, or something near it. She was surrounded by the clunk of knees against wood, the scrape of rubber on logs, the grunting of lambdas fighting through pain.

He wished she'd take training more seriously. She had the makings of a good soldier, but she also had the makings of a court-martial. He'd known when she'd snuck out of her barracks to find him at night, and he'd made sure he was hidden from view. Not that he didn't want to see her—he wanted to see her every minute of the day. He didn't want her to get into trouble. If she got in trouble, then she could be pulled from their team. They wouldn't be together.

But maybe a court-martial would be better. Maybe he

should encourage Aubrey to get thrown in lockup. He heard everything that was said at the base—he could hear and see and smell it all. And he'd heard about the attack in the North Pacific. The three carriers that had sunk. The invasion force that was making its way toward Washington State. The Tomahawk missiles that blew up midflight, for no apparent reason. The squadrons of fighter jets that had simply fallen out of the sky.

There were plenty of theories about the Russians' secret weapon—something that acted like an EMP, an electromagnetic pulse. Weapons like that could fry every piece of electrical equipment for miles and miles.

But it couldn't be an EMP. Those were caused by exploding a nuke in the high atmosphere, and no one had reported a nuke. In fact, Jack heard the generals say that both sides in this war were doing everything they could to avoid nuclear strikes. The Russians wouldn't use them freely—that would give the Americans an excuse to use their own, and then the world would be over.

It had to be something else. Some kind of targeted EMP-like device, probably mounted on the prow of Russian ships—something to fire when they came close to the American fleet. Would they be able to use it on land, too? They must be able to—there was no way the Russians would attack the biggest superpower in the world without being supremely confident in their abilities.

That had been the scariest thing Jack had heard: the commanders of this base were pinning a lot of hopes on the lambdas. Even though most of them weren't much better than regular soldiers. Jack could do amazing things, but he wasn't a weapon. He was a spy. Same with Aubrey: she was a spy who was being forced to learn the art of soldiering.

Jack had been pulled from basic training to attend a mini air-assault school, learning to rappel from a helicopter with a group of other lambdas.

"What do you hear?" Josi asked, as they sat at the bottom of the rappelling wall.

Jack looked at her. She was one of the few lambdas he'd met in the Dugway testing facility who'd ended up at this training camp in Oregon. Krezi, a fifteen-year-old from Las Vegas, was another. The three of them, and a young kid named Rich, had spent a week together training.

"What do you mean?" Jack asked with a smile.

"Whenever you get quiet," Josi said, "I know you're listening to something."

"You eavesdrop as much as I do," he said.

"Ugh." She grimaced. "Imagine if I could hear everything you did."

Josi took photographic memory to a new level. She remembered everything she'd ever heard—every word, every cough, every gust of wind—and everything she'd ever seen, down to every single leaf on every single tree. It was a good thing she didn't seem to have any physical debilitations accompanying her powers, because the mental stuff was already overwhelming.

"I know what he was listening to," Krezi taunted. "Au-brey."

"I was not," he said, though he could feel his face flush. "If you must know, I was listening to them talk about this mission. They might be canceling it."

Rich leaned back and swore. "You're kidding me. After all of this? After missing out on the real training?"

Jack shrugged. "The Russians have something that can knock planes and missiles out of the sky. You really want to try to fly a helicopter behind enemy lines?"

Josi let out a breath. "I've been thinking about that."

"Good," Krezi said. "Maybe we'll be somewhere safe. In case no one noticed, Rich and I aren't even old enough to be drafted, and yet here we are."

"You're a girl," Josi said. "You wouldn't be signed up for selective service anyway. Jack is the only one who could get the call from Uncle Sam."

"I'm seventeen, Photographic Memory Girl. You're the eighteen-year-old."

Josi rubbed her eyes and sighed. "Just because I know everything doesn't mean I remember it."

"I'll use that excuse the next time I'm taking a test." Jack laughed and bumped her arm. He only had eyes for Aubrey, but he couldn't help noticing how Josi could make even the battle-dress ACUs look good.

"Can I ask a question?" Josi said through red, tired eyes. "Why the Russians? I mean, does this feel a little *Red Dawn* to you?"

"I overheard General Penrod and Colonel Montgomery talking about that yesterday," Jack said. "It sounds like the Russians' goal isn't to conquer us and make us bow before them. Their goal is to make America cry. It's to make us not be a superpower anymore—to bring us down a few notches. They figure if we're weak, then maybe Mexico will come over the borders in the South and claim land. Maybe Cuba will go after Florida. And we'll be too dang busy stopping an invasion to plug the leaks everywhere."

"Okay, but back to the here and now. What are we doing instead of rappelling out of helicopters?" Rich asked. "My skills are kinda limited."

"They want you most of all," Jack said, wondering how much of this he should be telling them. It probably didn't hurt anything—their commanding officers had to know that Jack overheard everything. They'd never told him *not* to listen. "The Russians have some device that can disable planes and ships. You're a mechanical genius. They want you to figure out what that is."

"Oh, perfect," Rich said. "That doesn't sound like I'll be a target at all."

"Or on the front lines," Krezi said.

"Speaking of which," Jack continued, "they want you involved, too, Krezi. This device can disable electronics, but there's no reason to think it can disable you. You'll be the best weapon we have."

She rolled her eyes. "Better than a gun? Those don't have electronics."

"Depends on the gun," Josi said, still rubbing her eyes.

"You can cut through a tank," Jack said. "That beats an M16."

"I can cut through a tank if I'm right next to it and focus on it, like a welding torch. How many tanks am I going to get close to?"

"It's still better than a gun."

"And don't forget," Rich said, with more than a twinge of disgust in his voice, "we don't get guns. You and me, I mean."

Krezi and Rich were still considered too young to be trusted with rifles or sidearms. It was a decision that made the younger lambdas furious; they were being asked—forced, some said—to help the army, but they weren't allowed to defend themselves.

Not that Krezi needed a gun to defend herself. Jack had seen her blast a tree to splinters using just the power that came out of her hands. He'd seen her cut through half-inch steel plate, and blow a cement wall to pieces.

And Rich could innately understand and use any machine, be it a calculator or a backhoe. Jack had to assume the same skill would apply to understanding and using a rifle, if Rich ever got his hands on one.

"We should join the rebellion," Krezi said.

"Don't even joke about that," Josi replied.

"Who said I was joking?"

Jack leaned forward, resting his elbows on his knees. "You'd better be joking. If the wrong person heard you talking about the rebellion, you'd be dealing with the military police pretty quick."

"They overran a base in South Dakota," Rich said. "Someone said there were hundreds of them."

"And how many people died?" Josi asked sternly.

"I didn't hear that," Rich said.

"I did," Jack said. Sometimes he wished he had Josi's perfect memory. He'd recite the conversation word for word. "The rebels killed eighteen soldiers, plus three lambdas."

"The rebels are traitors." Josi tugged idly at a tuft of grass. "They're American teens—just like us—killing other Americans."

"I don't know," Krezi said, irritation in her voice. "It wasn't a military base they attacked—it was one of those concentration camps they sent us to."

"They're not concentration camps," Jack said. "They're quarantine centers for teenagers who have the virus. Do you really think that someone should have broken into Dugway and killed soldiers to get us out of there?"

"Maybe," Krezi said.

"Of course not," Josi said.

"But they forced us to go to war," Krezi protested.

"Wrong again," Josi said. "I remember you standing up and saying that you'd join the fight. I remember the Utah Jazz T-shirt you were wearing when you said it, and the skinny jeans with a hole in the knee. Thank you, photographic memory."

Krezi shook her head. "It was agree to join the army or get left in the camp forever."

"Not forever," Jack said. "Just until all of the infected were found."

"Yeah, right," Krezi snapped, and pointed her finger at the dry autumn grass in front of her. A moment later it burst into flame. Krezi watched it for a few seconds and then patted the fire out with her hand. "Do you really think they'd let me go home? Or would they send me to a lab somewhere to get tested?"

"I think we're all going to get tested before this is through," Rich said. "The army just needs us right now."

"I hate to get all chest-thumping and patriotic," Josi said, "but the US is being invaded. We can't pretend like that isn't happening. I'm glad I joined."

"Me too," Rich said.

"Ugh." Krezi sighed. "I don't hate America either. And yes, I think it was a bad thing that the rebels killed soldiers. I just wish none of this had happened in the first place."

FOUR

FROM A THOUSAND FEET UP, Zasha could see both shores of the Strait of Juan de Fuca, which was the pathway to both Seattle and Vancouver, Canada, two of the biggest port cities on the Pacific. This would be the landing area for the invasion force, and Zasha was flying ahead of an enormous convoy of hastily repurposed cargo ships, each one loaded with tanks, equipment, and soldiers.

The Russian fleet wasn't what it used to be—it didn't have the strength of the Soviet Union during the height of the arms race—but it wasn't flat-footed or impotent either. And if anyone on the shore got ideas about defending the strait, Zasha and Fyodor would be there to render them useless.

"How much can you see?" she asked Fyodor, who was dangling in his harness.

"I can see you," he said weakly. "I can see the sky."

"This is America," she said. "And Canada's over there. We're finally here."

"What day is it?"

She didn't know. She'd spent too many days in the hold of a boat without the sun, and too many nights flying with Fyodor strapped to her, to keep track of the calendar.

"It's Invasion Day," she said. "The day America crumbles before us."

Fyodor forced a pained laugh. "You're always very grandiose."

"Don't you feel it?" she asked, looking down at him. His face was so gaunt now; this wasn't the Fyodor she'd grown up with. "Don't you feel the energy of today?"

"I feel tired," he said. "And nauseated."

"You should see what I see," she said, gazing out at the forested shores. There were towns there—American towns.

"You should see what I see," Fyodor replied, and then chuckled.

Zasha blushed, though she knew it didn't mean anything. Fyodor was always making comments like that. Even if he did have a crush on her, it would never go anywhere. Not with what faced them. Not with the drugs that ravaged him.

"There are American homes," she said, changing his subject. "They will soon be Russian homes."

"We're not going to settle here," he said.

"We will eventually."

"They won't leave peacefully," he said. "Americans love their guns."

"That's why we won't let them stay. We're not going to be an occupying force. We've learned from our occupation of Afghanistan—and their occupation of Afghanistan. They will all have to leave and eventually our people will claim these cities."

He nodded tiredly. He knew the plan. Right now, Russian diplomats were delivering simple ultimatums: We are taking these territories and your people must leave. Do that or face annihilation.

"They're not going to like it," he said.

"It's war." She shook her head and looked down at him. "They're not supposed to like it. But it's not as if we're trying to take their country from them. We're just taking a few pieces."

"Do you know what I was reading?" Fyodor's voice was scratchy. "When the Americans took Alaska from us, they bought it for two cents an acre."

"If you can call that buying," Zasha said, getting angry. "That's why we've come to take it back."

This wasn't a landgrab, though. The Russian Federation hardly needed more land. This was about damaging the United States. The Russian terrorists had already done a fine job of bringing the so-called last superpower to its knees.

This invasion would make that damage more permanent.

And really, most of the attack was focused on Canada. Yes, they were attacking into Washington and Oregon, but the Canadian oil reserves were the real target. Once the Russians were sitting right on top of the Americans, and were controlling oil reserves as large as those of Saudi Arabia, the United States would know fear. They'd know what it meant to have your enemies at your front door.

Zasha looked down at Fyodor. "Do you realize how valuable you are?"

"Do you realize how valuable *we* are?" he corrected. "We're partners."

As they neared Port Angeles, artillery fire opened up on the northern side—the American military in a desperate defense. She heard the dull thud as the guns fired.

"It looks like we're back to work," she said.

Fyodor groaned. "I'm tired."

"I'm sorry," she said, pulling a syringe from the Velcro pouch on her chest.

"Do it quick."

"Soon we'll reach Seattle," she said. "Once the landing is over, we're sure to get some rest."

She plunged the needle into his arm, and at once his back arched and he writhed in pain.

She turned a wide curve and flew toward the sound of the battery. The Americans were hidden well, in a forest she thought she remembered as being a national monument of some kind. But the smoke and flame from their howitzers were clearly visible from her vantage point.

The soldiers must have known it was a suicide mission. There were maybe twenty guns against an entire fleet. The weapons were an improvement over previous artillery pieces the Americans had used, but that made them all the more vulnerable to Zasha's tactics.

These new artillery pieces had digital fire-control systems, and they used a GPS-guided munition. She'd have to kiss everyone in the logistics and analysis team. None of that would work anymore. They were essentially firing blind, without even radio communication from forward spotters.

Zasha kept moving, placing herself thirteen kilometers behind the artillery. This way, Fyodor's electronic disruption would stop the Americans, and the Russian fleet could fire back, since their targeting computers were working just fine. Zasha could see Russian aircraft above the action, staying well away from her, but sending recon information back to the big guns on half a dozen cruisers.

Zasha wished she could see it, be on the ground, close, when the bombs fell. She wanted to feel the earth shake.

She'd been raised for this. Chosen when she was three years old, picked for her good genes, high aptitude-test scores, and psychological evaluation. She'd trained in some of the same facilities where the Soviet Olympic athletes used to train, physical fitness in the day and studies at night.

The plan—the *maskirovka*—hadn't been clear from the beginning, at least not to her. She knew that she was being raised to be a soldier, but she never left the compound. She didn't know that this was a secret from the people of Russia, even from many in the regular military. She didn't know that she was special.

And back then, she wasn't. She was one of a thousand girls and a thousand boys, all training, all studying, all expecting to be *Spetsnaz*—special forces. It wasn't until she was ten that she was injected with the mutagen, and it wasn't until a year later that her true powers began to develop. The military weeded out the less useful and retrained them for more specialized assignments. Zasha had lost her best friend then— Anya, a girl who couldn't be burned. She couldn't create fire, couldn't control it—she could merely withstand it. Zasha had no idea what had happened to Anya; Zasha was transferred to a higher-security training facility with the rest of the more-advanced children.

From that point on, it was a new kind of training. Flying with weights. Flying long distances over the vast expanses of empty Russian countryside. She pushed herself, and with every challenge her commanders gave her, she gave herself an even harder one. She told herself she was not going to be another Anya. She was going to become essential. She was going to prove her worth. Exceed expectations.

The American forest was now a raging wildfire, the exploding shells sounding like distant thuds and pops.

It didn't have to be like this, Zasha knew. The invasion could be bloodless if the citizens would simply leave. America and Canada both had plenty of unused land where the refugees could settle.

Russian bombers had flown over Seattle yesterday, with Zasha and Fyodor strategically placed on the ground to keep surface-to-air missiles at bay, and had dropped pamphlets urging the people to leave. Whether they did or not was up to them, but the Russians were not here to slaughter. They were here to capture, to seize resources, to cripple a superpower.

That said, Zasha loved watching the flames below her. Stupid soldiers. What were they hoping to accomplish? A hit or two on a convoy ship? A lucky shot into an ammo magazine? It was foolish desperation, and they deserved to burn.

FIVE

AUBREY DISAPPEARED WHILE CARRYING HER dinner tray and crossed the mess hall to where Jack was sitting alone. She set her tray across from him, and then flickered back to view.

Jack started. "You nearly made me spill my water."

"You're not so tough when a sneaky girl shows up, are you?"

"You call that sneaky?" he asked, meeting her eyes. "I had you pegged the minute you walked in. You talked to Josi—I tried not to listen, but I did hear you saying something like, 'Where's the hottest guy in the army?' and then Josi told you I was over here."

Aubrey grinned and tore a piece of bread in half, dipping it in her bowl of beef stew. "I don't remember the conversation going that way at all."

"So you're denying it?" he said.

"I'm not denying I talked to Josi."

"But you are denying that I'm the hottest guy in the army?"

"What if there was a lambda," she said, "whose power was irresistible charm?"

"There is. You're looking at him. It's a lesser-known side effect of super hearing."

Her brow furrowed, but the smile didn't leave her face. "I didn't realize my eyes were getting that bad."

"Well," he said, "I'm here to tell you: it's me. You can trust me on that, because I have super sight and I look in the mirror at least once a day and—my goodness—what a fine specimen I am."

"I see super humility isn't a trait you've developed."

"When you've got it, flaunt it."

Aubrey laughed and took a bite of her stew-soaked bread. It was crusty and hard, even after dipping it.

"I don't see you around very much," she said.

"Secret mission."

"It had better be a secret mission that I get to come on." There was no joking in her voice now.

"It's a secret mission that's been canceled," Jack said. "We got the official word today."

Aubrey felt like a weight had been lifted off her chest. "Will you graduate with us tomorrow?"

He shook his head. "I don't think so." His voice was serious and he wouldn't look her in the eyes. "We're nine days short of the training you guys have had. We haven't done field ops. We haven't spent time on the gun range. There're a lot of things we haven't done."

"That's stupid," Aubrey said. "They know that you and I work together well. We're a perfect fit."

"Yeah," he said. "They're talking about keeping Rich and Krezi together."

"I don't know Rich," she said.

"Little guy. Fifteen. Black. You'd recognize him."

"What does he do?"

"He understands machines."

"I think I've heard of him."

Jack took a bite of stew and made a face.

"Army food is the worst," Aubrey said.

"All food is the worst. Do you know how much weight I've lost since I manifested? And I didn't have much weight to lose."

"You look good to me," she said, though she could see his face looked thinner, his cheeks sunken slightly and his skin a little gray. Still, she did think he was handsome—especially in his uniform. Besides, everyone in training camp had lost weight. She knew she'd slimmed down, losing some of her baby fat and gaining muscle tone.

"You look good to me, too," Jack replied.

She blushed. "So tell me the truth. Do you know where we're going after graduation tomorrow?"

He shook his head. "All I know is that virtually everyone here is headed north." He lowered his voice to a whisper. "The Russians have a three-pronged attack—they're hitting Portland, Seattle, and Vancouver."

Aubrey scrunched up her nose. "What do they want with the Northwest?"

"Ports," Jack said. "And they've taken Alaska; they're driving everyone out of there—like, all the citizens, everybody. Probably so there will be no one to fight back against them—no insurgents."

"But why do they want ports?" She reached across the table to take his hand. "What will they be transporting?"

He looked a little uncomfortable at the contact. Socializing like that was against the rules, and this was a very public place. But Aubrey didn't care. She didn't know if they'd get shipped to the same place. She didn't know when the next time would be that she could hold his hand.

"One of the generals thinks that they want the ports for oil—that they're going to push all the way into Alberta and take the oil deposits there."

"There's oil in Alberta?"

"The second-biggest reserve in the world," Jack said. "At least that's what the general said. There's another guy—a colonel—who thinks this is just another way to cripple us.

He thinks they'll take these port cities, head down the coast to take San Francisco, then move all the way south to San Diego. Cut us off from the Pacific entirely."

She squeezed his hand. "Do you think they can do it?"

"That colonel thinks they can. The general is still sold on oil in Canada. But it's not like either of those guys is making any of the decisions. Their job is to prep recruits to fight."

"Get a room." Aubrey let go of Jack's hand as Tabitha sat down next to her.

"Jack," Aubrey said, trying not to sound as annoyed as she was. "This is Tabitha. Tabitha, Jack."

Tabitha spoke, a coy smile on her lips. "I assume this is why you sneak out at night?"

Aubrey didn't answer.

"Doing some extra obstacle courses?" Jack asked, and he winked at Aubrey.

"Something like that," Aubrey said.

"Is it true you can hear anything?" Tabitha asked Jack, taking a big bite of stew.

"I can hear a lot," he said. "I can smell a lot, too, and this soup is making me a little sick. I think I'm going to find an apple or something. See you guys later." He stood up and left, taking his tray with him.

Aubrey hated watching him go. It didn't feel fair—he always had a connection to her; he could always listen to her, or see her, or smell her. But her only connection to him was talking to empty air, hoping he was listening.

"He's cute," Tabitha said.

"Yeah," Aubrey answered. "Too bad he won't get to graduate with us. And that means we probably won't be assigned together—which is stupid, because we're a great team."

"You and I are a great team, too," Tabitha said. "Think of everything we've done."

Aubrey disagreed. They were a good team, she thought. Not great. Tabitha was a telepath: she could talk to you with her mind. They'd been training together in a few field ops—Aubrey moving invisibly and Tabitha hanging back to relay orders. It was a useful combination, but not as useful as Aubrey being able to communicate forward—that could only be done by talking to Jack, or by using radios. With Tabitha, Aubrey felt like she was always being ordered around. With Jack, Aubrey felt like she was in control, like she could make her own decisions.

"We're fine," Aubrey said, and took a bite of bread.

"But you'd rather have Jack," Tabitha said. "I can understand that. If you want my opinion, neither one of us should be here—in the army, I mean."

"Too late for that. We graduate tomorrow."

"Don't remind me. Remember, we didn't sign up for this."

Aubrey hated this argument. She'd heard it a hundred times—half the time she'd been the one making it. "We didn't *not* sign up for it, either. I volunteered to fight the terrorists."

"It was coercion," Tabitha said. "We were minors, and we didn't know what we were getting ourselves into. And besides, I wasn't fighting terrorists—my assignment had me fighting our own citizens."

"The rebellion," Aubrey said.

"Yeah."

"And even after you saw what the rebels were doing, you still think being in the army is a worse alternative?"

Tabitha thought for a long minute, taking a bite of stew and chewing slowly. "Why does it have to be one or the other? Why can't we just go back to normal life and not fight anybody?"

Aubrey laughed. "We have to fight because we're being invaded. And it's not like they're coming in to free us from the shackles of an oppressive government. How many people have died since the first terror attacks? Two hundred and fifty thousand? And that number might get much higher. These are Russians, on our home soil."

"They can't attack civilians. It's against the Geneva convention."

"So you're willing to live in a world where there is no America anymore, just as long as you don't have to fight? What are you going to do when the Russians take control and find out about your powers?"

"I don't know, okay?" Tabitha snapped. "I have no idea. I just want things to go back to normal. I have friends and I have a family, and I wish none of this had happened in the first place."

Aubrey dabbed at her stew with a crust of bread. "I don't think anyone wants war. But it's here. And we can help. I told you what Jack and I did to help break up the terrorists' plan. I really think we can make a difference."

"I hope you're right," Tabitha said. "Because I'm starting to wonder who the bad guys are: the people who are invading or the people who are using teenagers as human shields."

SIX

JACK LAY AWAKE IN BED, staring at the ceiling of the Quonset hut. Aubrey was outside. She'd been outside for ten minutes and he'd spent that whole time wishing she'd leave. It wasn't that he didn't want to see her. He wanted to see her more than anything. He just didn't want her to get caught and not graduate tomorrow with the rest of her class. But she wasn't going anywhere.

Jack sat up in bed and pulled on his pants and jacket.

"Everything okay?" Rich asked, rolling onto one side.

"I think so," Jack said. "I'm going out to get some air."

"Liar," Rich said with a hushed laugh. "That's just something people say in movies when they want an excuse to leave the building. There's plenty of air in here."

Jack smiled. "The air in here smells like your dirty socks."

"Whatever, man. Ten bucks says you're going to talk to Aubrey."

"You don't have to be so loud about it," Jack said.

"Don't worry. I've got your back. I'm good at pretending to be dumb."

"Don't pretend to be anything," Jack said, lacing his boots. "Just go to sleep."

"I'll see what I can do."

Jack left the hut, entering the frosty November night. He shoved his hands into his pockets to ward off the cold and walked around to the back side of the building, to a spot where the floodlights created a shadow. He could see Aubrey plain as day, but knew that she'd be virtually invisible to anyone else. His heightened senses gave him almost perfect night vision. It was even better than night-vision goggles, because he could distinguish colors—not just the monochromatic green that the goggles gave.

"Hey," she said with a grin. "Took your sweet time."

"You shouldn't be out here," he answered. "Graduation is in the morning."

"That's why I had to come. What if . . . what if we get split up?"

He wrapped his arms around her in a hug. She felt like ice. "If we get split up, then our job is to survive until this thing is over and we get to go home to be together."

"Have you heard anything more about our assignments?"

"Not a word. My guess is that the decision is being made by some authority higher than here."

"That's not fair. They won't know how well we work together."

He shook his head. "That's not true. They all know about us taking down the terrorists. They know what you did to get Dan and Laura to fight each other. And they know that you need to have some way of communicating back to the rest of your team."

Aubrey let go of Jack, and then took him by both hands.

"You've heard about the rebellion, right?"

"Has Tabitha been after you about it?"

"Every minute of the day. She swears she's just talking, but I think it's more than that."

"You know what I want?" Jack said.

Aubrey groaned. "Don't tell me it's to join a rebellion."

Jack grinned. "No. I want to watch a football game."

Aubrey laughed. "You don't even like football."

"That's not true. I was just always busy after school so I never got to go. But I'd love to go to one right now. Bundle up, sit on those cold metal benches, eat corn dogs. I don't even care who's playing."

"I'd go with you."

"It's a date."

"When the war is over."

Jack smiled and pulled her in for another hug. "Then we

have all the more incentive to win this stupid thing."

He could have stood there all night, holding her close, smelling the stringent army soap, his cheek touching her loose hair. He closed his eyes and tried to pretend that he wasn't headed toward the battle, that he wasn't in Oregon, that he wasn't only a few hundred miles from the battle zone. He tried to draw on memories of home—of Mount Pleasant in the autumn, the big cottonwoods dropping their leaves, the crunch of frost on the grass, Aubrey in that old orange sweater she used to wear before she started shoplifting all her clothes.

He heard footsteps and let go of her instantly.

"Disappear," he said. She didn't hesitate.

A moment later, two soldiers on a nightly patrol turned the corner and saw him. One of them pointed his flashlight right into Jack's eyes. "Where are you going, soldier?" he barked.

Jack reached over and patted the Quonset hut. "Had to use the latrine."

"Taking the scenic route to get there," the other soldier said.

"Disorientation." Jack absently pointed to the lambda insignia on his jacket. "One of the side effects of my ability. It's worse when I first wake up."

One of the soldiers pointed in the other direction. "Straight that way, two buildings down, on your right. You shouldn't miss it, unless your nose doesn't work."

"Thanks," Jack said. He paused, hoping the soldiers would leave, but they didn't. So he whispered a quick good-bye to Aubrey and headed to the latrine.

By the time he was out of the bathroom, Aubrey's scent had moved back to her barracks. It was so easy for him to eavesdrop, but he avoided the temptation and returned to his own bed. The lights were off, except for a few lambdas who were reading with flashlights. One of them was Edgar, a kid who never got tired and never slept—ever. He didn't have super speed or super strength, but he could run forever and never break a sweat or have his heart rate increase. Jack wondered what the army would do with him. Another kid had a knack for languages. After two weeks of reading dictionaries, he was fluent in Russian, plus half a dozen dialects like Chechen and Avar.

Jack lay down on his bed. It always took him a while to tune out the noise around him and fall asleep. He'd tried earplugs, but they'd made him able to hear the blood flowing through his own ears, and that was maddening.

"We're leaving tomorrow," Rich said quietly from the next cot over.

"Tomorrow's graduation," Jack said.

"I know, but they're moving us all out. Bringing in a new bunch of recruits."

Jack sat up on one elbow. "How do you know that? I didn't even know that."

Rich grinned. "Technology defeats super senses!"

"Where did you find access to a computer?"

"The mess hall. They have one in the back office for ordering supplies and that kind of thing."

"Do you know where we're going?"

"No. All it said was that assignments were going to be made by General Freeman, but he hasn't input them yet. I got the impression that he doesn't like computers."

"So this is it," Jack said, rolling onto his back. "I wish we'd gotten more training. I don't know if you and I will be assigned to the same unit, but I'm a spy and you're a guy who is searching for the EMP device. That means both of us will be going to the front."

"I wish they could just keep me back in the Pentagon or something," Rich said, "and have me wage a cyberwar on the Russians with some drones. I'd be so much more effective."

"But somebody needs to find the EMP device," Jack said. "It's all they talk about—HQ, I mean. It's taking down planes and tanks and missiles and everything. If we don't stop the Russians here, before they can cross the Cascade mountains, they'll have a free pass to, well, anywhere they want to go. And did you hear they're forcing everyone out of Alaska? It's the end of November, and they're making people leave their houses. That's got to be a war crime."

"At least it's been a mild season so far," Rich said.

"Thank God for that," Jack said. "Seriously, I think God is looking down on these refugees and helping them out. I just hope he'll be on our side when we start attacking."

"You still believe in God after all this?" Rich asked quietly.

"Sure," Jack said. "Why shouldn't I?"

"It seems like a lot of crap is going on. Have you heard the saying about how there are no atheists in a foxhole? I don't know if that's strictly true. This war doesn't make me want to go to church—it makes me want God to step in and smite the wicked. But I know he won't."

Jack paused. He could think of a handful of scriptures that might apply, but he knew that he was in over his head. He wasn't prepared to have this kind of conversation—did that mean he didn't truly believe?

"I don't know," Jack finally said. "Maybe God will smite the wicked. Maybe he'll send them all to hell when they die. I don't know how it's supposed to work."

"Neither do I," Rich said. "Maybe God doesn't help out either army. Maybe he just helps the refugees."

Jack closed his eyes and prayed. He didn't know if it would do any good. He drifted to sleep thinking of Aubrey and of right and wrong, and whether he should go AWOL to go home to be with his family.

SEVEN

GRADUATION WAS ON THE WIDE lawn that served as the makeshift parade ground. Aubrey wore her Army Combat Uniform, with the quirky insignia of a single chevron above a lower-case lambda. She was a private now, but a lambda private. Supposedly the two ranks were equal, but everyone wondered how it would play out in the real world.

She could see Jack standing at the edge of the parade ground, where families would be if this weren't a time of war. As if her dad would come to see her graduate. Jack had a family that cared. Aubrey had a drunk father who used her to get welfare and shoplift their meals. Well, he didn't know she was shoplifting—just that she came riding home every couple of days with a backpack full of food.

Aubrey smiled slightly at Jack, and he smiled back. His

uniform was identical to hers, with the exception of the insignia. His merely bore the lambda, not the chevron. He was still called a private, but he was a PV1, not a PV2.

"This is a new experience for me," Brigadier General Freeman said as he stood at the front of the parade ground. "It's a new experience for all of us. You're the first of what will likely be many graduating classes from the Lambda Program. Training facilities like this one are being established all across the nation, and we'll soon be sending out waves of recruits to aid in the war effort—a war effort that is less than five hundred miles from this camp.

"You've heard the scuttlebutt. Russian forces have landed, and I don't just mean in Alaska, but in Washington State. Not since the Mexican-American War has the United States been invaded by a hostile nation, and yet here you are, right in the middle of it."

Aubrey swallowed as the words hit her. She knew she was going to war, but this suddenly seemed very final. She felt the panicked urge to disappear and hide.

"If this were a regular graduation, your parents and brothers and sisters would be here to cheer you on. And if this were a regular graduation, I'd have a lot more eloquent things to say. I'd talk about your fighting spirit. I'd talk about your dedication to home and country. I'd talk about how you are better for doing this than all of the naysayers and those too scared to pick up a rifle and defend their homeland."

A voice sounded in Aubrey's head. "Can you believe this guy? It sounds like a pep rally before a football game."

It was Tabitha, using her telepathy.

The general continued. "Normally a graduating class would be moving out together, getting their assignments, and working as a company. But—"

"But you're special," Tabitha said in a mocking tone. "Seriously, can we just be done already?"

Aubrey tried to push Tabitha's voice out of her mind and focus on the general's words.

"Even some of the nongraduating privates will be moving out with you today. Some of them will finish their training at other facilities, and some will finish in the field as time allows."

The people around Jack seemed surprised by this news, but he stared back at Aubrey and smiled again. Yesterday he said he didn't know what was going to happen. Maybe something had changed during the night.

"You're young," General Freeman said, turning slightly so he was addressing both the graduates and nongraduates. "And I know that this isn't where many of you thought your lives would be going. But I promise you—the Lambda Program will make a decisive difference on the battlefield. Those are not simply words. We've seen what the Russians did with their equivalent of lambdas. We're playing catch-up, but we also have something the Russians don't have."

"Spirit!" Tabitha mocked. Her snark seemed to catalyze Aubrey and make her all the more attuned to the general's words.

"We're defending our homes, our families, and our freedom. There isn't a soldier here today who wouldn't lay down his or her life for their country."

Aubrey felt the spark of patriotism rising in her, and it was easier to push away her panic.

"We may have seemed hard on you," General Freeman said. "But you'll never regret the thousands of push-ups you did, the hundreds of rounds you fired, and the lifesaving skills you've learned."

"Ugh," Tabitha said. "Let's just go to war already."

"It will be my pleasure to serve alongside each and every one of you." He nodded to the graduating company, and then to the nongraduates. "Thank you."

"You knew you weren't staying for training?" Aubrey asked, hugging Jack tightly.

"I'd heard something," he said, holding her by the shoulders to look at her. "You outrank me now."

She grinned. "That's right. You have to do what I say, Private."

"Sounds terrible," he said with a wink.

"So where are we going?" Aubrey asked.

Jack shrugged. "I don't know."

She punched him in the shoulder, and he recoiled. She'd exercised a lot in the last seven weeks.

"Honestly, I don't know," he insisted. "If they've made the decision, they didn't make it here, or I was paying attention to the wrong conversation. I have to sleep sometimes."

Aubrey felt a knot in her stomach. "I hope they keep us together," she said, almost more to herself, and then instinctively reached for his hand before stopping herself.

"Me too," Jack said. "I bet they will. We have a proven track record."

"Will they think our"—she paused to choose the most deliberate word—"*relationship* is a liability?"

"I've never heard them say that. And I've been listening any time your name comes up."

"What else have they said?" She felt defeated, not knowing her future.

"That you're a good shot."

"The best," she said.

"The best in your platoon," he replied. "There's someone in third platoon who has you beat. Still, second place isn't bad, especially for a girl with bad eyes." He smiled at the last remark, and she moved to punch him again before, oddly, she wasn't there anymore.

She could see that it took him a second to realize what was going on—it was always confusing, no matter how many times she did it.

A moment later she reappeared and watched him blink away the confusion muddling his brain.

Her voice was quiet, so even the people standing a few feet away couldn't hear the words she whispered in his ear. "I couldn't let this day go by without a congratulations kiss."

"One day," he said, shaking his head, "someone is going to be looking across the field at just the wrong time."

"I've got a hundred and forty yards. Unless they have binocular eyes like you, they wouldn't be able to tell what that was."

"It can't have been the best ever. I couldn't even kiss you back." He was standing closer to her now so no one else could hear.

"I enjoyed it."

There was a shout, and one of the drill instructors called for attention. Aubrey and Jack watched as General Freeman strode out in front of the group.

"I hate to break up the party," he said, and he looked sincere. "But orders are in. No rest for the weary."

EIGHT

JACK LISTENED TO THE GENERAL read through names, but he was listening to Aubrey's heart, too. He'd taken to doing it whenever they stood at attention—he found it calming.

He heard another sound, coming in close. Helicopters, approaching from the northeast. He could pick out the distinct rotor noises of at least four smaller ones—Black Hawks, probably—and one big beast, maybe a Chinook. It had two rotors. He loved that he was getting better at identifying military vehicles by their sound, but this seemed ominous. He wanted to reach out and take Aubrey's hand. He didn't want them to be separated. His heart told him that they wouldn't be—they couldn't be—because they worked together so well. But his head told him otherwise: Why would they be assigned together if she hadn't been brought on his special training week?

The helicopters were close enough that he could have seen them even if he didn't have hypersensitive vision, but they were behind them, and he was standing at attention.

"Lyon, Holmes, Savage, Staheli, Eden," the sergeant called out. "Please step forward. Go get your rucks and your full ACUs and gear. You're moving out. Report to the helipad in ten. Dismissed."

The five of them—four graduates and one fourteen-year-old redhead—tentatively stepped forward, and then, realizing the urgency, began jogging back to barracks.

"Allred, Fisher, Paterson, Shaw, Flynn. Same thing. Rucks and gear and get to the helipad. Dismissed."

He called three more names—three people Jack assumed wouldn't ever be on the front lines: someone who could make plants grow, someone who could control the movement of water, and someone who could draw any image with pinpoint accuracy, like a photograph.

"Get your gear and get to the parking lot. There's a truck waiting for you."

Jack changed the direction of his hearing—even he couldn't explain how he could focus on different areas, but he could—and found four idling trucks at the front of the base.

"Cooper," the sergeant called, and Jack was pulled back to attention. Cooper. That was him. "Torreon, Jefferson, Sola—" That was his helicopter crew, all of them nongrads. Krezi, Rich, and Josi. The sergeant continued. "Tyler, Parsons."

Aubrey didn't follow the rules. He heard her exhale loudly and felt her hand grab his.

"Gear and the helipad. Get moving."

Jack's heart felt like an enormous weight had been lifted. He was with Aubrey. And he was with the team that he'd come to trust in their week of jump training, even though, presumably, that part of the mission was called off.

"So we're with Tabitha, huh?" Jack asked as they ran.

"Yeah," Aubrey said, wincing. "She can be annoying."

"Everyone else is good," Jack said. "Too young for a fight, but good."

"Josi's not too young," Aubrey said. "She's eighteen."

"Rich and Krezi are fifteen. They don't even get to carry guns."

"Maybe that's good," Aubrey said. "Maybe that means we won't be on the front lines."

"I doubt it. You and I were made for the front lines."

"But we were made for recon. Not for shooting."

He glanced over at her. "I wish we weren't in the middle of this."

"Where would you rather be?"

"Mexico. We could still do it. Skip out and go."

Aubrey laughed, as though he was joking. She didn't realize how serious he was.

"I'll come visit you in Leavenworth," she said, referring to the military prison. He knew the risks of going AWOL. He also knew that no one could find Aubrey if she didn't want to be found. But he was a different matter. They'd track him down easily, even without her help.

"You could probably sneak in and say hello."

"No. Too many cameras." She always showed up on cameras—her power only affected brains nearby, not security cameras.

She had to turn left to go to her barracks; his were straight ahead.

"Hey," she said, stopping him and grabbing his arm. "You okay?"

"Yeah. It's just—it's real now, you know?"

"I know. But we're going together."

A group of four lambda privates ran past them.

"I wish I could hug you again," he said.

Aubrey smiled. "Like I said, we're going together. I'll probably be sitting next to you on the helicopter. Speaking of which, have you ever flown in one?"

He nodded. "A few times."

She made a face. "Do they make you throw up?"

"They're worse than a plane," he said. "Get a seat by the window."

She took his hand again. He knew that was going to get them in trouble sometime.

"We'd better hurry," she said. "I'll see you there."

"'Kay." He paused as though he was going to kiss her

good-bye, but of course he wasn't. She liked to break the rules, but he didn't.

He let go of her hand. "See you there."

She grinned at him and then turned and jogged away toward her barracks. Time was ticking for him, he knew, but he watched her run for a good twenty seconds. She was why he was doing all of this. She always had been.

The barracks were buzzing with energy when he got back. There wasn't much to do—all the guys had packed their rucks that morning in anticipation of shipping out—but Jack needed to get dressed in his full combat uniform, not just the greens he wore to graduation. He pulled on his vest and fixed it into place.

"This is it," Rich said from across the row of beds.

"It is," Jack said.

Rich was already fully dressed and was checking the straps on his ruck. "It's kind of nice that we'll all be together. The four of us, I mean."

"Yeah." Rich, Jack, Krezi, and Josi had spent every waking minute together for the past week. And Jack suspected Rich had a bit of a crush on Krezi. Not that Jack was one to talk.

"Have you heard where we'll be going?" Rich asked.

Jack pulled on his helmet and began adjusting the straps. "Nope. But I think it's safe to say we're on recon. That's what Aubrey's good at, too. I'm not sure about Tabitha."

"You still think they'll want me to get up close and

personal?" Rich said, and struggled to pull on his pack. It was enormous on him—made for a full-grown man, not a fifteen-year-old. At least the army had made some allowances so that it wasn't as heavy, plus Rich didn't have a weapon to worry about.

Jack nodded. "That's what I heard—that they want you to help figure out what technology is knocking out the power."

Rich stood there quietly, waiting as Jack finished getting packed and dressed. Rich was a good kid. He was young, but he never used his age as an excuse—unlike Krezi, who was always letting people know she was only fifteen. Not that Jack could blame her. He wondered whether he'd be more like her than like Rich if this had happened a few years ago. After all, Jack still had his own doubts about himself as a soldier.

Jack pulled on his rucksack. All together, the ruck and his weapon and his body armor and everything else weighed close to a hundred pounds. He'd done plenty of physical training in his time at the camp— he'd slogged through swamps carrying all of this—but the weight was still hard to bear. It seemed like he was in a movie, he thought. Like he didn't belong, and was looking at everything from the outside.

"Ready?" he asked Rich.

"I guess."

By the time Aubrey got back to her tent, Tabitha, Krezi, and Josi were already there.

"You know what we are?" Tabitha asked, folding a shirt and putting it in her ruck.

"Our team, you mean?" Aubrey asked.

"Yeah. The Fantastic Six. They're going to have us go after the device. You, me, and Jack make the greatest recon team ever, Rich can understand any machine, so he can figure out what it is and how to stop it, and Krezi can shoot when the power's turned off."

Josi looked up from her packing. "What about me?"

"I haven't figured you out yet," Tabitha said.

"At least we'll have something exciting to do," Aubrey said. "I'd hate to be the guy stuck in the back who can count really well, or girl who can make plants grow faster."

"If you call getting shot at exciting," Krezi said. "At least you can turn invisible. Some of us don't have that luxury."

Josi wrapped up a bag of toiletries and put them in her rucksack. "You can shoot. My superpower is getting massive post-traumatic stress disorder. Seriously, I think that's all I'll be good at."

"What would the therapist say about that?" Aubrey asked, scratching her chin. "Something about how you need to find a creative outlet for all the bad energy you're absorbing." She laughed. "You could take up flower arranging."

"Ooh—or cooking," Krezi said. "We could use a better chef. We could use *any* chef. All we have now is a guy who knows how to use a can opener and a microwave."

Aubrey put the last of her belongings in the rucksack. "You guys ready? Because we're going to war in"—she checked her watch—"four minutes."

"Ready," Josi replied, slinging her rucksack onto her shoulder.

Tabitha groaned. "I'll be done in two minutes."

"You guys go ahead," Krezi said, nodding to Aubrey and Josi. "I'll wait for Tabitha."

Aubrey smiled. "Okay. Enjoy your last few minutes of peace."

NINE

"DID YOU EVER THINK YOU'D be here, getting ready to go into combat?" Tabitha asked as she put the final items into her bag.

"Not really," Krezi said. "I mean, my brother's in the air force, but he's a mechanic. He never sees any action, and everyone is pretty happy about that."

Tabitha bent down to tie her shoes. She wanted to have a long, personal conversation, but she knew they had to get to the helicopter. "Does he have any kind of special ability?"

"I don't think so. He's twenty-six. Wasn't the quarantine just for people twelve to twenty?"

Tabitha nodded. "I feel bad," she said. "We've been living in the same room for six weeks and we hardly know each other."

Krezi shrugged. "Different training, different schedules."

"I'm sorry you didn't get to graduate," Tabitha said.

"No biggie." Krezi headed outside, with Tabitha a few steps behind her.

They weren't supposed to cross the parade lawn, but they did anyway. It was the fastest way to get to the helipad, and Tabitha knew they were running late.

She wanted just one person from the team to start questioning things, but they were all so patriotic that they couldn't see common sense.

"You've heard about the rebellion, right?"

Krezi glanced over. "Sure."

"What would you say if I was thinking of joining it?"

There was a long pause. It dragged out until they'd crossed the lawn and were heading up the road.

"I'm not," Tabitha finally said. "I was just wondering what you would do if you thought I was. Obviously you're not a fan of the idea."

"If I could make a custom-built rebellion where I called all the shots, then I might join," Krezi said. "Right now they're too violent."

"I heard they're democratic. They vote on every action they take."

"But I don't want violence at all. I want a peaceful protest. And I'm only one vote."

"Wrong—they use the same system that the military uses.

You're a category Five-D, right? That means you're a powerful weapon, so you get five votes. The strongest get the most power."

"How do you know?"

"*Time* magazine," Tabitha lied. "They had a whole article about it. It was all anonymous, of course." The truth was that the rebels had tried to recruit Tabitha and she'd turned them down. They told her to contact them if she'd had a change of heart. She wasn't sure, but she thought she might be having one. Maybe it was because she was afraid of the Russians. But she told herself she was afraid of the Americans. She'd seen Americans get killed by Americans.

The helipad came into view. Tabitha touched Krezi's arm, and when the girl met her gaze, she mouthed the word *Jack*.

They were silent the rest of the way to the helicopter.

TEN

ZASHA STOOD ON THE ROOFTOP of a Seattle skyscraper. Fyodor
lay sleeping on the hard surface of a helicopter platform
beside her, exhausted from the drugs.

It had been a long day —a constant fight against the
American air force in the skies, coming at them from every
direction in an attempt to pierce Fyodor's bubble, and the
army units positioned on the ground to defend the harbor.

But now the Russian fleet had landed and was offload-
ing its cargo, creating a foothold in the city. Russian fighters
were patrolling the skies. And Zasha and Fyodor were finally
able to rest.

The others like Zasha—enhanced soldiers who had been
raised and trained to participate in the *maskirovka*—would be
taking over much of the work now. There was Otto, a boy

with power over the weather, who would be heading south for the attack into Portland. Ekaterina, a girl who couldn't exactly fly but was intensely strong and tough and could leap long distances, would be going north into Canada along with Natalya and Lyubov and a handful of others.

Zasha was heading east with the main force, through a narrow pass in the Cascade mountains. She could see the peaks in the distance.

Fyodor stirred. Zasha sat down on the helipad next to him and laid a hand on his shoulder.

"Zasha Litvyak," he murmured, his words slurred. "Flying ace. How many Americans have you killed?"

"You have killed them," she said, the breeze whipping at her hair. "You're the hero."

ELEVEN

TWO MEN STOOD IN THE apartment building's lobby, holding Alec's ID between them and scowling. They'd done all they could to verify his identity; Alec didn't speak a word of Russian. Back in Denver it was his job to blend in—to look like the all-American boy he was supposed to be. His "parents"—his handlers—had smuggled him across the border and now were living a perfectly average life: he was a dentist and she was a midlevel manager at a railroad. No one had ever slipped up and spoken Russian in the home, or eaten any food that could have been thought of as Russian.

That was not to say they hadn't trained him. Some of the training was simple: how to build a house, so that Alec would be able to understand how to knock one down. Or the lunch when he and his mom had eaten in the grassy area by the power substation, while she described how each part of it worked. The harder thing was convincing Alec that America was a bad place. He'd only known the training school back home, and America seemed like a land of plenty. So they worked on that most of all. His dad came into his bedroom every night with newspaper clippings—stories about murders where the police used excessive force, about poverty, even a combination of the two: police violence against the homeless. Then his dad would speak wistfully about Russia, and the control their homeland had against crime.

"You," one of the men down the hall called. "Alec Moore."

Alec stood up.

"Vy govorite na russkom yazyke?"

Alec stood there and shook his head slightly.

"Then we'll have to do this in English," the man said in a heavily accented voice. "Come with me."

He led Alec around a corner, another man falling into step behind them. Alec realized they were afraid of him. He could tell them they didn't need to be, but that wouldn't do any good. He could look like a spy easily, and be shot on sight.

They led him into a cinder-block room and handcuffed one of his wrists to a radiator. It was hot, and he knew his wrist would burn soon.

"My hand," Alec said. "It will scald."

"Then it would be best if you answer the commandant's questions."

The two men left and Alec stood up, looking everywhere for the pressure-relief valve. It was on the far side.

He picked up his metal folding chair in one hand and swung it down against the valve. He missed. He tried again. A blister was already beginning to form on his cuffed hand. This time the chair hit the valve, but the little brass fitting held.

He swung and swung again, the pain in his hand excruciating. Finally, on his seventh attempt, the valve broke, blasting steam like a geyser into the room.

Alec set the chair back where it belonged, and sat down. There were four large blisters just below his wristband that declared him "healthy."

The door opened, and a tall man strode in.

"It's like a sauna in here," the commandant said.

"Broken radiator."

The commandant took a seat across from Alec. "Alexi Petrovich."

Alec had never been called that, not even by his fake parents. His surprise must have shown on his face.

"New name for you?"

"Yes, sir."

"Let's set out some ground rules. You don't play with my mind, and I tell you the truth."

"It's a deal," Alec said.

The commandant began reading through the file. "You were assigned to Denver with Maria Proponov and Peter

Ivanovich. Raised there since you were five. You have the power to implant memories in people's heads. Most impressive."

"We all do what we can for the motherland," Alec said.

"Your last mission didn't go as planned."

"My last mission? Oh, you mean with Dan and Laura. I considered the fires I started at the Bremerton oil reserves as my last mission."

"Tell me about Dan and Laura."

Alec frowned. "Betrayal. The American military was moving in. Dan created an avalanche and Laura was supposed to pick me up and run. She never did. I was caught in the quarantine."

"How long did you wait for them?"

"I pulled myself loose from the rubble after an hour or two, but there was no sign of either of them."

"You'll be pleased to know that they both—independent of each other—infiltrated a Green Beret team. Sabotaged the groups from the inside."

"Are they alive?" Alec asked. If they were alive, he'd kill them himself. You don't abandon your leader.

"They're either dead or on the run. They tried to fill the entrance to a naval base with another avalanche. That was the plan, at least. According to highly placed sources we've been able to gather, they were fighting each other, and Dan created the avalanche to bury Laura. The Americans don't have the manpower to clean up that landslide yet—every piece of work equipment is being used elsewhere. No one wants to dig through a few hundred feet of dirt to see if they survived."

Alec had tried to kill Laura, had blamed her for leaving him in the first avalanche. The fact that she had been trying to take down a naval base didn't make him forgive her. He was her commanding officer.

His eyes met the commandant's. "What do you want me to do? Send me out there. Give me a job."

"You can implant memories, eh?"

"Yes, sir."

"Find a car. I want you to join the exodus of people who are leaving Seattle. I especially want trouble caused at the mouth of Snowqualmie Pass. As long as that road is packed with civilians, the Americans won't bomb it. Put roadblocks on alert. Tell them there's a spy among them; tell them we— those damned Russians—have broken through in the south and are heading over to flank them."

"Is that true, sir?"

"Of course not." He unwrapped a stick of Rolaids and ate half of them.

"Yes, sir."

TWELVE

AUBREY DIDN'T THROW UP ON the helicopter ride, though it took all her willpower. She hated everything about it—the pounding of the rotors, the sharp banks, the sudden drops. It didn't help that the pilot said this was one of the smoother helicopters to ride in—that just made her feel worse.

Her eyesight grew blurry and she got all the same feelings as when she strained against invisibility—the fatigue, the clumsiness, the body aches. She clutched Jack's arm through the whole flight, and she didn't care who saw.

If there was one person onboard who looked worse than Aubrey felt, it was Josi. She spent most of her time huddled forward, head in her hands. Aubrey still didn't know how Josi's powers worked, but if she had such a complete, all-encompassing memory, did that mean that she wasn't able to block out any of the sensations?

Rich seemed thrilled by the whole thing, completely at ease, like he'd flown in helicopters his whole life. Krezi also seemed relatively unperturbed.

For her part, Tabitha wasn't as annoying as usual. She was probably feeling airsick, too, and it cut her snark down. Or maybe she was using her telepathy to talk to someone else.

It was dark by the time the helicopter landed. The pilot said something that Aubrey couldn't hear as the door slid open and they all hurried out, hauling their heavy gear with them. Aubrey was wobbly on her feet, and Josi finally did throw up, just outside the door. Aubrey let go of Jack and put her hand on Josi's side while Jack grabbed Josi's ruck and hauled it with him toward the officer waiting at the edge of the helipad. Josi spit and coughed, and then moved along with Aubrey.

"I'm okay," she mouthed.

"I'm impressed you waited until we landed." Aubrey had to shout to be heard over the rotor blades. Already the door was being closed, and the Black Hawk was taking to the air.

"I'm still vibrating," Josi said with a weak laugh.

The officer at the edge of the pad was a Green Beret. Aubrey had worked with the Green Berets before and she had learned to respect them. What they did was hard, and they got assigned tough jobs—like working with lamb-das—because they were trained for it. These were guys who trained the Afghanis to fight; supposedly they could train fifteen-year-old lambdas, too.

"Parsons and Cooper," the man said, reading Aubrey and Jack's Velcro name badges as they approached. He had a hard, boxy face and a slight New England accent. There was no disdain in his eyes the way there had been with her previous Green Beret captain. This soldier seemed to be taking in the whole scene, assessing the situation like it was a puzzle to be solved.

"Let's get out of the cold," he said, and took Josi's ruck from Jack. He flung it over his shoulder like it was a child's kindergarten backpack, and led the way toward a collection of darkened tents five hundred yards to the—was it the south? Aubrey felt turned around.

"What direction are we headed?" she asked Josi, not because she really needed to know, but because she thought it might help Josi to get her mind off the helicopter ride. If her mind was ever really off something.

Josi stretched out an arm. "That's north," she said weakly. She seemed to be embarrassed she wasn't carrying her own rucksack. "So we're going southeast. Ish."

"The map in your head doesn't happen to know where we are, does it?" Aubrey asked, a smile in her voice.

"I couldn't see how fast the helicopter was going," Josi said, her voice finding a little strength. "But my best guess is we're somewhere west of Yakima."

"How close is that to Seattle?" Aubrey asked.

"About a hundred and fifty miles. It's mostly mountains between here and there. You ever seen the Cascades? A couple of giant volcanoes with smaller mountains all around them. Fun."

The captain was holding open the door to one of the tents, and the six of them hurried inside. Rich looked like he was dragging already. He had as much gear as the rest of them, minus the weapons, and he was the smallest member of the group, even shorter than Krezi.

Inside were two long tables, and the captain ordered them to drop their gear and take a seat. Six of the chairs were already taken by Green Berets. Josi sat next to Aubrey on her right, and Tabitha on her left. Rich and Krezi sat by Jack on the other side. Aubrey looked over at Jack. With his helmet on, she couldn't see the scar on the side of his head that he had gotten on their last Green Beret detachment, when the team had been sabotaged.

"Welcome to Operation Detachment Alpha nine-one-one-nine," the captain said, addressing everyone in the room. "I'm Captain Gillett. We don't have a lot of time for touchy-feely, get-to-know-you games, but if all goes well, we'll get to know each other a lot better later. For now, I'll just explain how this first op is going to work."

He pointed to one of the Green Berets, a man with a baby face and bright red hair—the Green Berets weren't wearing their helmets.

"This is Sergeant Sharps. He's the youngest looking of the bunch, and he's going to be leading this mission on the ground. Basically, we're sending you in as a group of refugee kids, turned around and heading the wrong way."

"The wrong way?" Krezi said. "As in, toward the battlefield?"

Aubrey froze. Krezi hadn't asked for permission to speak, and Aubrey could see the crease form in the captain's forehead as he debated whether or not to call out the infraction.

Captain Gillett leaned forward, resting his knuckles on the table, and looked at Krezi.

"You're how old?"

"Almost sixteen." After a moment she added, "Sir."

"Fifteen," he said, and stared down at her. She seemed to shrink in her seat under his gaze. Finally, he looked up at the rest of the team. "I want you all to start addressing each other the way that Lambda Torreon addressed me—without asking permission to speak, and without saying *sir*. For this assignment you are not soldiers and you're not to act like soldiers. There will be no saluting, no military decorum of any kind. This is a recon mission."

He pointed to Sergeant Sharps. "You can call him Nick. Like I said, he's going to be leading you on the ground, and yes, Torreon—Lucretia—you are headed toward the front lines. That's to be expected from a group of Green Berets, even when you're fifteen."

"Krezi," she said quietly. "Not Lucretia."

Gillett nodded slowly, his face expressionless. "Okay. Well, let's start with you, Krezi. As you may know, the war effort is being seriously hindered by some unknown weapon that the Russians have that disables electronics."

"Like an EMP?" Rich asked.

"No," Gillett replied. "An EMP is an electromagnetic pulse that destroys electronics. This just turns everything off for a while. And when I say everything, I mean everything. Cars don't work because their spark plugs don't spark. Lightbulbs, wristwatches, computers, tanks, jeeps, airplanes, everything. Whatever this is, it has to have an impressive and mobile power source."

"What does this have to do with me?" Krezi asked. "You said you were starting with me."

Gillett pulled a plastic pen from his pocket and set it on the table.

"Show the team what you can do."

Krezi grinned. "I can do a lot of things to that pen."

"Surprise me," Gillett said.

Krezi pointed one finger at the pen. Aubrey had heard about Krezi's powers, but hadn't seen them in action.

There was no flash of light, no explosion. Instead, the pen simply softened, like melting chocolate, losing its shape and turning from white to tan to brown, until it finally caught fire and burned in a slow, mellow mess.

Tabitha's voice appeared in Aubrey's head. "That's . . . not impressive."

Gillett looked up at the group. "What you just saw is the beginner course in Lucretia—I mean Krezi—Torreon. Krezi, what you bring to this group is firepower. When the power is out, you have power. They can't fire their big guns at you, but you can fire at them. I'm told you can cut through plate steel?"

She nodded. "Slowly, but I can."

"Slowly might be all that it takes. Plus, you're much faster on smaller blasts. You can blow up a truck?"

Krezi thought for a moment. "I never have, but sure. I've split boulders in half."

Tabitha's voice came again. "Then maybe that's what you should have done. Melting a pen? I'm really scared."

Gillett spoke, his words cutting through Tabitha's. "Krezi's our artillery during a power outage. Next is the Trio, our primary recon team: Aubrey Parsons, Jack Cooper, and Tabitha Tyler." Gillette looked at Aubrey. "Give us a taste of what you can do."

"It's not spectacular to watch," she said.

"I don't know how it couldn't be."

He didn't understand how it worked. It wasn't like she blipped out of existence.

"Here goes," she said, and she disappeared.

There were all the usual looks of confusion on faces—not

startled surprise, just the effects of her brain messing with theirs. She stood up and walked around to Jack's side of the table. She watched as they began to look for her, but then got distracted as if she had never been there, and wanted to move forward with the meeting.

She reappeared. "Hi," she said, with a little wave.

"What was that?" asked one of the confused Green Berets.

Aubrey shrugged. "I told you it's not much to watch."

"They don't get it," Tabitha said in Aubrey's mind. Aubrey wished she could turn her off.

"She becomes invisible," Gillett said, his face pleased but still stony. "Or more accurately, her brain sends the signal to your brain that she's not there."

"That's why you were confused," Aubrey said, returning to her chair and feeling a little embarrassed. "My brain confuses your brain."

Sharps— Nick, the Green Beret, nodded approvingly. "Invisibility."

"Limited invisibility," Gillett corrected. "She still shows up on cameras, and her brainpowers only extend approximately one hundred and forty yards. If she's farther away than that, you can see her."

"Even so," said another of the Berets, the name on his chest reading VanderHorst, "that's killer recon."

"Exactly." Gillett pointed to Tabitha and Jack. "And with

a spotting team like this, she's a perfect spy. Jack Cooper, hypersensitivity. He can track Aubrey anywhere she goes, by sound and by smell—she wears perfume when she goes on a mission, if you can believe that." He reached into his gear and pulled out a square box and handed it to her. "Your brand, I've been told?"

Flowerbomb. Just sniffing the box brought memories flooding back. Her first assignment catching a "demon" lambda; the catastrophe at the Space Needle; the avalanche.

She exchanged a smile with Jack, and set it down.

"Jack and Aubrey work well together—the two of them helped break the terror network—and now we have an added bonus: Tabitha Tyler. Tabitha is a telepath. So Jack can watch Aubrey, and Tabitha can pass intel and orders back to her. The perfect team."

The Green Berets nodded, and Aubrey tried not to look disappointed. She didn't want Tabitha in her head. The moments when Aubrey was alone and whispering to Jack—so far away that only he could hear—were some of their most intimate times together. Now Tabitha would be in the middle of that. Granted, Aubrey would be safer and more effective, but it was hard for her to let go of what had been.

"Next we have Richard Jefferson," Gillett said. "He's going to be central to everything we're doing."

Rich's dark skin flushed, and he looked straight ahead—not

at the captain or at the Green Berets.

"Richard can—well, how would you explain it? You can talk to machines?"

"Kind of," Rich said.

"It's just *Rich*," Krezi said.

"Rich," Gillett repeated, his face still mostly expressionless.

"It's not that I can talk to machines," Rich said, scratching under his helmet. "It's that I can understand how they work. Just by touching them. I mean, give me any computer, and I can run it—I know the passwords, how to navigate the system, everything."

Gillett nodded. "Or give you a car and you can drive it, or a clock full of gears and you can fix it, am I right?"

"Right."

Gillett looked at the group, and then rapped on the table with the knuckles of his right hand. "Rich is going to solve our problem for us. We're going to find the Russian device—this electronic-interference device—and Rich is going to explain how it works."

There was a pause, and then Nick Sharps pointed at Josi. "What about the sick one?"

"Josi Sola," Gillett said, nodding to her. "Imagine a photographic memory that isn't just photographic but audio and sensory recording as well. She can't forget a thing. I think she's still trying to process the sensory input of the chopper ride, aren't you?"

Josi nodded.

"Look at me," he said, and she stared at him with weak eyes. "Tell me the names of all the Green Berets, their hair color, and something else about them."

"Nick Sharps," Josi began, and seemed to be fighting the urge to throw up. "Red hair with a little brown at the temples. He has an ink stain on his left index finger—I think he's left-handed."

"Good," Gillett said.

"Chase-Dunn. Brown hair. Crooked nose like it was broken, I think. VanderHorst. Brown hair—kind of a muddy brown—and a mole under his right eye. Ehlers. Shaved head, but the stubble is light, probably blond. Tattoo of a sword on his wrist."

"That's Excalibur," Ehlers said proudly.

"Lytle. Black hair. Scar along his chin. And Uhrey. Black hair and he's cracked his knuckles eight times since we've been in this room."

No one spoke for a moment, and then Lytle leaned forward. "So what is that for? I mean, no offense, darlin', but do we need a Sherlock Holmes on our team?"

Gillett finally sat down at the end of the table. "She memorizes what Rich tells her. Let me lay out the plan for tomorrow. First of all, the goal: we want to get Rich in contact with one of the Russian vehicles. We figure that there's something about their vehicles that keeps them immune to the effects of whatever device is interfering with our electronics. So Rich touches a truck or a jeep or a tank and figures out how it works and what makes it so special. You can do that, Rich?"

Rich nodded and opened his mouth to speak, but Gillett cut him off.

"Rich relays the schematics of the machine to Josi, who won't forget a word."

Lytle spoke up again. "Can't we just use a camera and a voice recorder?"

"Not if the power's out," Gillett said. "This team is designed to operate without electricity. We wouldn't need Tabitha if we could rely on radios. We wouldn't need Jack if we could rely on night vision. We wouldn't need Krezi if we could rely on heavy firepower. As for Aubrey—well, she can turn invisible, and that's useful whether the power's on or not."

Rich raised his hand. It made him look very young, like a kid in school. Which was exactly where they all should have been, Aubrey thought.

"Yes," Gillett said, nodding to Rich.

"This may be a dumb question, but how am I going to touch a Russian truck? Isn't there a war going on?"

Aubrey was glad that Rich asked it, because she'd been thinking the same thing. She could sneak up on a truck, but she couldn't bring someone with her.

"It should actually be easy. Well, relatively easy. There's no war front near Seattle—not anymore, not after the landing. There're too many civilians, and they're clogging the streets trying to get out of town. The Russians have pledged to drive all Americans out of Washington. In fact, rumor has it that they've asked us nicely to just leave."

"How does that make it easy?" Rich asked again, clearly nervous.

"Because it's not like you're sneaking up on the front lines of World War Three. We're going to be sneaking up—if you can call it that—on a roadblock in Snowqualmie Pass. Our forces are waiting until the civilians clear out and until we can isolate this electronic device to counterattack. There's no shooting going on up there, except for the citizens who have taken up resistance fighting."

It was Tabitha who spoke next. "So we're just driving up to a roadblock—to the place where they're looking specifically for soldiers?"

"It'll be a panicked nightmare," Gillett said. "A steady line of refugees on one side of the road and you guys on the other. You'll run into the roadblock, they'll probably turn you around, and you'll mix into the sea of evacuees. Only Sergeant Sparks—*Nick*—is going with you. He looks young. The Russians will think you're just another pack of teenagers in a minivan."

"Do we have a cover story?" Jack asked.

"I don't suppose you'll need much of one," Gillett said, "but we can hammer that out." He unfolded a map across the table. Aubrey recognized the city names from when they'd fled Seattle, just over two months ago. It felt like she was going back into the lion's den.

THIRTEEN

"JACK, I DON'T LIKE THIS."

Jack had been listening for Aubrey all night but knew she wasn't getting a lot of privacy. The girls' tent was a hive of activity, with soldiers coming and going from several different units. It was only now, as Jack heard the crunch of gravel under Aubrey's feet and smelled the splash of Flowerbomb perfume on her, that he could focus on her voice—and that he knew she could talk privately.

"I'm outside," she said, and then laughed. "I probably don't need to tell you that. I went for a walk. I can't sleep. I hope you're awake."

He wished he could answer her, wished that he had Tabitha's powers.

He wished he and Aubrey were getting in a car in the

morning and driving to Mexico, not into a potential combat situation.

"I don't like that Tabitha's in charge," Aubrey said. "I know that's petty. But she and I are the same rank, and I don't know why Captain Gillett chose her to be second-in-command."

Jack thought he knew. It was because Tabitha was the one giving the orders to Aubrey via telepathy. Supposedly Tabitha would be watching over everything. Not that it mattered. They had Sergeant Sparks—Nick—with them. He was really in charge. He'd be calling all the shots.

"But that's not the worst thing," Aubrey said. "I'm supposed to clear a path for Rich to approach a Russian vehicle. What does that mean? Shoot people while I'm invisible? That doesn't make me a soldier—it makes me an assassin. A cold-blooded killer. That's not what I agreed to."

It had troubled Jack, too, but Aubrey was leaping to the worst possible scenario. Ideally, she could just cause commotion on one side of the roadblock—spill a little gas, start a fire. Or puncture the tires on a truck and get the soldiers working on repairing them while Rich snuck in from the other side. It would be dark, and hopefully the guys manning the roadblock would have too much to deal with to notice Rich and Josi.

Aubrey had stopped now, no more rocks crunching under her feet. She let out a long, slow breath that sounded like it had a little shiver to it. It was almost Thanksgiving, and there was snow in the mountains between the camp and their target.

"Did we agree to this?" Aubrey asked, her voice quieter. "I mean, I know we said yes, but did we really know what we were agreeing to? Did we do this because we wanted to join the army, or did we do it because we didn't want to be locked up in quarantine? I remember standing up and saying we'd join—we did it together—but why did we do it? Do you remember?"

He honestly didn't. Maybe it was a surge of patriotism. Maybe he was thinking that they needed to protect their homes and families. They'd been shown pictures of everything the terrorists had destroyed—the collapsed bridges and the burned malls and the fallen skyscrapers. But was that why they had joined? In his heart, Jack wondered if he had done it to stay close to Aubrey. And he wondered if she had joined because she had nowhere else to go. Her father had sold her out when the army had begun searching for scattered teens during the initial roundup. Jack doubted if she'd ever go back to him.

"Ugh," Aubrey said, and then laughed. "Sorry I'm so depressing. Maybe you're sleeping and not hearing any of this and I'm just talking to myself. As if I didn't already feel like a dork."

She started walking again and Jack imagined he was walking beside her, holding her hand.

"Josi is doing better. A medic came and checked her out.

Did you know they have medics who are assigned especially to the lambdas? They act like they have it figured out, although I don't believe it. Do you know what advice he gave her? To keep her eyes closed whenever she could, to sleep a lot, and to avoid stressful situations. Seriously. We're going to the front lines in an hour and she's supposed to avoid stressful situations.

"Anyway, you probably need to sleep and not listen to me. I should be sleeping, but I figure I can do that in the van on the way."

She paused for a long time, not walking or talking. Just standing still. "I can't believe it's starting again," Aubrey finally said. "We're going to see people die again, Jack. We might die. You might die."

Jack closed his eyes and wished he could say something to her. Something comforting and soothing. Something to make everything better. But there was nothing. She was right.

She might die.

"I'm going to get in out of the cold. Sleep good, Jack."

Jack drove the van, with Nick sitting in the passenger seat. They were on the interstate headed through the mountains. The clock on the dash read 3:15 a.m., and they hoped to hit a roadblock sometime around five.

There were thousands of cars on the other side of the

median, all fleeing from the invasion, but the westbound lanes were empty. Occasionally they'd hit a roadblock of American forces, and Nick would give them the proper pass-words and authorization to get them through.

None of them were carrying any official papers, and they'd all removed their dog tags and left them with Captain Gillett back at the base. They were spies. If they were found out, they could all be shot according to the rules of war. Jack didn't know whether that thought gave him any more or less fear than their mission.

Nick turned the heat up. He was wearing a sweater and jeans. Everyone else had coats—all commandeered from a department store in Yakima.

"I bet you didn't know this," he said, staring out the front window, "but it gets cold as hell in Afghanistan. You always think about it as a desert, but those are some high frigging mountains, and the wind can blow like a son of a bitch."

"I've never thought about it," Jack said. He glanced in the mirror. Aubrey's head was against a window and her eyes were closed. Only Rich and Tabitha looked like they were awake.

"Neither did I till I was in the middle of it. Fortunately you're always walking—I spent five months going up and down mountains. Your hands get chapped, but your body stays warm."

"And Green Berets don't get cold," Jack joked.

"Damn straight."

"How old are you, anyway?"

Nick laughed. "You're asking because I look like I just got out of junior high, right? I'm twenty-four. Started out as a grunt in Iraq and did that for four years before I went in for the Green Berets. Coldest decision of my life."

"You seen a lot of action?" Jack asked.

"Depends on what you call *action* and how you define *a lot*. Are you asking if I've fired my gun much?"

Jack shrugged. "I'm just talking."

Nick laughed. "I understand you've seen plenty of action for your short time in the army."

"Plenty," Jack said.

"Well, you're going to see even more."

"I know."

Nick brought his foot up and put it against the dash, leaning back in his seat.

"He doesn't seem worried," a voice said. It startled Jack. He was so used to his hypersensitivity that he knew how sounds rang around in his ears, and this was different. It was a voice in his head—Tabitha.

"I can't believe they're sending in six kids and one soldier," she said. "It's suicide."

It wasn't suicide, Jack thought. He looked in the rearview mirror and met her eyes. Then he gave a small shake of his head.

"You're saying it's not suicide? Are you kidding? We're unarmed, driving straight toward a roadblock that is specifically looking for people like us. There might even be Russian spy planes watching us right now."

Going into a situation unarmed was their job. They were spies.

"You know," she said, "not all lambdas are doing this. Not all of them are just going along with everything that the military is telling them to do, and getting in the middle of a fight when they're totally unprepared."

Jack wanted to respond. To argue. For starters, Tabitha wasn't "totally unprepared." She was a full private. She'd gone through basic training—or, the rushed lambda version of it. And more than that, she had volunteered to join the army. Just like the rest of them.

He looked at her in the mirror again and Tabitha's blue eyes stared back at him. Even though it was dark in the van, he could see every bit of her face—every strand of hair and eyelash. She was smiling. Maybe so little that she didn't think anyone could see it, but Jack knew faces. He knew how the muscles pulled around the lips and along the cheek, how tiny creases formed about the eyes and mouth, how the eyes dilated ever so slightly, how the teeth were revealed. He observed it all.

If they were really going into a suicide mission, why would she be smiling?

Jack's first thought was that she was a traitor, like the lambdas he'd known before—the lambdas who had been terrorists.

But Tabitha wasn't like that, he told himself. It had taken nearly all of their time at basic training for Jack to learn to trust people again, but he'd convinced himself he could. The terrorists had been hunted down. Even the army had stopped forcing the lambdas to wear the horrible bombs around their ankles—that was as close to a stamp of approval as Jack could get. The military believed the terrorists were rooted out. He had to agree.

"If we survive this," Tabitha said, "then we should talk about it. I shouldn't have brought it up when we're getting ready for a mission."

Brought what up? That lambdas shouldn't be in the army? There was no point in talking about that. They were already there. Already assigned to a Green Beret ODA on the front lines of a war on American soil. There wasn't anything else to talk about.

Jack glanced back at Aubrey. She was still sleeping, her lips slightly parted.

"She's going to be all right," Tabitha said, and Jack's eyes darted to Tabitha's face. "We're the Trio, remember? She's in good hands."

Jack gave a slight nod in the mirror, and then focused on the road.

"She's talked about you, Jack. She's told me a million good things. How you used to hunt together back home. How you were always there for her. She cares about you a lot."

He didn't look back. He didn't like that Tabitha could just get into his head, and he didn't like that she was talking about Aubrey. It felt too personal. Too intrusive.

He focused on the street, staring at the road ahead of them. He could see the curves and contours of the mountain highway, far beyond the reach of the headlights. And he saw the seemingly never-ending line of cars headed in their direction, driving away from danger. Danger that he was driving into.

Jack thought back to Aubrey's question. What had made them decide to join the army?

FOURTEEN

AUBREY WAS NUDGED IN THE ribs, and she sat up with a start. She glanced first at Krezi, who had woken her, and then looked forward at the shapes appearing in the headlights.

She adjusted her glasses and saw three vehicles blocking the road: two large six-wheeled trucks and one single tracked vehicle that looked like a small tank with a fixed fifty-cal machine gun mounted on the low-sloping turret.

She recognized it from training, but the name escaped her.

Jack was continuing to drive toward the roadblock, but a Russian soldier was lowering his hand, signaling for them to slow.

A floodlight in the back of one of the trucks burst on and filled the van with light so bright she had to shield her eyes. The van slowed and came to a stop.

As they'd planned, Nick opened his door and stepped outside, causing immediate shouts from the Russians. Aubrey disappeared and slipped between the driver and passenger seats—pausing to kiss Jack on the cheek—then climbed out into the light.

They were well within one hundred and forty yards of the Russian vehicles, and she knew she was safe. Half a dozen Russians were pointing assault rifles at Nick, who had his arms up in the air and looked as nervous as a teenager facing down the Russian army was supposed to look.

"Get in your car!" a man called with a thick accent.

"We have to get to Seattle!" Nick called back, his voice shaking. "Our families are there. We have to get them out."

"Get in your car!" the man shouted again.

Aubrey began walking toward the armored vehicle, watching as its turret pivoted and aimed at the van. This was it. This was the first real contact with the enemy. She felt a wave of nausea and fought to stay calm.

"We need to get into the city," Nick continued, his voice pleading.

Aubrey walked past the soldiers to the back of the roadblock and looked behind it. She didn't see any reinforcements. She raised a set of binoculars to her eyes and searched the darkness farther down the road, but there was nothing there either. That wasn't saying much—it was dark and she'd just been blinded by the floodlight. She'd have to wait until the white spots disappeared from the center of her eyes.

She reached into her coat pocket and pulled out the bottle of Flowerbomb perfume. She sprayed it on her wrists, and then misted her neck.

The Russians were continuing to shout and Aubrey glanced back at them, getting a full count. There were eight men on the street, all pointing their rifles at Nick and the van. Another man stood up in the turret of the tracked vehicle—a BMP! That was what it was called!—and another man sat in the driver's seat, his head sticking up through a hatch in the front. From what she remembered, there would be one more crew member inside, with passenger room for a squad of infantrymen. They were probably the guys out on the street.

There was a man standing in the back of one of the trucks, pointing the floodlight, but there were no soldiers in the cabs of either truck. So that was a grand total of twelve men.

She felt for the gun at her hip, and the grenades she wore on a harness inside her long coat. Just the thought of using them made her feel sick again.

The commander of the BMP was talking on a radio, saying something in Russian. In the street Nick was starting to get back into the van.

"Turn around!" the lead soldier ordered.

"Where are we supposed to go?" Nick said.

"*Mnyeh vsyo ravn.* I don't care. Turn around and go."

"Our families are there," Nick said.

"Your family is on road," the soldier argued. "You go back. Find them there."

"We don't know where to go."

"You go back," the soldier said again. "Or we shoot."

Nick held his hands up higher and nodded. It really was a convincing performance, Aubrey thought. He looked young and innocent and totally intimidated.

He got back into the van, but didn't close the door.

"You go," the soldier said, taking a step forward.

"We're trying to figure out where we're going!" Nick said, his voice pleading.

"You go. *Idi ot suda!* You go."

Nick pulled the door shut, and Jack started the engine.

Aubrey suddenly felt very alone. Jack turned the van around on the empty street and pulled away. He drove slowly, hugging the shoulder, and after a hundred yards or so he turned off the median and into the trees that separated the eastbound lanes from the westbound.

"Aubrey, you okay?" Tabitha's voice appeared in her head.

"I'm good, Jack," Aubrey said, relieved to be communicating with them.

There was a pause. "Jack says you're okay. Can you give Nick a sitrep?"

"Twelve soldiers," Aubrey said, watching the Russians. "I think the main cannon is still aimed at you guys, but I don't think they can see you. No one is wearing night-vision goggles, and I can't make out much of the van through the trees. But, you know, my eyes aren't the best. Still, I think you're okay to send Josi and Rich."

The plan was for Josi and Rich to trek through the thick pines until they got close to the roadblock. Then Aubrey would create a diversion. What the diversion was going to be was something Nick was supposed to decide, and Aubrey didn't like that she couldn't make her own choice.

"Roger that, Aubrey," Tabitha said. "Josi and Rich are changing clothes."

FIFTEEN

JACK HAD HIS EYES CLOSED, focusing all his attention on Aubrey. The perfume was strong, and he was pulled to her location—it was almost like he could picture her in his head: she was close to an exhaust pipe of one of the trucks and a soldier with body odor. He could hear the low conversation of the Russians and he wished he could understand the language. That was something they needed on their team—a translator.

Josi and Rich had taken off their coats. They were wearing all-black clothing underneath. They both pulled on ski masks, and then waited for Nick to give them the order.

"Ask her if we're clear to send them," Nick said, and Tabitha, who was leaning against the side of the van, nodded.

A moment later Jack heard Aubrey's voice. "It's clear. I can still see a little bit of the van, but they don't seem concerned about you. It looks like you're trying to get into that traffic jam on the other side."

"They're good to go," Jack said.

"Just like we talked about," Nick said to Josi. She nodded, and then, crouching, began moving into the trees toward the soldiers.

Nick turned to Tabitha. "Find out if there's anything she can do about that light."

Jack listened as Aubrey moved—she got higher, like she was climbing. The wind carried her perfume more.

"The floodlight is run by a generator in the back of the truck," she said. "It's weird and all the instructions are in Russian, but it looks like the gas ones back home, like at Nicole's cabin."

Jack turned to Nick. "She can turn off the generator. That would look like an accident."

Nick nodded. "Do it."

Tabitha was motionless.

"Okay," Aubrey said.

Jack listened to the hum of the generator motor, and Aubrey's scuffing footsteps as she got closer to it. He could smell the exhaust coming off of it.

Someone lit a cigarette.

"This is weird, Jack," she said. "Not the generator. I mean, it's weird being right here with all the Russians."

He couldn't help but think it was strange, too, and it made him nervous. She'd been face-to-face with the bad guys before, with terrorists, and even with Green Berets who thought she was the enemy.

But this was war. That was an armored personnel carrier. These were Russians.

It still blew his mind that Russians were the enemy.

He could hear her doing something—moving something metallic. There was a scrape, and a heavy thud.

He held his breath.

"Ask her if she's all right," Jack said to Tabitha.

"I'm okay," Aubrey said, slightly out of breath. "I had to push the generator away from the side of the truck. The soldier up here looks confused, but he's not drawing his gun or anything."

"She's okay," Jack repeated to Nick. When Aubrey moved something while invisible, whether it was opening a door, or picking something up, or even pushing a person, the confusion that her brain created always seemed to cover it up—people assumed there was a gust of wind, or that they'd stumbled, or that something had been off-balance to begin with.

"I'm going to unhook the battery," she said. "That should work, right? You know motors better than I do."

"Tell her yes," Jack said.

"Got it," Aubrey said a moment later.

He heard a pop—probably the plastic cover coming off the battery terminal.

"Tell her not to electrocute herself."

There was a scrape of metal on metal.

Aubrey laughed nervously. "I'm not dumb, Jack. And tell Tabitha she's not funny."

The metal continued to scrape—to squeal. It was a tiny sound, but he was hyperattuned to it. She was pulling the cable off the terminal. He could hear her breath get heavier.

"This is tight," she gasped. "Hang on."

Nick interrupted his thoughts. "How are Josi and Rich?"

Jack was shaken from the moment, and opened his eyes. He tried to refocus, hearing the sound of feet sliding over rock and past brush. Compared to the battery cable they sounded like elephants.

And then the generator motor puttered.

The light immediately dimmed down to the flicker of a candle.

"*Blyad!*"

"*Schto sluchilos?*"

Jack breathed a sigh of relief, and he heard Aubrey say, "Thanks." Tabitha must have congratulated her.

He focused back on Josi and Rich, who sped up now that the light was out.

"They're okay," Jack said. "Maybe fifty more feet to go. Josi's in the lead; Rich is following."

"Now what?" Aubrey asked.

"Now what?" Jack asked Nick.

"Where are the Russians?"

He didn't have to ask Aubrey that, but Tabitha apparently did, because Aubrey started talking just as Jack opened his mouth. He paused to listen to her, and then repeated the information to Nick.

"Four of them are in the bed of the truck. The others are still standing around the BMP. There's a lot of talking."

Nick had his arms folded, his thumb in his teeth. "How long before they can get that light back on?"

"All they need to do is replace the battery cable and restart it. Not long if they have a wrench."

"I want Rich to touch that BMP, not the trucks," Nick said. "They might not be hardened like it is."

Jack took in a sharp breath. It would take a big diversion to get everyone on the other side of the road.

"What?" Aubrey said. "The BMP?"

Tabitha had been talking.

"What do you propose?" Jack asked, feeling tightness in his chest. This was the part they were supposed to play by ear, and it could go any number of ways.

"A gun misfire," Nick said. "Someone on the far side of the road. I want a gun to go off and for it to hit someone."

There was hardly a pause before Aubrey responded. "He wants me to shoot someone?"

"How?" Jack asked. "With her gun?"

"No," Nick said. "Pull the trigger on one of their AKs. Fire a burst. Hit someone in the leg."

"That's not going to be easy," Aubrey said almost immediately. "And I don't like it, Jack. I told you, I don't want to be an assassin."

"What if she can think of something else?" Jack asked.

Nick chewed on his thumb, thinking.

"Jack," a whispered voice said. Josi. "We're as close as I dare to get."

"Josi's in place."

"Tell them to wait," Nick said to Tabitha.

There was a pause.

Josi barely breathed her words. "Roger that." She was probably twenty feet from the nearest truck—the truck full of Russians.

"I don't want to shoot anyone, Jack," Aubrey said.

"Ask Aubrey if there's a target," Nick said. Jack already knew there was. There were three soldiers standing close together, on the far side of the road.

"A target?" she asked defiantly. "There are soldiers. They look like you, Jack. They're just teenagers—maybe a little older. I'm supposed to shoot one?"

Jack didn't repeat what she'd said, but turned to Tabitha. "Ask her if there's anything else."

"There's dry grass," she said, and then started to move. He followed her movements as she crossed the pavement to the three soldiers.

"She's going to try something else," Jack said.

Nick unfolded his arms. "What?"

"I think she's going to start a fire."

"Hang on, Jack," she said.

"A fire will just create more light," Nick said. "Tell her to shoot him in the damn leg."

She didn't answer.

"What did she say?" Nick demanded.

"Nothing," Jack said.

Nick grabbed Tabitha's arm. "Tell her that's an order."

"Watch this," Aubrey said. Jack couldn't see her through the trees, but he knew she was right next to the group of soldiers.

"Ask her what she's doing," Jack said.

"No, damn it," Nick said. "Tell her to follow orders."

"Flick," Aubrey said.

"*Chyort!*"

"Ask her what she's doing," Jack said, but then he smelled it. Aubrey was moving toward the brush on the far side of the road, carrying the cigarette with her.

"Come on," she whispered. "Come on."

"What's she doing, Jack?" Nick demanded.

"I was right. She's starting a fire."

Jack heard the Russian say something that sounded like it was probably a swearword, and the two other men laughed. Jack focused on the cigarette. The smell of burning tobacco was pungent and smelled gross next to Aubrey's perfume.

"Damn it," Nick said. "Tell her to fire the gun."

But then Jack smelled it—the softer, subtler smell of burning weeds.

"Too late," Jack said.

"Distraction started," Aubrey said triumphantly. "I'm getting tired, Jack. And seriously, tell Tabitha to shut up."

For a moment—a long moment—everyone was quiet.

"The wind caught his cigarette," Aubrey said, obviously pleased. "Blew it in the weeds."

"Pozhar!"

And then suddenly all the Russians were talking at once, and moving toward the fire. Jack heard them getting out of the back of the truck, and the commander in the BMP turret was saying something that sounded urgent.

"Nobody needs to get shot," Aubrey said.

"They're all moving to the fire," Jack said to Nick. "It's a good distraction."

"They're going to put it out fast. There are probably fire extinguishers in all three of those vehicles."

"What do we tell Josi and Rich?"

"Damn it," Nick said, pacing back and forth behind the cover of pines. "Ask them if they have a clear path."

"We do," Josi said. "But the guy's still in his turret. We'll be right under him."

"They do," Jack told Nick. "But what about the guys in the BMP?"

"Tell Aubrey to get her butt over to the BMP, and get

ready to drop a grenade in the hatch. And tell her that's an effing order."

Tabitha nodded.

"He's kidding, right?"

Jack turned to Tabitha. "Tell her Jack says to do it."

Nick spun. "What's that supposed to mean? She listens to you, but not me? Isn't this the frigging army?"

"Just tell her," Jack said. He looked at Nick. "We're running out of time."

Nick shook his head. "Send in Josi and Rich. And tell Aubrey they're coming."

Jack listened as Josi and Rich darted from the wood line and up onto the road. They ran to the base of the BMP; he could tell they were on their knees by the tracks.

Aubrey was moving away from the fire and toward the big vehicle, too. Jack heard her unzip her coat.

"A grenade?" she said. "Jack, I just saved someone from getting a bullet in the leg, and now he wants me to drop a grenade in the BMP? And tell Tabitha that yes, I'm going, and shut up."

"She's going," Jack said.

Nick was looking at Tabitha. "Tell her to be ready to drop that grenade inside if there's any sign that Rich and Josi have been spotted."

Aubrey was next to the BMP now, and Jack could hear her unclip a grenade from the vest inside her coat.

"This is a stupid plan," Aubrey said. "I could drop this in an empty truck cab just as easily and no one would get hurt. And yes, Tabitha, I know we're at war; people are going to get hurt. But these particular people don't have to get hurt right now."

Jack could hear Rich whispering to Josi.

"Eight-cylinder diesel engine . . . fourteen-point-eight liters displacement . . ."

"I don't know if you can see this, Jack," Aubrey said, "but I was right. This whole roadside is going up, and they're chasing it with fire extinguishers."

"Is she doing it?" Nick demanded.

Jack nodded that she was as Aubrey kept talking.

"Who is being the bigger jerk? Tabitha or Nick? Because I can take it if it's Nick, but if Tabitha thinks she can boss me around like this then we're going to have words."

Something felt wrong. Jack was overloaded with sensory information—the smoke from the fire, the fizzing of the extinguishers, the specs Rich was reciting to Josi, the angry calls in Russian—but something else was happening and Jack couldn't put his finger on it.

He looked at Nick, staring as he listened.

"What is it?" Nick said, running his fingers through his red hair.

Krezi, who'd been quiet this whole time, stood up.

"Guys?" she said.

Jack looked at her, still knowing that he was missing something.

She pointed a finger toward the endless row of cars heading east on the freeway. Jack turned to see what she was pointing at, and saw that the endless row was . . . ending. Disappearing into the blackness. It was as if the world was falling away, car after car falling off the end of the world.

His eyes adjusted and he saw that the cars were still there, but they had gone completely dark—and the edge of darkness was moving toward them rapidly.

"Nick," Jack said. "That electronic interference—we're about to be right in the middle of it."

Nick stepped forward and watched the approaching line of darkness.

"Tell Rich," he said urgently, turning to Tabitha. "See what happens to the BMP."

"Does this mean we're going to get attacked?" Jack asked.

"We need to give Rich and Josi more time." Nick grabbed Krezi's arm. "Get up there in the trees, and watch over them. Shoot anyone that spots them."

She nodded and stripped off her coat to reveal the black sweater underneath. She pulled on her ski mask and then hurried forward, almost running through the woods.

SIXTEEN

"THE LIGHTS ARE GOING TO go out," Tabitha said. "That Russian thing is coming here."

"Is it coming for us?" Aubrey asked, suddenly tense. Her arm was getting tired from holding the grenade out beside the BMP driver's head.

It wasn't the high explosive grenade— the M67—that she'd learned to throw in basic training. Instead, she'd chosen an M84, a so-called "flashbang" grenade because it made a deafening noise and a blinding flash. She'd been armed with both types, but Aubrey didn't want to drop a high explosive into the BMP—and she hadn't been ordered to. This would have the same effect. It would render it, and the people inside, useless, and she wouldn't be killing anyone.

She hoped. She was dropping it right into the driver's lap,

and she had no idea what kind of damage it would cause that close.

And now the lights were going out.

"Stay there until we give the order," Tabitha said, her tone authoritative and annoying. "We have to make sure that Josi and Rich have time."

Aubrey looked at the fire, which was getting under control. The soldiers weren't as concerned about it anymore, now that they'd extinguished the bushes closest to the truck. Only three of the nine men had extinguishers, and one man unzipped his pants and began to pee on the flames. The others laughed.

She could take them all with one grenade, she thought, and she was glad Nick wasn't here to offer that as a suggestion.

"Jack, what does it mean that the lights are going out?" Their team could blend in with the mass of citizens on the freeway, but Aubrey would have to get rid of her grenades and sidearm. The Beretta M9 seemed to weigh heavily on her hip, though it was still covered by her long coat.

Everything seemed heavier. She always forgot how much being invisible wore her out until she was forced to do it for a long time.

"We don't know about invasion," Tabitha said, finally answering her question. "Hold there until you get further orders."

And then their lights went out. The dim floodlight that

was still running off the remaining charge in the generator flickered out, and the controls in the hatch of the BMP went dark.

"Schto zdyes proeshodit?"

"Prover rahdyo."

"Jack," Aubrey said. "The BMP lost power. I thought the whole point of this was that the BMP doesn't lose power when the electronic interference comes. Isn't that why we're here?"

There was no answer for a long time. The driver ducked lower in his seat and began messing with switches.

"Stay in position," Tabitha said. "We don't know what's going on."

The Russian in the turret stood up taller and called to the men on the side of the road. Everyone except the ones with extinguishers hurried back, the one man zipping his fly.

"Jack," Aubrey said. "I think they're getting organized again. Josi and Rich need to get out of here."

"Roger that," Tabitha said. "Hold on, Aubrey."

There was a long pause, and then Tabitha added, "Maybe they wouldn't be getting organized if you'd shot one of them."

Aubrey exhaled long and slow to keep her temper, and she tightened her grip on the grenade.

The commander was giving orders, pointing all around. He gestured in a big circle around the BMP.

"Jack, they're calm. They're getting in a defensive formation, but they're calm," Aubrey said. "What does that mean?"

A moment later Tabitha spoke. "Josi and Rich *need* to move."

The Russians started to spread out, and Aubrey strained to see over the BMP to the other side, where Josi and Rich were still crouched. She saw a flicker of blackness against the white line at the edge of the road.

Tabitha's voice came to her. "We've pulled them."

"Vot oni tahm!" the commander called, and pointed toward where the two had just run into the forest.

"Dang it," Aubrey said, more to herself than to Jack, but then she spoke out loud. "I think they were spotted. We've got two—no, four—soldiers going after them. They're at the tree line—the soldiers, I mean."

She wished her eyes were better, and she cursed the darkness. Her arm ached from holding it out, so she pulled it back, clipping the grenade to her vest inside her coat. She took out her Beretta, chambered a round, and flicked off the safety. This was not where she wanted to be.

"What do I do, Jack?"

Tabitha's response was quick. "Don't let Josi and Rich get followed."

Aubrey skirted the edge of the BMP. No one could see her—certainly not the big gun, which was motionless. It sounded like the engine had failed—the Russian commander was shouting down at his driver, and the driver was shouting back at him.

The four Russians stood at the tree line. Aubrey ran past them, hurtling into the darkness, only to catch her foot on something and fall to one knee. Her eyesight was getting worse—she'd been invisible for too long.

But she could see what she'd caught her foot on.

It was Rich. He was less than ten feet from the Russians, facedown in the bushes and holding perfectly still.

"Oh no," she whispered. "Jack, they're right here, right in front of the Russians."

She looked up at the four men. They had their automatic rifles pointed right at her. They'd probably heard her stumble over Rich. Maybe he'd made a noise. She didn't know.

"Jack, what do I do?"

"You shoot them," Tabitha said, her words slow and deliberate. "You're a soldier. This is what you signed up for."

Aubrey was at a loss for words.

She held her gun up, pointing it at the chest of one of the men. He was wearing a Kevlar vest, and she adjusted her aim to his head.

Her hand shook.

"Jack, Tabitha said you want me to shoot these guys. Can you confirm that for me?"

"You have to trust me," Tabitha said. "This is coming from Nick. We have to get Josi and Rich out."

Aubrey still stared. One of the men took a step forward, and the others did the same. They took another step.

There was a brilliant beam of blue-white light that blasted from somewhere behind Aubrey, hitting one of the men full in the chest. He flew backward in what seemed like slow motion.

Krezi.

And then Aubrey's training finally kicked in.

She fired two shots into the next man, only ten feet from her. He dropped like a stone. Krezi blasted at another, and then Aubrey fired again, dropping the fourth.

She reached into her coat and grabbed a grenade—it was round in her hand, not cylindrical. High explosive. She yanked the pin and threw it toward the BMP and the remaining soldiers.

Aubrey dropped to the ground, covering her head, and the grenade cracked with a concussive *whump!*

"Go," she said, shoving Rich and Josi before she realized she was still invisible.

"Jack, get them out of here." She stood up and pointed her Beretta back toward the BMP. There were no men visible.

Josi moved, and grabbed Rich, shouting, "Come on!"

Aubrey's hands were shaking, and she could feel sweat dripping down her back despite the cold.

"Take the rest of them out," Tabitha said. "You and Krezi."

"Why?" Aubrey asked, staring blankly at the side of the

BMP, knowing five soldiers were hiding on the other side, and three more waited inside.

"They can't call for backup if their radios are down," Tabitha said, sounding far too calm. "But they'll be up again soon. We can't let anyone get that chance."

Something flew over the top of the BMP, and Aubrey ran forward, slamming her shoulder into the vehicle and dropping to her knees.

The Russian grenade exploded in the forest, and a jolt of white-hot pain scared through Aubrey's leg. She gritted her teeth, unclipped another high explosive from her vest, and stood up long enough to drop it into the open turret. She ducked again, and the blast was muffled by the heavy steel of the vehicle's walls.

She'd had to kill three more, she thought. "Three more," she said out loud. And she started to cry.

But she didn't stop.

A man appeared around the edge of the BMP, firing blindly into the forest. Aubrey turned to shoot him, but Krezi hit him first. He flew backward and out of sight. Aubrey took a breath and marched around the backside of the BMP to where four soldiers sat crouched.

They never saw her. Probably never heard the pop of her pistol as she tore through them. Together, the four of them slumped against the tracks of the BMP, unmoving.

"Oh God."

SEVENTEEN

"AUBREY," TABITHA SAID. "AUBREY, ARE you okay?"

She looked at Jack, whose face was white as a sheet. He shook his head. "No answer. But she's alive. I can hear her breathing."

"Krezi," Tabitha tried. "Honey, are you okay?"

There was a pause and then Jack spoke.

"Krezi's good," he said. "She sounds shaken up."

Josi and Rich appeared out of the trees, black silhouettes in the darkness. Josi had pulled off her ski mask, and her brown hair was a mess in all directions. Rich simply walked to the van and sat down in the open door.

"You okay?" Jack asked him.

He nodded, and then looked up, tears on his face. "You know what?"

"What?"

"There was nothing special about the BMP. Its power went out like everything else. It was hardened for an EMP, the way our tanks are, but that's it. Just standard stuff. Old stuff."

Josi stuffed her ski mask into her pocket. "We did all of this for nothing."

There was silence, then Jack held out his hands. "Do me a favor. Don't say that to Aubrey."

"She's going to find out," Tabitha said.

"I know," Jack said, "but she doesn't need to find out right now, and not like this." He looked toward the roadblock where Nick had gone to try to round up Krezi and Aubrey. "I'll be back."

He took off toward the carnage of battle.

"Krezi," Tabitha called with her mind. "You coming, honey?"

"I thought we were dead," Rich said, leaning forward, elbows on his knees. "I thought they had us."

"I did, too," Josi said, looking only moderately more composed than Rich.

"What happened out there?" Tabitha asked. Jack had narrated some of it, but everything happened so fast.

"I killed people," Krezi said, her face expressionless as she emerged from the woods. "Three people. Aubrey killed the rest."

"The rest?" Tabitha said, stunned. There were twelve Russians up there. That left Aubrey with . . . "Nine? That's—"

"Amazing," Rich said, rubbing his chest. "She saved my life. Our lives," he amended, looking up at Josi.

Josi nodded, and then turned away. "I don't think that I can do this anymore."

"Just think of how Aubrey feels," Tabitha said.

Josi's eyes met hers for a moment, and she stammered to say something, but rushed to a bush and threw up.

"Krezi," Tabitha said. "Come sit down. Get warm. It's colder outside than it looks."

Krezi smiled an exhausted grin and climbed in past Rich, settling in the middle seat.

"Jack told us what you did," Tabitha said, coming to stand at the door. "That you took the first shot. If it wasn't for you, Aubrey might have stayed frozen."

Rich nodded emphatically, but didn't add anything.

"You practice this in training," Krezi said, stoic and calm, "but it doesn't prepare you. Not really."

"You did good," Tabitha said. Then, instead of talking out loud, she entered Krezi's mind. "It's a rotten world, and we got stuck with the crap lives. But you did good. You saved Rich and Josi. That's what matters."

Krezi took a deep breath, and a tired smile broke across her face. "It's not my first time." As soon as she said it the smile disappeared, but she continued talking. "I killed a terrorist, back when I was assigned to my first unit, before basic training. I killed a guy who could fly—shot him right out of the air."

Tabitha thought about that for a long moment. Krezi had killed four people in battle. A terrorist and three soldiers. In regular life Krezi would have been a freshman in high school; instead, she'd become a weapon. A lambda 5D, one of the rarest of the rare. The only lambda 5 in their squad, one of only eight in their training class.

Tabitha hated it. She hated what Krezi was going through. "I'm here for you," Tabitha said to Krezi with her mind. She hoped it felt more personal that way. "If you need to talk, I'm here."

There was a sound behind them in the trees, and the others appeared—Aubrey walking with a limp, one arm draped around each of the guys' shoulders. She'd been injured?

"What's wrong?" Josi said, rushing to them.

"Shrapnel in the leg," Nick said. "It's not bad, but we need to clean it up and get the hell away from here."

Krezi moved to the backseat of the van and Aubrey clumsily climbed onto the middle bench, her back against the window and her leg up.

Nick looked at Krezi. "I don't suppose you can just make something glow? I need a little light."

"Sorry," she said. "I make things glow and then they blow up. But I can light something on fire for you."

"Good enough," he said, and reached up into the glove box and found the van's owner's manual. He handed it to her. "Keep it burning."

By the light of Krezi's fire, Nick cut an X in Aubrey's jeans just above the knee, exposing a bleeding wound—fresh, bright-red blood surrounded by brown, dried blood. Her pants were soaked dark, and in the firelight they looked black. He folded his knife, revealing a pair of pliers.

"This is going to hurt a lot," Nick said.

Jack climbed into the front seat and reached out to take Aubrey's hand. She squeezed tight, her knuckles white around his fingers. As Tabitha watched she wished she had someone on this mission—someone anywhere—who would hold her hand as she gritted her teeth against pain.

"It's going to be okay," Josi said, sounding confident, watching beside Tabitha.

"Yeah," Tabitha said. "It's going to be okay."

Nick tugged and Aubrey grimaced as he pulled the shard of warped metal from her leg. Fresh blood poured from the wound and Aubrey let out a loud gasp, then closed her eyes and gritted her teeth again.

And then in an instant she was gone, and Tabitha didn't know where she had gone or even what she'd been watching—why were they gathered at the door?

Then she was back, and Tabitha couldn't be sure if she'd gone at all.

"What was that?" Nick said, an alcohol wipe in his hand.

"Sorry," she gasped. "Keep going."

He cleaned the wound the best he could, then mashed a stack of gauze pads onto it. "This will have to do," he said. "I don't have anything to use for stitches." He wrapped a long roll of surgical tape around her leg four times, securing the gauze in place. It looked terrible, but Nick didn't seem like he wanted to spend any more time on it.

"We need to get on the road," he said. "And by on the road, I mean on the road with all the people. Everyone take off any military gear and leave it here."

"Why can't we wait for the power to come back on?" Krezi asked.

"Because we have a wounded soldier, and because I don't want to be sitting in this van when someone comes around the mountain and finds a squad of dead Russians."

Just as they began to set off, Aubrey turned back to look at Josi. "Did you get it? The intel on the BMP?"

Tabitha held her breath, but Josi only hesitated a moment. "We got everything it had."

EIGHTEEN

JACK WALKED BESIDE AUBREY, HER left arm around his shoulders as she limped along. They were making their way down the side of the freeway, the cars beside them stopped and powerless. He searched for something to say to her, but he'd already asked the stupid questions: "Are you okay?" and "What can I do?" Of course she wasn't okay, and there was nothing he could do.

He replayed the final moments of the mission in his head, matching them with the images of the dead bodies he'd seen after it was all over. Aubrey was standing over the four dead soldiers when he reached her, pistol still extended, the slide locked back and empty. The look on her face was one of such intense pain that he'd assumed her leg wound was far worse than it was. She was broken and defeated, torn apart from the inside.

She'd told him that she didn't want to be an assassin, and that was when she was asked to drop a grenade into the BMP— when her target was just three men. She was also ordered to stare at a man, point-blank, and shoot him in the leg.

Three men. That number seemed so low now, but it was huge. He could understand exactly why she hadn't wanted to do it.

That was the trouble. He could understand all of it. He just couldn't *do* anything about it.

Suddenly he heard an engine, and then another, far away in front of them. He began to see taillights.

"Power's coming back on," he called back to Nick.

Nick nodded and kept walking.

Soon the cars around them lit up, and the people inside seemed thrilled as they revved their engines.

Why had the electronic interference been activated here? Had there been an attack somewhere nearby? Had American planes been sent in? Jack had eavesdropped enough to know that no American bombers were having success against this unseen device. And if what Rich found was accurate, the Russians weren't immune to the electronic interference. The BMP lost power just like everything else.

That was important information—vitally important information. Josi was wrong to think they had done this mission for nothing. Now they knew that when the Russians turned off the lights they turned themselves off, too.

"Hold on, guys," Nick said.

Aubrey and Jack stopped and faced him. The cars on the freeway hadn't started moving yet—it might take an hour for this endless traffic jam to get rolling again. Nick pounded on the door of a semitruck.

The driver rolled down his window, and Nick hopped up on the step.

"I don't have room for passengers," the grizzled man said tiredly.

"We're not hitchhiking," Nick said, his voice low. "We're US Army doing recon, and we've got a wounded soldier. Can I use your radio?"

"You're a bunch of kids," the driver said. His voice wasn't angry, just skeptical.

"I'm Sergeant Nick Sharps, Green Beret ODA nine-one-one-nine." He rolled up his sweater to reveal a tattoo on his arm—Jack couldn't see what it was. "We were on special assignment. Undercover."

The driver didn't look like he was entirely convinced, but he slowly nodded. "It's not like you're wasting my time, I guess. We're going nowhere fast."

Nick hopped down and the driver opened the door. A moment later Nick was in the driver's seat and Jack could hear the click of a knob being turned.

"Breaker breaker," Nick said. "This is Nightingale, how 'bout ya, Harlequin?"

There was a pause, maybe five seconds, then a voice crackled through the radio.

"Copy you, Nightingale, this is Harlequin. How's the road?"

"Clean clear to Flag Town, come on?" Nick said.

The driver snorted. Jack didn't know why.

"Road's clear up here," Harlequin responded. "You have a full load?"

"Yep. I'm about to put the hammer down."

"Copy that, Nightingale. See you in a short, good buddy."

Nick clipped the radio back, and switched the dial to its original position.

"The Green Berets use radio code from C. W. McCall?" the driver said, a smile in his voice.

Nick reached out to shake hands with the man. "The Green Berets were never here, okay?"

"Gotcha," he said. "You need anything? I've got food."

"You have any Gatorade?"

There was movement that Jack couldn't make out, but he heard the sound of a plastic cooler opening.

"Thanks," Nick said, and then he climbed down from the cab of the truck and handed a bottle of apple juice to Aubrey.

"Good luck," the driver called.

"Thanks," Josi said, and Tabitha gave him a wave.

"Drink that," Nick said to Aubrey. "All of it. You need the fluids."

She nodded and unscrewed the cap before putting her arm back around Jack's shoulders.

They started walking again.

"What was that about?" Rich asked.

"Helicopter's on its way," Nick said quietly.

Aubrey drank the apple juice slowly, tasting each mouthful for a long time before swallowing. Jack used to think it was gross that he could hear the sound of the inner workings of everyone's bodies, but he was used to it now. Aubrey's heart rate was up. Everyone's was, except Nick's. But Aubrey's heart was pumping harder than the others. She'd lost a lot of blood, and that might be the reason. Or maybe she was still full of adrenaline.

"How are you doing?" he asked her for the hundredth time.

"Okay."

He wanted to press her, to find out what was really going on inside her head, but he didn't know how to do that—especially with all these people around.

"How's the leg?"

"Not as bad," she said, and then she forced a smile. After a moment she added, "At least I didn't get shot in the head."

Jack touched the mark above his ear. The scar tissue was soft and slick. "I'm glad you didn't."

"This is going to limit my choice of skirts in the future," she said.

"We'll get you stitches back at the base and it'll heal up fine," Jack replied.

She looked at him doubtfully.

He gazed back at her, at her gray eyes that were so full of hidden color. "I mean it. My scar hasn't limited my choice of hats."

She let out a small laugh, and he thought it was the biggest victory of the night.

They walked in silence for another five hundred yards or so before she spoke again. "It was bad, Jack."

He pulled her tighter against him. "I know."

"I'm not sure you do."

How could he respond? She was right—he probably had no idea.

"So tell me," he finally said.

Aubrey didn't answer immediately. She swallowed the last of the juice.

"I don't think I can right now," she said.

"You need to talk about it." He tried to keep his voice as soothing as possible. He didn't want to pressure her, but he knew she was going through something terrible. If she wasn't going to talk to him, she needed to talk to someone.

He drew in a deep breath. Flowerbomb perfume. That scent wasn't regular Aubrey—it was warrior Aubrey. Soldier Aubrey. It smelled like danger and trouble.

And underneath it was the salty, copper scent of blood.

"I did it all wrong," she said, and he could hear the tremble in her voice. "I didn't follow orders. I thought I knew better."

"You did what you thought was right."

"No," she said sternly. "Don't make excuses for me. It all went to hell back there, and I did everything I wasn't supposed to do."

He opened his mouth to say something—to tell her that the mission went to hell because the power went out, which made the soldiers go into defensive positions—but he knew she didn't want to hear it. And he didn't know if it was true.

"Maybe if I'd—" she began and then stopped herself. "Maybe . . ."

"You can't second-guess yourself."

"Yes, I can," she said. "I have to." Aubrey was crying now. "Nine men are dead because of me. Maybe they didn't have to die. And don't tell me this is war. I know what war is, and it's not all about who can massacre the most people."

Massacre. Jack thought about the word. About what she was accusing herself of. About what it must be doing to her.

When she spoke again her voice was tense and strained. "So tell me what I'm supposed to do, Jack. If I'm not supposed to second-guess myself. Am I supposed to accept that I'm a mass murderer? Because I was there, and what I did wasn't heroic."

NINETEEN

IT HAD TAKEN THE BETTER part of seven hours of bumper-to-bumper traffic for Alec to cross the Snowqualmie Pass, from Seattle over the mountains to Yakima. It was the worst traffic jam he'd ever seen, even worse than the mass exodus out of Denver when the terrorist attacks started.

Alec was driving a stolen Honda Civic. He wasn't worried about them checking the registration at any of the American checkpoints. He could always lie his way through that.

What he needed was an American army uniform. A poor refugee fleeing a bad situation was one thing, but a soldier could feed all sorts of bad information up the chain of command.

He leaned back in his seat, knowing that he could fall asleep right there if he let himself. He'd been awake for how long—thirty hours? Thirty-six? But he was determined to prove his worth to his commanders, show them that he was better than just a terrorist—that he was a real soldier.

Ahead of him, Alec saw an American roadblock, and he knew this was his first big chance. The men guarding the roadblock were all probably low-ranking grunts, but so much the better. It would be hours before his lies got sorted out.

He crept his car forward as the army checked each vehicle for bombs and guns and hidden passengers. When he reached the front of the line, Alec started working on the man's mind before he'd even rolled the window down.

"Boy, am I glad to see you guys," Alec said. The soldier was wearing an American uniform that had the two chevrons of a corporal. He was followed by six men who began searching the car, without reading any rights or seeming to care about them. "It's chaos back there."

"Who are you with?"

Perfect. Not "Who are you?" but "Who are you with?" Alec's memories were already beginning to take hold. He rattled off a unit number.

The American corporal saluted. "Is there anything we can get you, sir?"

Alec spoke without looking at any of the men, as though they were beneath him. "Inspect these cars more thoroughly. Another roadblock said they found RPGs in an undercarriage.

Someone even found explosives behind a bumper. Take your time. Do it right."

"Yes, sir," said the corporal. "What I mean is, we are, sir. Did you not hear about the attack on one of the forward outposts?"

"Word travels fast," another man—a private first class—said. "Especially stories of the mutants. We thought we were the only ones that had them in our military, but there are more."

"Where can I find your commanding officer?"

"Two hundred yards back behind us," the taller of the two men said. "They're guarding the road in case we tell them there's trouble."

Alec was still working on the corporal's mind. There was so much fun he could have—he could make the corporal believe the private was a spy who needed to be killed. He could alter the man's brain so quickly between pain and plea sure that eventually he'd take his own life to stop it. But none of that would help his goal—disrupting the enemy lines. Alec would save his tricks for the commanding officer.

TWENTY

IT WAS ANOTHER MILE OF agony—mental and physical—before they walked across the median and onto the empty westbound freeway. A Black Hawk was setting down, and they hurried to get inside.

Aubrey's leg hurt, but at least the pain had distracted her from her thoughts. Now that she was in the helicopter and able to move her leg into a comfortable position, there was nothing more to keep her mind from replaying what had happened.

She'd shot two men, aiming for their necks and faces to keep the bullets above their Kevlar vests. She'd run to the BMP and dropped a grenade into the turret.

Why hadn't the Russians closed the turret? Shouldn't they have done that if they were under fire? Three men—the driver, the gunner, and the commander—were dead because they were too stupid to close the turret and block her grenade. She wouldn't have been able to kill them if they'd just closed that damned turret.

And then she'd run around to the other side, and unloaded her gun on four men who were huddled together for safety. Four men who had no idea that anyone was looking at them. Who couldn't even know where the bullets were coming from. Her gun held fifteen rounds, and she'd used every one. It was like an executioner's firing line.

Aubrey felt a tear roll down her cheek. She'd thought she was being so clever by starting the fire with the stolen cigarette. If she'd followed orders—if she'd made one of the guns appear to misfire and hit a soldier in the leg—then maybe the Russians would have stayed on the far side of the BMP. Maybe they never would have come near Josi and Rich. Maybe no one would have had to die.

It made so much sense now. A real diversion—a distraction that actually meant something to the soldiers. Nick had known what he was talking about, and Aubrey had thought that she knew better. That she was smarter. She had smiled when she'd done it—joked about flicking the cigarette away.

She'd even been smiling when she was holding a flash-bang grenade instead of a real one. Granted, she hadn't been ordered to use it, but would it have made a difference?

Would it have saved lives? Would it have made her less of a murderer?

Aubrey looked at Jack. She couldn't see much of his face in the darkness, but she could tell he was smiling at her. She didn't deserve that smile.

She focused on Nick, who was leaning back in his seat, his head tilted so he was staring at the ceiling. It was his orders she'd disobeyed, and he'd have to explain why the mission had gone to hell.

She moved her gaze to Tabitha. Aubrey had been upset that Tabitha was second-in-command—that she'd been chosen to lead the group if something had happened to Nick. Aubrey had thought she'd have done a better job. This all proved what a lie that was.

She looked at Rich.

"What did you find out?" she asked over the noise of the rotors.

He seemed uncomfortable, and he glanced at Jack before turning back to Aubrey.

"We found out how the BMP works," he said. "Everything. I could drive it myself."

"What about the device?" she asked, but before the words even escaped her lips, the thought struck her. The BMP had gone silent when everything else had. The turret hadn't pivoted to aim at Josi or Rich when the rest of the soldiers had. It was dead.

"There is no protection for their vehicles," Rich said. "They're just as vulnerable to electronic interference as everything else."

Aubrey's hand balled into a fist.

"This is good," Nick said. "I know what you're thinking, but this is good information."

Aubrey was seething. "How is this good? How could it possibly be good?"

"It's not just good," Nick said. "It's great. It tells us that they're disabling themselves whenever they disable us."

It was Jack who responded. "How is that possible? We've heard about how they're obliterating our forces."

Nick was smiling. "It means that they're bringing the device close to us. They're moving the device around. That has to be it."

"So we killed all those men to find out they're moving the device around?" Aubrey asked.

"I can guarantee you," Nick said, nearly shouting over the noise of the blades, "the brass will be thrilled to get this intel. Thrilled. Do you know how much easier it is to chase down a device than it is to fight against an army full of indestructible vehicles? That BMP is just a regular BMP, and their tanks are just regular tanks. This is great news."

This was good news? It didn't feel like good news. It felt more like failure.

Aubrey turned and looked out the window. They were

flying low—less than a hundred feet above the freeway. She assumed it was in case the power went out, so they could try to survive a crash landing.

She looked back at Nick. She wished she could talk to him privately. She wanted to apologize. To plead for forgiveness. But it would have to wait until they got back to the base.

She could talk to Jack, though.

She spoke quietly, her voice muffled completely by the rotors. "Jack, can you hear me?"

He nodded.

"I'm not going to let this happen again," she said. "I screwed up. Bad. I didn't follow orders, and I might have been the reason that all those men had to die."

He looked like he wanted to say something, but she was glad he couldn't—at least, not privately.

"I'm going to do better," she said, feeling another tear on her cheek. "I'm going to be better. A better soldier. I'm going to follow orders. No more screwing around thinking I know more than my commanding officer does. Because I don't."

He gave her a smile.

The distant horizon was turning a gray blue when the helicopter landed in a field next to a dozen other Black Hawks and three big Chinooks. Nick stood and slid the door open, and the team hurried out, Jack pausing to take Aubrey's hand and help her down.

Nick turned and pointed at Josi and Aubrey. Josi looked

green again from the flight. "Josi, I need you to come with me. They're going to want to hear your report ASAP. And Aubrey, get to the medic tent. You know where that is?"

Aubrey nodded.

"You need someone to help you?"

Even though she knew Jack was ready and eager to volunteer, Aubrey shook her head. "I'll be fine."

"Okay," Nick said. "The rest of you, get some sleep. We'll debrief later. Good work out there."

Everyone nodded and began leaving, but Jack paused, watching Aubrey. "Are you going to be okay?"

"I'm fine," she said. "Really."

"I don't believe you."

"I'm going to see the medics," she said. "I'll be okay."

He sighed. "Everything's fine. You're going to be fine."

"I know."

He turned and left, and Aubrey started toward the medic's tent. But as soon as Jack was out of sight—even though she knew he was probably listening—she took a right and headed toward the training area.

Her leg hurt, but she let the pain motivate her. She found what she was looking for in the center of the training field. It looked the same as the one back at her basic training camp. The obstacle-course wall.

She thought about saying something to Jack, but decided not to. This was for her. Something she needed to do.

Aubrey tested her weight on her bad leg, balancing on it. Pain shot from her knee to her hip, but it held her.

With a deep breath, she took a running start, gritting her teeth against the stabbing jolts coming from her muscles. When she reached the wall, she leapt.

Her fingers caught the top, and she clamped on tight, using the momentum to curl her biceps and bring her chin up above the top of the wooden planks. She gasped as her legs slapped the wall, but she didn't let the pain stop her. She swung one elbow over the top, then the other, and lifted herself up on the palms of her hands. When the peak of the wall was at her waist, she bent forward and turned, slinging her good leg up and over.

Straddling the top, she took a long breath. She flexed her bad leg, the pain still fierce but bearable. She could feel new wetness dripping near the bandage and knew she'd reopened the wound.

Let it bleed, she thought, and lifted that leg over. She clenched her teeth and then dropped, making sure to break her fall with her good leg.

Aubrey smiled, and limped to the medic station.

Aubrey woke to see Tabitha shaking her shoulder.

"Time to get up," she said. "We're meeting in twenty minutes."

Aubrey stood slowly, her muscles aching from the night's

activities. She looked down at the large white bandage wrapped around her thigh. There was a spot of red just above the cut, but that was all. The medics had given her eight stitches and some painkillers.

Josi was still sleeping, and Tabitha looked reluctant to wake her. Josi had come in even later than Aubrey had.

"What time is it?" Aubrey asked, rubbing her face with both hands.

"One thirty," Tabitha said.

Aubrey nodded and reached for her pants. Four hours of sleep. She felt like she could sleep another twelve.

"Do you think she remembers her dreams?" Tabitha asked. "The way she remembers everything else?"

"I hope not," Krezi said, pinning up her hair. "She needs a break."

Tabitha reached down and touched Josi's arm. She woke with a start, sitting up.

"What is it?" Josi asked.

"Meeting in twenty," Tabitha said, and then checked the clock. "Make that eighteen."

Josi flopped down again and covered her eyes with her arm.

There was something comforting about being back in ACUs. Aubrey felt like a real soldier again instead of a spy.

Josi uncovered one eye. "You guys already shower?"

"I did before they stitched me up," Aubrey said.

Tabitha shook her head, and ran her hands through her short blond hair. "I wish I did."

"We can't keep going at this pace forever." Josi swung her feet over the side of her cot. "I know. I know. We're at war. But don't the Russians have to take a break for showers and sleep?"

"Do you remember your dreams?" Krezi asked Josi.

"Every single one," Josi said without looking up. "It almost doesn't feel like being asleep."

"Is your brain going to explode one day?" Krezi asked, reaching for her patrol cap.

Josi groaned and stood up. "It feels like it is. They say after the war I'm going to get studied—they want to see if they can make everyone's brains work like mine. Which proves they don't get how awful it is."

"I think we're all going to get studied before we get out of this," Aubrey said. "We'll have lifetime careers as test subjects."

"But they're just using us while they can," Tabitha said. "We're tools. Krezi's a gun."

"Hottest gun you ever saw," Krezi said, and made a kissy face in the mirror.

Aubrey laughed. "Yeah, these ACUs are really hot."

Josi had pulled on her pants and was lacing up her boots. "I don't know about you guys, but I'm glad the ACUs are formless. The last thing we need is one more reason for the boys to stare at us."

"I don't mind," Krezi said.

"You're fifteen," Aubrey said.

"We don't all get to have our boyfriends on the team," Krezi shot back.

Tabitha laughed. "Jack and Aubrey are just friends. Isn't that what you told the drill sergeant back in training, Aubrey?"

"I've seen Rich looking at you, Krezi," Aubrey said, dodging the question.

"I've seen Rich looking at all of us," Krezi said. "He's a fifteen-year-old boy."

Aubrey finished buttoning her jacket and moved to the mirror to pin up her hair. Her eyes were better now that she'd slept.

"Jack isn't Aubrey's boyfriend," Josi said. "He's her puppy dog."

Aubrey turned and stuck out her tongue. "You're just jealous."

"I think we're all jealous," Tabitha said.

A moment later Josi joined Aubrey at the mirror. "I wish we could wear our hair down more often."

"I'm sure we will," Aubrey said. "We're spies, remember?"

"We're special ops," Josi corrected. "And if you want my guess, we won't be doing any spying for a while."

"Why do you say that?"

"Because the Russians are on the move. I'm sure that's what our meeting is about."

"Great."

"How do you know?" Krezi asked.

"I spent a lot of time in the library during basic training. I read Sun Tzu, Carl von Clausewitz, Jomini. All of the great classics. And every one of them says that if you want to win a war, you attack when the enemy is least ready. We're getting more ready every day—more of our soldiers are arriving, and from here we just have to get them on the train through Snowqualmie Pass, and they'll cross the mountain in a matter of hours. Who knows how many people we've already amassed on the front. But we're still not ready—not as ready as they are. According to every strategist I've read, the best plan is to attack now and don't give us time to get more troops dug in."

Aubrey grinned at Josi in the mirror. "And I thought you were just a pretty face."

Captain Gillett and the six other Green Berets were already in the tent when the girls arrived. Rich and Jack hadn't gotten there yet.

"I hear congratulations are in order," VanderHorst said as they took their seats. He was looking at Aubrey, and she felt instantly uncomfortable.

"Nick deserves all the credit," Aubrey said quietly, looking down at the table.

"That's not what I mean," VanderHorst said.

Gillett put his hand on Aubrey's shoulder. "What he means is that you're going to get a Purple Heart."

That stunned her. "Seriously? I'm walking around. I'm fine."

Rich and Jack entered the tent. Jack was smiling—he must have been listening.

"I read the medic's report this morning," Gillett said. "You took shrapnel from a Russian grenade."

"I only needed eight stitches." The last thing Aubrey wanted was an award for her own stupidity. For disobeying orders and getting a dozen men killed—even if they were the enemy.

"Eight stitches still qualifies," VanderHorst said. "You were injured in combat by an enemy weapon. Welcome to the club." He rolled up his sleeve and showed a jagged scar on his forearm. Then he began to clap and the rest of the room joined in.

Sergeant Lytle spoke up. "I hear you're not too bad with a gun either."

Aubrey looked down and shook her head.

The applause quieted, and Gillett took his place at the head of the table.

"I wish we had more time to debrief last night's mission. There are things that we need to talk about, but first I want to make you aware of a new situation that's arisen."

He unfolded a map on the table.

"We're here, just north of Yakima. The Russians are on the other side of the Cascade mountain range. That's good, because there aren't a lot of ways to cross the mountains, and under normal circumstances we would be able to pin them in the mountain passes and stop their advance."

"But," Rich said, "they have the device."

Gillett nodded. "This morning, an armored division tried to move into defensive positions around the mouth of Snowqualmie Pass and got stopped in its tracks—literally, I guess. Our satellite intel suggests that the Russians will be both moving through the pass and making use of the railroad."

"Isn't that the same thing?" Rich asked.

"No," Gillett said, and pointed again. "The railroad takes a slightly different course through the mountains."

"Can't we bomb the railroad?" Jack asked.

"If we could keep anything in the air long enough," Gillett said, frustration in his voice. "We should be able to bomb the pass, too. Our analysts expect the Russians to move fast. They want to take all of Washington, and they want to do it before we are able to get enough troops here to defend it."

"How far away are reinforcements?" Rich asked.

"We don't have that kind of information. We need to focus on our job, and right now our job is to find that damn device and destroy it."

"Captain," Chase-Dunn said. "If the Russians haven't

made it through the pass yet, then how did the device get up to stop our armor? Is it moving separately?"

"We don't know," Gillett answered. "At this point, we have no idea what this device looks like or how it's being moved or activated. Some have suggested that it's a satellite, or a high-altitude plane. Some have suggested that it's small and being moved in a civilian truck. Some have even suggested that it's a lambda."

"That would be one scary lambda," Chase-Dunn said.

"And that's why the lambda theory keeps getting shot down," Gillett said. "We've never encountered anyone with powers even remotely on the scale of this thing."

"So what are we supposed to do?" Aubrey asked.

"We're going to the front lines—for real this time," Gillett answered. "We're officially the recon team looking for the device."

He looked at the six lambdas. "You can all perform without power. And we can all fire our rifles without power. We're going to stop them."

TWENTY-ONE

ZASHA STOOD OVER FYODOR'S BED, watching him twitch and writhe under the effect of the drugs. They were in a farmhouse just off of I-90, in the town of Cle Elum, at the far east end of the pass through the mountains. She'd been told the name of the pass but it was some American Indian word she couldn't pronounce.

Two companies of armor and an artillery company were in the town now. All of them were immobilized by Fyodor, but he was positioned as the barrier blocking the American advance. Behind them, in the pass, hundreds more Russian vehicles were approaching. They were being covered by Russian fighter aircraft—Zasha couldn't be everywhere at once.

"We need to break through here—and soon," General Feklisov was saying in the other room. "Our northern and southern spearheads are struggling to cross the mountains.

If we can't do it with Zasha and Fyodor, then no one can do it."

Zasha sat down in the large overstuffed chair in the corner. This house seemed very American to her—the bedroom was a child's and it was decorated with posters of basketball players. It wasn't a sport she'd ever seen played, but she recognized the distinctive ball. There hadn't been much time for sports in her training camp, other than the occasional game of football— what did Americans call it? She couldn't remember.

This child seemed to have a lot of toys. More than one child should need. He certainly didn't have enough books. Those had been her childhood entertainments, and the piti- fully small shelf above this boy's bed made her disgusted with him. Or with his parents. They were probably the ones to blame for a boy who cared more for toys and basketball than for books. She looked at Fyodor's twisted, emaciated body. He loved to read, even more than she did.

Doctor Safin entered the room, and Zasha stood.

"He's been on the drugs too long," she said.

Doctor Safin nodded. "Yes. But it will have to be a little bit longer."

The doctor took Fyodor's pulse, and then his blood pres- sure. He checked his temperature and his pupils. All the things he normally did. Zasha wondered if there would ever be a time when Fyodor's health would override the general's demands. She doubted it.

And why should it? Fyodor's powers were immense. If he

wasn't utilized for his powers, then what good was he to the country? He was just an invalid boy.

No, he was a friend. A powerful tool, but a friend. She wished that he were awake so he could speak.

"When do we move out?" she asked the doctor. She rarely spoke with the generals directly—she worked with Doctor Safin. "And are we bringing in the glider?"

"Are you feeling overworked?" the doctor asked, looking up at her.

"The generals are talking about a full ground attack, aren't they? We ought to have the glider ready."

"If you're positioned well you won't need to move about too much," he said.

"When are we moving out?" she asked again.

"There is already American armor at the edge of Fyodor's bubble," he said. "Quite a bit. And more is coming. We'll wait until more of our artillery has been brought into position."

She knew what her role would be then: get thirteen kilometers behind enemy lines, so that the front of Fyodor's bubble extended to the front of the American lines. Then, just as they had done with the Navy, the Russian guns would open up on a sea of powerless targets.

"We're going to give you the drug," Doctor Safin said, and Zasha winced at the words.

"I know you don't like it," he said, "but the battle will be long."

"That's why we need the glider."

"You know you're better than the glider," he said. "And the glider can only be used at night."

"How long will Fyodor be active?"

"No longer than he's been active in the past."

She stood and walked to the window. A platoon of infantry was there, preparing surface-to-air defenses. When Zasha moved forward, they'd be vulnerable to any plane that didn't fly through Fyodor's bubble.

"When do we move?" she asked, checking her antique watch.

"Tonight."

TWENTY-TWO

AUBREY WAS DRESSED IN HER full ACU, including helmet and heavy Kevlar vest. She was carrying her M16 and a full complement of ammunition, grenades, and equipment.

Everyone in the passenger compartment of the armored personnel carrier—a Bradley—was also in uniform: Jack, Tabitha, Sharps, Chase-Dunn, and Lytle. The rest of the group was in another Bradley following out on the battlefield, though they couldn't tell where without windows. It felt claustrophobic in the tiny compartment, three on each side, their knees touching. There were no windows; light came from the open turret, and even that was minimal. It was five o'clock, and that was late enough this time of year to turn the sky a dull gray.

"When is Thanksgiving?" she asked as the Bradley rumbled forward.

"Five days," Jack said.

"You've been counting down?"

"Gotta keep sight of something," Jack said.

"I don't think we're going to be home for turkey dinner," Tabitha said.

"Probably won't be home for Christmas either," Lytle said.

Aubrey adjusted her glasses. The movement of the vehicle kept making them slip down her nose. "You think this war is going to last through Christmas?"

"You know as much about this war as I do," Lytle said. "But I do know this: I've never been in a short war."

"If we can stop them here, won't that be a big deal?" Aubrey asked. "If we can keep them west of the Cascades?"

Nick answered. "There are three main ways they can get out of the Cascades—up by Vancouver, down by Portland, or right here."

"Or can't they just go straight down the West Coast?" Tabitha asked.

"They could," Nick said.

"If they wanted to do that, wouldn't they have landed farther south?" Aubrey asked.

"That question's above my pay grade," Nick said. "For all we know, they have landed or will land to the south."

Lytle grunted approval. "That's one thing you have to get used to. In a war, you only know what your unit is supposed to do. You don't worry about what everyone else is doing."

Nick and Chase-Dunn nodded.

Rumbling started. It sounded like distant thunder, but within moments it began to roar all around them.

Aubrey tensed, and she wished she could hold Jack's hand. Instead she gripped her rifle.

"Is that ours or theirs?" Tabitha asked nervously.

"Ours," Jack answered. "It's coming from behind us. I can hear planes, too."

Lytle looked at the ceiling of the tight compartment as though he could see the stars. "Let's hope to hell they stay up in the sky."

The commander standing in the turret climbed down and closed the hatch, leaving them with the few lights glowing inside the Bradley.

The worst part of this mission was that they didn't know what they were looking for. They were part of the offensive—part of the overall attack on the mouth of Snowqualmie Pass to stop the Russians from breaking through their lines to the geographic freedom of the east—but Aubrey didn't know what she was going to be doing. This wasn't like the infiltration at the roadblock, where Aubrey would be listening to Tabitha and reporting to Jack, and they knew they had to create a distraction and sneak up on the vehicles. This wasn't organized at all. There was no real plan.

She noticed she was shaking, and not from the movement of the vehicle. She clutched her rifle tightly again, feeling the trembling moving up her forearm.

The roar of the artillery was louder, and getting louder still. Aubrey was certain they had to be close to the battle.

"How are we supposed to find the device?" Tabitha asked, a note of panic in her voice.

"We've already talked about that. We don't know," Nick said, his voice more calm than his words would suggest. "We're going to find it because we have to find it. We're moving toward the center of their lines, which is where we expect them to move the device when the battle gets in full swing."

"We think it's like a spray bottle, radiating out in a cone," Lytle said. "So, if it's at the front of their lines they can still use it, but it stops us cold."

Tabitha's voice appeared in Aubrey's mind. She sounded frightened. "This is suicide. We don't even have a plan."

Aubrey looked at Tabitha, but she had her eyes closed. It looked like she was grimacing against every loud rumble of artillery fire.

"If they disable us, they'll disable themselves, too, right?" Aubrey said. "Will this turn into an infantry fight?"

"In the dark with no night vision," Tabitha said out loud.

"We don't know what to expect," Nick said. "So far our artillery is firing, which means they must have targets and we're not disabled yet."

Just as he finished the sentence, all the lights in the Bradley went out, and it came to a sudden stop.

Lytle swore.

"What do we do now?" Tabitha asked, plainly terrified.

There was silence. Complete silence.

The commander climbed up and opened the hatch on the turret. A little light trickled in, but they were still mostly in darkness.

"Everything's out," the commander called down to his crew.

"What do we do?" Tabitha asked again.

Aubrey watched the commander, who was scanning the horizon with binoculars.

"Hold tight, darlin'," Lytle said.

"Don't call me that," Tabitha snapped, but it was obvious her concerns had nothing to do with the word *darlin'*.

"Nothing's moving," the commander relayed down to them. "It's like the whole world just turned off."

The gunner called out, "Chain gun's down."

"Get up here on the machine gun."

"This isn't good," Tabitha said telepathically to Aubrey. "We're sitting ducks."

Aubrey searched the darkness for Nick's face, but she couldn't see well enough to make out an expression.

"I'm seventeen years old," Tabitha continued. "I shouldn't be here. Not like this. Not in the middle of a war."

Aubrey wanted to say that Tabitha was a private—that she'd been through the same shortened basic training just like

Aubrey—but the words were frozen in her mouth. It wasn't even Tabitha's telepathic thoughts that prevented Aubrey from talking. It was her own fear.

She wanted to disappear, but there was nowhere to go.

"Shit," the commander yelled. "Get down! Close the hatch! Incoming!"

There was a long moment of deadly silence, of intense quiet that was so heavy it squeezed all the air out of Aubrey's chest.

And then the world exploded.

The Bradley rocked as artillery shells seemed to detonate right on top of them.

Tabitha screamed, and Jack grabbed Aubrey's arm. She fumbled with his hand until their fingers were laced together. It was completely, utterly black inside the vehicle, but it felt as if they were in an earthquake.

"What do we do?" Aubrey shouted, but her cries were covered up by the noise. She doubted even Jack could hear her.

There was nothing they could do, and she knew it. They were under heavy artillery fire. If they went outside they'd be torn to shreds by shrapnel. Already she could hear flecks of metal scraping the sides of the vehicle, and the thought seemed to make her leg flare with pain.

"No one's answering me," Tabitha said in Aubrey's mind, her telepathic voice cutting through the deafening noise. "What are we supposed to do? We're going to die!"

Aubrey let go of Jack's hand and reached across him to where Tabitha sat. She grabbed at Tabitha's jacket and then their hands met. They clutched each other for a moment, fingertips to fingertips, until an enormous explosion seemed to lift the Bradley a few feet and drop it again. Their hands were torn apart.

"We're going to die," Tabitha repeated. "We're going to die."

Aubrey wished she could get Tabitha out of her head, but there was nothing she could do.

"They're going to keep firing. Nothing can stop them. We can't get out of here."

"Calm down," Aubrey shouted, her voice smothered by the noise of the artillery.

Aubrey reached for Jack's hand again, and found he was covering his ears. She grabbed his leg instead.

She didn't want yesterday to be the last thing she did with her life—the killing of nine men. She had resolved to be so much more, to make her life more meaningful. To be a better soldier, a better person.

She couldn't die here.

And then the darkness turned into bright yellow light, and the noise was so loud that it didn't even seem like noise—it felt like weight, like heat, like death.

TWENTY-THREE

JACK'S WORLD EXPLODED IN PAIN as all his senses overloaded in an instant—too bright, too loud, too pungent, too bitter. Too everything.

For a moment he couldn't hear, couldn't think. He saw the fire in the front of the compartment. Aubrey was on her feet, the closest to the flames and desperate to get out.

Lytle was next to the back hatch. He should have been opening it. But he wasn't moving. By the light of the blaze Jack saw slick wetness running down the front of Lytle's unmoving body.

Tabitha jumped up, pounding on the door, panicking, no idea how to get it open.

Nick was dazed, unable to stand because Aubrey was in front of him, filling up the tiny aisle space. Chase-Dunn stood and shoved Tabitha back into her seat, and then began yanking on the handle to open the hatch. Something was stuck.

Jack's hearing came back all at once, and for a moment the world seemed to be moving in double time to catch up with what he had missed.

"Come on, Nick," Aubrey was shouting, yanking at the Green Beret's vest straps. "Get up. We have to get out."

"It's not opening!" Tabitha cried.

Jack glanced back at the fire and saw the slumped, lifeless body of the Bradley commander. The gunner was nowhere to be seen.

Then Jack noticed he could see outside—through a split of twisted metal in the turret.

"Open, damn it," Chase-Dunn bellowed.

"We're going to die." Tabitha was standing, her back pressed against the damaged wall. "We're going to burn in here."

"We're not going to die," Jack said, and climbed over Aubrey's seat toward the turret.

The heat was tremendous, and he wondered if he had started to blister. He stepped over the fallen commander— what was left of him—and climbed up the ladder to where the top hatch was blown wide open.

"This way," Jack shouted, his hands stinging on the hot metal.

No one heard him and he jumped back down and grabbed Aubrey. "We can get out through the turret!"

Nick nodded in groggy agreement, and Aubrey turned to reach for Chase-Dunn. "The turret," she yelled. "Hurry."

Jack turned back around and darted up the ladder, fighting to ignore the bloody mess around him and the pain in his fingers. When he reached the top he pushed what was remaining of the hatch out of the way.

Outside was a nightmare of flames and explosions. He stopped on top of the Bradley, looking down into the turret as Aubrey climbed out and quickly jumped to the ground. The front of the vehicle was a gaping hole spitting fire and sparks.

After Aubrey came Nick. He was tottering on the ladder, moving in shaky, uncertain motions. Jack grabbed him by the forearm and pulled him out. Tabitha came next, darting as fast as her feet would carry her, and jumping off the Bradley as soon as she could.

There was a long pause before Chase-Dunn appeared at the bottom of the ladder, and Jack could only assume he was taking a final check of the other soldiers. Finally, after Jack was sure he was starting to roast in his Kevlar suit, Chase-Dunn jumped onto the ladder and scrambled up. He waved Jack's outstretched hand away.

"Get on the ground," he said, pain on his face. "Everyone needs to get down."

Jack checked his gear and then jumped over the edge of the Bradley, hitting the hard earth and stumbling forward. A moment later, Nick landed behind him, and then Chase-Dunn followed.

There was a sudden screech across the sky and a firework show of explosions lit up the Russian lines. Jack recognized the shapes he had memorized during training. Four F-22 Raptors—stealth fighters—had just dropped bombs on the Russians, seemingly unaffected by the power outage.

Instantly, the artillery bombardment from the Russians slowed.

Chase-Dunn grabbed Jack and pulled him to the rear of the vehicle where the team was gathered.

"What's everyone's status?" Nick asked, breathing heavily.

"I'm okay," Aubrey said.

"Me too," Jack answered.

"Freaking out," Tabitha said, but tried to keep a calm face on.

"Lytle's gone," Chase-Dunn said. "Shrapnel to the neck. I'm good. How about you?"

"Hit my head," Nick said, "but I'll be okay. Do we know the status of the other guys?"

Jack turned and leaned out from behind the Bradley, searching the devastation for the second half of their ODA. There were burning vehicles everywhere, providing the only light on a motionless, powerless field.

Up ahead was the other Bradley—maybe three hundred yards in front of them. It was stopped, but didn't appear to be damaged.

"It's okay," Jack said. "I think. It's not on fire."

The American planes appeared again, flying in a line parallel to the Russian battle lines. Jack saw a rocket fly up and miss one of the fighters, and then they each dropped another bomb.

"Wherever the device is," Jack said, returning to the relative safety of the back of the Bradley, "it's not over there. The Russians are able to fire their artillery, and their tanks are firing on ours. And our planes are making it through."

"How can the planes make it through?" Nick asked.

"They're not flying over us. I think that's the key—they're not flying above the device, so the device isn't affecting them."

"So it's over here somewhere?" Chase-Dunn asked, his face full of fury for his dead brother-in-arms.

"It's got to be," Jack said. "That's how it's stopping all of us."

"Well, let's go find that son of a bitch."

Nick nodded sluggishly, obviously more injured than he was saying. "Everybody, rifles up. Follow Chase-Dunn. I'll take the rear. Let's get the rest of our team."

"We're going out there?" Tabitha said incredulously.

"It's no safer here," Chase-Dunn said, and then turned

and began jogging across the churned earth. "Let's go free our compadres from their coffin."

Aubrey shared a look with Jack and then followed. Jack ran after her, and listened to the frightened protests as Tabitha came behind. Nick's footfalls were irregular, like he wasn't running in a straight line, but Jack focused on Aubrey in front of him and tried to keep up. She didn't run like someone who had eight stitches in her leg. She didn't run like she was carrying almost a hundred pounds of gear and body armor.

An explosion rocked the ground beneath them and Jack stumbled, nearly falling on his face. Clods of dirt landed all around, and Jack turned back quickly to make sure everyone was still standing. Nick was steadying himself, but Tabitha was right behind Jack, running like the devil himself was chasing her.

There was a scream of engines—much louder this time— and two more planes came strafing the enemy. These were Warthogs, one of the most heavily armed attack aircraft in the air force. They dropped their payload, blasting with rockets and cannon while surface-to-air missiles flew up all around them. None of the Russians' defensive missiles hit their mark, and the Warthogs disappeared over hills to the north.

Jack was out of breath by the time they reached the second Bradley. Chase-Dunn pounded on the back hatch with his fist, but Jack was sure the people inside wouldn't be able to hear it above all the other noise.

"Tabitha," Nick said, catching up. "Tell them to open up. And get out of the way—that door is going to hit you when it opens." Jack noted a slight slur in his speech. Did he have a concussion?

Tabitha stared at the door for a long moment, and then the small hatch on the back cracked open, revealing Captain Gillett.

"We got hit, sir," Nick said, trying to straighten up. "We lost the crew and Sergeant Lytle."

There was a roar of engines again, and Jack watched the Warthogs coming back for another pass. Their cannons lit up for a moment and then went dark. Instead of flying over the enemy, the two planes drifted, powerless, and then crashed into the enemy lines.

"The device moved," Jack said urgently, turning to Nick and then to the captain. "Those planes just went down and they were flying in the same track both times."

"What are you talking about?" the captain asked, stepping through the hatch and outside.

"Two Warthogs," Jack said. "They flew north and were fine, but when they tried to fly south along the same course they were knocked out of the sky. The device is moving."

"You're sure it wasn't just anti-aircraft fire?"

"I watched the whole thing, sir."

The captain turned back to the hatch. "Come on, guys. Let's hoof it." He looked at Jack. "It's moving west?"

Jack nodded. "Yes, sir."

"Then we head west," the captain said.

"Toward the enemy?" Tabitha asked.

"Going the other way is called retreating," he said as the rest of the team climbed out of the Bradley.

The artillery was falling sporadically now, and Jack could hear the gunshots slowing—or maybe there were fewer guns.

"Best guess for how they're moving it?" Gillett asked, taking out binoculars and scanning the enemy lines.

"Could be someone invisible," Aubrey said.

"It's moving fast," Jack responded. "Or it did move fast last night when we were at the roadblock." He remembered watching the headlights wink out as the device neared them. "It had to be going at least twenty or thirty miles an hour. Maybe more."

"Someone on a motorcycle?" VanderHorst guessed.

"Motorcycles would be turned off like everything else," Nick answered. "Bikes?"

Gillett nodded. "Keep your eyes and ears open. Watch for anything unusual." He adjusted the straps on his vest. "Let's move, people."

The group hurried away from the Bradley in a loose line, like they'd been taught in basic training.

Jack stared at the enemy's front—it was far in the distance, maybe two or three miles away, but he could see the Russian tanks as plain as day. There was infantry fighting—grenades exploding and the muzzle flashes from a hundred rifles—but none of the tanks was engaging.

"They've disabled their own stuff," Jack said, running to catch up with Gillett, who was leading the group. "Probably to stop the planes from hitting them."

Jack looked out again. There were still Russian vehicles moving, but they were in the rear ranks—several more miles back. In the distance, flying over what had to be Snowqualmie Pass, were Russian fighters.

"They don't want their own planes to get too close to the front—don't want them to get caught up in the . . . what do we call it, the blast arc of the device?"

Gillett stopped and turned to face Jack. "How far back before you see anything electric?"

Jack pivoted and stared toward the far eastern side of their lines. He could see a farmhouse with lights on. A streetlight.

"I'm not great at judging distances," Jack said.

"You called it a blast arc, right?" Gillett said.

"Assuming it is an arc," Jack said with a nod.

"Then we need to get to the starting point," he said. "Look at the front lines and then look for the farthest distance that the power is out. Think of that like the tip of a spray bottle. Everything is arcing out from there."

Jack turned and gazed at the Russian line. There were

rows of tanks—not exactly rows, but staggered groups. Some of them were firing and some were not.

"That's where it will be," Gillett murmured as he looked through the binoculars.

"You want us to go up there?" Jack said, trying to shove away his fear. "Behind enemy lines."

"We've got to find the device."

He turned his gaze back toward the Russian front.

"I think their infantry is advancing," Jack said. "They don't need power."

Captain Gillett nodded. "Then our boys'll be advancing, too. And we need to cross through the line if we're going to get behind it. Let's get up there."

TWENTY-FOUR

AUBREY RAN IN FORMATION ALONG with the ODA. Captain Gillett was in the lead, followed closely by Jack. Chase-Dunn and Nick were bringing up the rear. Aubrey didn't think Nick should be running. Aubrey had seen football players try to run with concussions, and that was what Nick looked like.

She couldn't believe Lytle was dead—couldn't believe what she had seen, what she had stepped over in her scramble to escape the Bradley. She was glad Josi hadn't been in that Bradley—she'd never get the pictures out of her head.

It was pitch-dark, with the exception of burning vehicles. If there was one good thing, it was that the majority of the vehicles—Bradleys and Abramses and Strykers—seemed to have avoided the artillery. Most were simply disabled by the device. Soldiers were piling out and awaiting the incoming infantry assault. Aubrey saw one man look at their team quiz-zically, probably wondering why they were running toward the enemy.

"This is the dumbest thing we've done tonight," Tabitha said in Aubrey's head. "We need to get the hell away from this battle, not try to get in the middle of it."

Tabitha was twenty paces ahead of her, too far for Aubrey to respond.

"Did you see the bodies?" Tabitha asked. "Did you see Sergeant Lytle's neck? He was right in front of me. It could have been any one of us. If that artillery shell had landed six feet back, we'd all be dead."

"Get out of my head," Aubrey said, but she was sure Tabitha couldn't hear her breathless words.

"Not every lambda is fighting in this war," Tabitha said. "They let a lot of them go home—the ones with weak pow-ers. And they didn't force everyone to fight. I bet if we'd said no back when all of this started that we'd be home right now. I'm from Oklahoma, for God's sake. I shouldn't be here."

They hadn't let anyone go home that Aubrey had seen. She didn't know if that was good or bad, but that's what she'd seen. A life as a prisoner in a quarantine camp, or a life in the army.

"Jack, if you can hear me, Tabitha won't shut up."

And then Aubrey laughed—a tired, exhausted laugh.

"Maybe you say the same thing about me," Aubrey said.

"'Aubrey won't shut up. She talks to me all the time and complains and I can't get her to shut up.'"

Tabitha's voice sounded in Aubrey's head again. "I keep thinking about the rebellion," she said. "The lambda rebels aren't like the terrorists. They're not fighting the good guys. They're just trying to stand up for the rights of kids who don't want to be used as weapons."

"I know," Aubrey said. "For the last time: we all know."

Tabitha seemed to love talking about the rebellion. Aubrey wondered where she was getting her information, because they'd all been essentially out of communication with the outside world since they'd started basic training.

Up ahead, Aubrey could see Gillett talking with Jack, and they changed direction—just slightly. There were hundreds of soldiers ahead of them, from both nations.

She felt a gust of wind fly past her face. And then another.

"Get down!" Nick yelled.

She stood for a moment, frozen like a deer in headlights. Another gust of wind.

Not wind. Bullets.

She dropped to her knees and raised her rifle. She couldn't see any targets.

Their entire group was on the ground now.

"Jack," Aubrey said. "I'm going to go invisible, but I'll be right here."

They hadn't practiced combat maneuvers with the Green

Berets, but this was what she'd always done in lambda training—what she'd been taught to do by her drill instructors. She disappeared and went prone. One of her lenses had cracked when the Bradley was hit, but fortunately, the cracked lens was her left eye, not the one she used for looking in her scope.

Bullets began to hit the ground around them. Aubrey strained to find a target, but all she could see were outlines—silhouettes against the fires of burning vehicles. She couldn't tell whether they were looking at her or away, and she didn't dare fire.

"We have to keep going," Gillett yelled back. "The device is on the move."

Nick and Chase-Dunn got up and began moving in a crouch, their rifles pointed toward the enemy. Aubrey did the same, staying invisible.

Krezi was next in line, and she was still lying down. Aubrey grabbed her by the vest, pulling her up.

"What the hell?"

Aubrey reappeared just long enough for Krezi to see her. "The enemy's over there," she said, and faded out again.

Even though she was invisible, she kept her head down. Anyone more than one hundred forty yards away could still see her.

A thought occurred to her. She stopped where she was, staring downrange, and then took off running toward Gillett.

She reached him just as he and Jack were stopping at the bottom of a crater. Jack was looking around, trying to spot the device.

Aubrey appeared.

"What are you doing up here?" Gillett said.

Aubrey was out of breath. "It's a bubble," she wheezed.

"What?"

"My invisibility. They measured it at training camp. It's a bubble that radiates from me—forward and back and up and down. I'm the center of a bubble."

"So what?" he asked, watching as Jack searched.

"So what if it *is* a lambda? What if it's some lambda's brain, and it's sending out signals in a perfect sphere, shutting everything down."

"That'd be one hell of a lambda," the captain said skeptically.

Aubrey could hear bullets flying over their heads. Outside of the crater the rest of their team was under fire.

"Okay," Gillett said, peering up and over the edge. "If it's a lambda, and there's a bubble around that lambda, what does that mean?"

"It means it's behind our lines," Aubrey said. "It's behind us, not in front of us. Jack, look up front to where the power starts, and then look back to where the power starts, and right in the middle of that is where we'll find the lambda."

Jack climbed up the side of the crater and looked forward,

then back. He stared for a long time, and Aubrey wished he'd get his head down—infantry was fighting only a hundred yards away.

"If she's right," Jack said, "then the lambda is miles behind us. I'd guess this bubble—if it is a bubble—is close to twenty miles wide."

"Is it still moving west?" Gillett asked.

Aubrey could hear the Green Berets—and maybe Josi and Tabitha, too—firing.

"It's stopped for the moment."

Gillett looked through his binoculars again. "So it's a question of moving forward or moving backward."

"If we go backward," Jack said, "it'll be miles to the center of the bubble. But we have to get back there to find the lambda." There was a rumble across the sky, and Aubrey looked up. She didn't see the planes, but brilliant explosions rocked the Russian lines.

She sighted her rifle on the nearing Russian infantry, looking down the scope and trying to identify uniforms. There was an outline that was clearly someone carrying a Russian AK-74 rifle. She lined up the crosshairs—and then saw him fall from someone else's bullet.

"I can't tell who's on our side," she said.

"Wait," Jack said, but when she looked he was talking to the captain. "The bubble or the arc or whatever it is just moved farther back toward the Russians. Maybe two or three hundred yards. No, closer to five hundred."

"It's protecting their lines from bombs," Gillett said.

"It's stopped all their artillery," Jack said. "And most of their tanks. They're all quiet."

"It moved fast."

"Really fast," Jack agreed. "And I didn't see anything move up there—no vehicles."

"So you think it's the bubble."

"I just think it moved really fast."

The infantry assault was pushing the Americans back— the Russians were getting closer every minute.

Images from last night flashed in Aubrey's mind. Her insubordination. Her pledge to be a better soldier—a pledge that she made to no one but herself, but a pledge that she intended to keep.

"Permission to engage the enemy?" she asked.

"Of course," Gillett said.

Aubrey disappeared, and ran up the side of the crater and over the top. She jogged forward. She was determined to make up for her poor choices yesterday.

Aubrey dropped to a knee, alone in a stretch of farmland. Ahead of her, American soldiers were pinned down, fighting a losing battle against a stronger force.

She lifted her gun to her shoulder and sighted a Russian. They were easier for her to identify now—they were close, and there were so many of them.

She let out a breath and squeezed the trigger, firing a burst of three rounds, dropping him. She flicked the selector switch to semiautomatic, and sighted another soldier. She let out a breath and squeezed.

TWENTY-FIVE

"WHERE DID SHE GO?" GILLETT asked, but Jack could only shake his head. She wasn't close enough that he could smell or hear her.

Jack raised his own rifle, hoping he wouldn't hit her in the back.

Beside him, Gillett began to fire, too.

There was a flash of light as Krezi blasted a burst of energy. It hit the ground in front of a soldier and he fell back.

The American soldiers ahead of them seemed to be doing a little better.

The two American fighters—Super Hornets—screamed out of the night sky again and strafed the enemy. Jack lowered his gun and watched, and a moment later he saw it—more Russian vehicles went dark and powerless.

"It moved again," Jack said. "The planes are forcing it to. It goes really fast."

Ahead of him, the battle was raging, and the Americans began to push the Russians back. Lying in the crater and watching the fight, Jack felt almost like he was in the nineteenth century. No tanks were moving. No artillery fell on them. No planes were in the sky. It was just rifle versus rifle. Granted, they were automatic rifles and everyone was wearing body armor and helmets, but this was a different kind of war, somehow more primal, more ancient.

"Let's try to find that lambda," Captain Gillett said. "You think you can locate the center of the bubble?"

"I can try," Jack said. "But it might move."

"That's why we should go now." He turned and yelled down the line. "Everyone get ready to move on me. Aubrey, that means you, too."

There was a long pause. Jack wondered if Aubrey had tried to do something heroic—tried to get over into the enemy lines and win this fight single-handedly. Jack had known her long enough to know that last night had to be affecting her, and affecting her hard. Aubrey was still dealing with the guilt of a home life based on lies.

Would something like this push her over the edge?

And then she was back in the crater with them, loading a new magazine into her M16 and breathing heavily.

"We're heading out," Gillett said.

"Okay," she said, her face flushed.

Gillett checked his own gun, and then clapped Jack's arm. "We're following you."

Jack took a breath and then nodded. This was so much guesswork. He could really only see lights in the distance in both directions. In every direction. And he was somehow supposed to find the center of a circle of darkness?

At the very least he knew he had to head east.

He scrambled up and out of the crater, jogging at a decent pace. He worried he was going too fast for Aubrey—she'd just been invisible and that made her tired. But he forced himself not to think about that. That was for the captain to deal with. Jack just needed to find the lambda.

As he ran he dodged around more craters, around lifeless tanks with bewildered crews, around infantry squads who didn't know where they were supposed to be or what they should be doing. He crossed dirt roads and fields. It was cold, but he was sweating gallons under his gear.

He listened to Aubrey run, listened to her breathing. She was panting for air, but so was he.

Jack refocused on the area in front of him. There were miles to go before they would get to the center of the circle, and that was if he could find it. This was why they'd been forced to run so much in basic training with all their gear. Somehow it seemed easier here—probably because real bullets were flying.

He took a moment to listen to Rich, and then to Krezi. They were pushing hard. Harder than anyone should have expected of them. Even so, Jack kept running. He would let Gillett decide when it was time to break.

"Jack, I need to talk to you," Aubrey said, her words coming out in short, strained breaths.

He waited for her to say more. The muscles in his calves, thighs, and back all stung. It felt like he was carrying another person on his shoulders.

"Not now," she gasped. "Later."

And then Jack stopped, coming to almost a dead halt and staring up in the sky.

A figure—a girl—flew up from a stand of trees. Jack had seen flying lambdas before, but not like this. Below her, in some kind of harness, she carried a second person—a small, thin boy.

Before Jack could even point to her, she was launching forward—westward, toward the Russian lines. He followed her path as she rocketed away.

"What is it?" Gillett said, stopping beside him. He was sucking in gulps of air.

"Did you see her?" Jack asked.

"See who?"

Jack looked down at his watch. It was ticking again.

TWENTY-SIX

TABITHA LEANED AGAINST A WOODEN fence, her gun slung across her chest.

Captain Gillett was on the radio calling in for a helicopter to pull them out.

"Finally," Tabitha said telepathically to Krezi.

Krezi looked back at her and rolled her eyes.

"I hurt everywhere," Tabitha said. "I swear, there are going to be blisters on my blisters."

Krezi nodded and leaned against the fence, too. She wasn't carrying a gun, and she folded her arms across her chest.

"You should have seen it," Tabitha said. "The inside of our Bradley, I mean. It was horrible. Sergeant Lytle was sitting right across from me and he got hit with a piece of shrapnel. It was long and jagged. It looked like a dagger, and it was just there in his neck. It was like he never had a chance, you know?"

Krezi didn't meet her eyes. She stared into the middle distance.

"It could have been me," Tabitha said. "It could have been any one of us. Just luck. Luck of the draw. One second you're alive, and the next second you're dead, right through the jugular. This was Sergeant Lytle, you know? I mean, it's not like we were friends, but we knew him, right? He called me *darlin'*. I think that's probably against some rule, like it's sexual harassment or not politically correct or something, but I liked it, and now he's dead, somewhere back there.

"And it's not like he's the only one. The whole crew of our Bradley was blown to bits. Gone. I can't even tell you what it was like. We had to step over one of them to get out. And one of them was so . . . I don't know. It was like he wasn't even there anymore, like there was no part of him that I could see. I don't know how it happened."

Krezi knelt in the cold grass. The captain was off the radio. A helicopter was coming.

"No, I do know how it happened," Tabitha continued. "We were hit by a goddamned artillery shell. Right in the nose. I'm amazed any of us survived. I couldn't hear a thing for five minutes, my head was ringing so much. And there was nothing any of us could do. Nothing. We were just sitting in that tin can, waiting to get shot at.

"That's the worst of it. They knew that the Russians had something that could shut down every vehicle. And they have us looking for it in a Bradley? I mean, it's better than making us walk out in that hellstorm, but that was really the best thing they could think of?"

Tabitha struggled against her sore muscles and sat down. The Green Berets were still on alert, but the battle was over. She hadn't heard a shot in the last fifteen minutes.

"I don't know about you, but I didn't sign up for this so I could be target practice for the Russians. I signed up because they said if we didn't sign up we'd be stuck in the quarantine until further notice. And you know what that *until further notice* means? Probably means forever. It means that instead of assigning us to combat they were going to experiment on us and see how we worked.

"And look at you. You didn't get to finish basic training. You're not a private—you're a private lambda, which is the bottom of everything, and they have you out here fighting. They think that even without basic training they can just use you to shoot your lasers or whatever.

"Look, Krezi, I know I shouldn't be talking like this. Our country was just hit by terrorists, and now it's being invaded. But what about the constitution? What about our rights? Why are we protecting a country that would act like this?"

Tabitha paused. Maybe she'd said too much. Maybe she shouldn't be venting to Krezi.

Or maybe she hadn't said enough. Everyone had the right to know what they were facing. What the world was really like. Tabitha had tried talking to the others. Tried talking to Jack, but Tabitha could never say anything to Jack that wouldn't eventually make it back to Aubrey, and Aubrey was such a loose cannon.

"You and I have talked about the rebellion," Tabitha said, almost afraid to mention it again. She'd already brought it up once tonight only to be brushed away by Aubrey—pretending she couldn't hear. "I shouldn't even call it a rebellion. It's more like a movement. Or a protest. I heard about it at the quarantine, and then when I was assigned to my first unit we saw them—they were trying to get more lambdas to join them."

Tabitha didn't tell Krezi that the rebel lambdas had tried to free the teens from a quarantine center. Tabitha's first mission with the Green Berets had been to ferret out the rebels and stop them. They got to the quarantine center at the same time a lambda, a big guy who had grown into some kind of monster with scales and spines, was trying to tear down the fence. Tabitha's Green Berets killed him. All he was trying to do was free teenagers from unconstitutional incarceration, and they'd shot him a dozen times. Maybe more.

"I don't know where the rebels are anymore," Tabitha said nervously. "I don't know how we'd find them. But I'd rather be with them than on the front lines of World War Three. It's not like they even need me here. You know what I've done tonight? I used my amazing powers to get someone in your Bradley to open the door. That was my contribution. And you—you shot at people, but were you more effective than any private with a rifle? My point is, it's not like us leaving is going to hurt the war effort. Nothing's going to fall apart just because we're not around."

She looked into the distance, to where dozens of vehicles burned. Maybe hundreds. So much death. And so much of it pointless—their soldiers had died as sitting ducks. Lytle had just happened to be sitting in the seat where the shrapnel flew. It could have been any one of them. It could have been her.

She touched her throat—the smooth, bare skin that was exposed above her Kevlar vest. She could see the chunk of metal in her mind, see the blood pouring down her chest.

It could have been her. She was sitting right across from him.

"I don't know about you," Tabitha said, "but I'm not doing this anymore. I don't care if they lock me up for going AWOL—at least I won't be out here, on the front lines, waiting for artillery to land on me.

"You can come if you want, Krezi. I can't promise you'll be safe. But it'll be better than this. We can get home. We can see our families."

There was the steady sound of helicopter blades coming in

behind her, and Tabitha glanced over her shoulder to see the approaching Black Hawk.

She looked at Krezi, who hadn't turned to face her this whole time. Was Krezi going to report everything? Turn her in?

Gillett shouted, "Everybody, move. I don't want this bird to go powerless while we're on it."

Tabitha stood up and checked her rifle out of habit.

"You can ignore everything I just said," Tabitha told Krezi. "But I mean it. I'll take you with me. We can get out of here."

Tabitha followed VanderHorst to where the Black Hawk was coming in to land. She had to shield her face from the flying dirt it kicked up.

She felt a hand grab her sleeve, and she turned to see Krezi. Even in the dark, she could tell the girl had been crying.

Krezi's voice sounded like a whisper against the noise of the helicopter.

"Yes."

TWENTY-SEVEN

ALEC WAS NO LONGER ALEC. He was Sergeant Moore. He had tricked a man into going into the clump of bushes beside a stream, where Alec had then choked him until he no longer struggled. The guy could easily have beaten him in a fair fight, but Alec was carrying a garrote—two sticks with a wire between them. He took the man's uniform and boots, all of which were a size or two too big.

Fortunately, ACUs looked baggy on everyone, so Alec was no different. He fished in the pocket of his own pants and pulled out a black armband with the letters *MP* emblazoned on it. Military police. All the vehicles that survived were retreating from the battlefield, or heading to defensive positions, and Alec was standing at a central intersection, giving completely fake orders to all the men who were returning, directing one infantry company back north, sending tanks on a wild-goose chase down a westward road until they saw a big pink water tower—for all Alec knew, no such water tower existed.

He stayed at that intersection long enough to spread chaos, then pulled off his MP badge, stuffed it in a pocket, and followed a tired-looking infantry platoon that was heading back to base. After a few minutes he was able to bum a ride on a Bradley.

There weren't enough medals for all the things he'd done. He hadn't been properly thanked for his work at Bremerton, for setting the whole city on fire. Granted, he hadn't done the grunt work, but it was his plan, and he'd watched from across the water as his people did their jobs—giving their lives for one final victory. And what a victory it had been! It had sent the American fleet scurrying into the sea, where the Russian fleet destroyed it. Alec didn't know how they'd done it, but it had to be a lambda. Some ultrapowerful lambda. The Russian Federation wouldn't have created this wondrous gift and then not expected the blessed to use their powers to serve their nation. Of course the lambdas would serve. That was what they had to do—what they must do.

It hurt Alec's pride a little to know that there were others like him—others who were better than him in so many ways. But now he was on the ground, getting close to the Americans' base of operations. His people would see who the real hero was.

TWENTY-EIGHT

"WE HAVE TWO FLYERS AMONG our lambda group," Major Brookes said, sitting at the head of the table. "But both are male. From that lambda base out in South Dakota."

"This one was definitely a girl," Jack said. He'd seen her clearly. She'd been wearing a formfitting black combat suit. "Somewhere between eighteen and twenty."

The major had command over all of the lambda teams at the Yakima base. It had taken hours for Gillett to get a meeting with him, and Jack was exhausted. They'd been debriefing from their evening's events for a solid hour. Jack's watch was wrong—he hadn't been able to fix it since their time inside the electrical interference—but he guessed it had to be close to two in the morning.

Jack was alone with Gillett and the major. The rest of the

team had gone back to get some rest. Gillett seemed completely impervious to fatigue. He hadn't yawned once. Even the major looked miserable—eyes red and lethargic.

"I'm going to take this up the chain of command," Brookes said. "If their lambda is a flyer, then we should be able to track her down. Our radar can pick up flyers if they're not too close to land—and if we know what we're looking for."

"It makes sense," Jack said. "I've only heard rumors about the invasion and landing, but the concept of a flyer, and the concept of a bubble, all seem to fit what we know."

Brookes nodded. "I like this bubble idea." He scooped up his handful of papers and tapped them into a neat stack. "Now, I know you need sleep, but I want you to talk to one more person—our lambda doctor. Tonight was rough and I'm worried about all of the lambda teams."

Jack nodded.

"Good work," Major Brookes said, and stood. Jack and Gillett stood as well and watched as the major left the tent.

Gillett put a hand on Jack's shoulder. "You all right for another hour of debrief?"

Jack forced a smile. "I'm dead on my feet."

"One more hour," Gillett said. "I'm sure that the doc is as tired as you."

"Then that's one tired doctor," Jack said. He tried to straighten his posture. "I'll manage."

"You did good work today. Get to bed as soon as you can."

"Yes, sir."

Gillett headed out the door and Jack slumped back down into the chair. Because the enemy was so near—some sixty miles or so, Jack guessed—they were all still wearing their ACUs, including vest and helmet. He felt like he was carrying sandbags on his shoulders. Even his boots seemed to weigh fifty pounds.

And he had a headache. It was more than the usual buzz, the constant input of information that made his head ring. This was developing into a full-blown migraine. He'd almost thought he'd lost his hearing when that artillery shell had hit the Bradley, but now it seemed that all of that sound—and the sound of every explosion and gunshot since—had built up in his head, filling his brain and expanding outward to make his skull swell and ache. He felt like his ears were going to bleed, like pressure was building up behind his eyes to make them pop out of his head.

"Hey, Jack."

He turned to see Aubrey sitting beside him.

"What are you doing?" he asked.

She smiled, pushing her glasses up on her nose. She'd changed into her second pair since the first were broken. These frames were more stylish, not the simple wire ovals she usually wore, but a thicker, squarer frame, and violet instead of silver.

"I need to talk to you."

"The doctor's coming in to see me," Jack said.

"I know. You listen for him," Aubrey said. "When he comes, I'll disappear."

Jack wanted to think that Aubrey was coming to see him because they hadn't spent much time together lately, but he could see on her face that it wasn't about that. She wasn't happy. Her eyes looked just as tired and red rimmed as the major's had, and her hair was coming unpinned, drooping down under her helmet.

"What's wrong?" Jack asked. It was a silly question. Everything was wrong. They'd just been in the middle of a firefight. Just seen a member of their team killed, and seen all the crew members of the Bradley blown apart in a vicious explosion. They knew more was ahead.

She looked at the floor, and put her hands on the side of her face. He could hear her heart pounding, and smell the salty wetness of a tear.

He reached for her hands, but she didn't move to meet him, so he rested his palm on her knee. He could feel the softness of the gauze bandage beneath his hand.

"Thirty-one," she said, and looked up at him through tearstained eyes.

"Thirty-one what?"

"Kills. Thirty-one. Nine yesterday. Twenty-two today."

Jack froze.

Thirty-one kills. Aubrey Parsons. The same Aubrey Parsons who he'd played with since elementary school, who he'd gone to church with, who he . . . loved. Loved like a sister at first, and then more than a sister.

Now there was a dark emptiness in her eyes. A hardness that seemed so foreign on her gentle face.

"Say something, Jack," she pleaded. "And don't tell me I'm a soldier. I know I'm a soldier."

He took a breath. "You're a good person. You're one of the best people I know. This doesn't change that."

"I'm not, though," she said, and the tears began to flow freely. "I had to kill the nine people yesterday because I disobeyed orders."

"You don't know that Nick's plan was better than yours," Jack said. "It was just different."

"It was better," she said. "It would have put more people on the far side of that BMP, and farther away from Josi and Rich."

"You can't be sure of that."

She shook her head and wiped at her cheeks.

"It's not just that, though. It's not just yesterday. What about today?"

"You didn't break orders today," Jack said firmly. "You asked permission to fire, even though you knew we already had authorization to engage. We were being shot at."

"But," she said, and then stopped. She pulled off her glasses and wiped her eyes. Jack loved her eyes, especially now that he could see so much better. They appeared gray when you first looked at them, but they were filled with color—with greens and blues and streaks of yellow and white.

She put her glasses back on. "Do you think it matters—in war, I mean? Do you think it matters why you kill people?"

"Matters to who?" Jack asked. "To God?"

"To God. To other people. To humanity. To yourself."

"You're not a murderer," Jack said. "They were shooting back at you."

She spoke quick and sharp. "They weren't shooting at me. They couldn't even see me."

"Then they were shooting at Americans. They were shooting at your ODA. You were saving lives."

"I wasn't trying to save lives," she said, suddenly quiet.

He didn't answer, but waited. He didn't know what was going on inside her head, but he knew she had something she wanted to get out.

"I wasn't trying to save lives," she repeated. "I was trying to prove that I was a good soldier. I was trying to be everything that I wasn't yesterday. Trying to follow orders and kill as many Russians as I possibly could."

"You said it yourself," Jack said softly. "You were trying to follow orders."

She met his eyes. "But I was doing it for me. Don't you get it? I wasn't doing it to save lives or be patriotic or help the war effort. I did it so I'd feel better about myself. And you know what? I don't. I don't feel any better about myself.

I feel worse. I feel like I killed twenty-two men today all for my own gain."

He shook his head. "I don't know how else to tell you this, but you did the right thing. Everyone fires their guns for different reasons. Some fire because they're scared of dying. Some fire because they're angry. Some fire because their training kicks in and they're on autopilot. I can't read minds, but I can hear what they whisper to themselves while they're fighting. Some are praying. Some are swearing. Some are scared. But it's all just war."

"That doesn't make it okay," she said, and wiped at another tear. "Does it? Isn't that just another excuse?"

"War isn't good," Jack said. "I don't think anyone would say it's good unless they're a psychopath. Some wars are more justified than others—and I think this is a justified war. We're being invaded. They're taking our homes. But that doesn't make killing any easier, and nothing makes killing good. You're not going to find a peaceful solution on the battlefield."

"I don't like that answer, Jack," she said. "I don't feel like a soldier is supposed to feel."

"I don't think we know how a soldier is supposed to feel," Jack said. "Maybe this is it."

"But it's different for me," she said, rubbing her neck. "Because I'm not a soldier. I'm an assassin. I shoot people when they can't see me. That's how I killed those nine men yesterday. And that's how I killed so many tonight. I would have killed more, but I ran out of bullets."

Jack reached out and took her hand. It was cold and sweaty, and he clasped it between both of his.

"You were saving lives. I know you can't see it, and I know you don't like it, but you were saving lives. Every one of those men you killed is one fewer man who would be pointing a gun at me or Josi or Krezi or any other soldier."

She squeezed his hand back and nodded, close to sobbing.

"This sucks," Jack said. "War sucks. Our being here sucks. Do you know what I kept thinking the whole time that you were out there tonight, shooting? I was terrified that one of us would accidentally shoot you in the back. Or that a stray bullet would find you even though you were invisible."

"I was being careful," she said.

"Is it possible to be that careful? We're all in danger, all the time. Any one of us could be like Sergeant Lytle today."

She nodded again and reached her other hand out to his.

"I apologized to Captain Gillett," she said. "For disobeying orders yesterday. I wish he punished me, but all he said was, 'Don't do it again.' I apologized to Nick and he just told me what's done is done. I wish there was someone who I could be accountable to."

"They told you the right thing," Jack said.

"I'm going to report to you from now on, Jack. I'm trying to do things right. I'm trying to be a good soldier, but I can't see what's good and what's bad. Can I be accountable to you?"

"Sure."

"I know it might sound stupid, but I don't care. When I kill people—because I know I'm going to kill more people—I'm going to talk to you about it. I'm going to tell you why I did it. There's not going to be any more killing just to prove I'm not a coward, or for my own pride. If I'm going to be in this war, I'm going to do it on my own terms. But I need you to be my backbone. Can you do that?"

"I can do that."

They sat there in the tent for a solid minute without saying a word. Aubrey had stopped crying, but Jack was sure she wasn't done for the night. He felt like he was going to crash at any minute, the weight of everything toppling in on him.

He looked at her, wondering where the easy days had gone and whether they would ever be back again.

"I love you, you know."

"I love you, too."

TWENTY-NINE

ZASHA BURST INTO THE BEDROOM of the sprawling house in Cle Elum, sweat gluing her hair to her forehead and the sides of her face.

"He needs to rest," she said, striding to the bed and putting a hand on Fyodor's heaving chest. "This is killing him."

Fyodor looked up at her. His mouth moved, but no words came out. There was pain in his eyes, a deep, haunted pain. They'd had him boosted with drugs for nearly sixteen hours and were only now in the process of flushing his system. An IV ran into his arm, and she could see—and smell—where he had vomited onto the bedding.

Dr. Safin didn't say anything, but raised his eyes to the corner of the room. Zasha turned and saw General Gromyko standing beside the lamp. She started and then saluted.

He returned the salute slowly, staring at her as if he was deciding what to say. Eventually he just nodded to the doctor.

"His vital signs are returning to normal," Dr. Safin said, after clearing his throat. "He's fatigued, but this isn't killing him. He's made of stronger stuff than that."

"Forgive me," Zasha said, the general's presence making her nervous. "But I know Fyodor better than anyone, and he wasn't acting the same on today's mission. He was convulsing. I believe he was having seizures."

It had been worse than that. She *knew* he was having seizures—she'd seen it before in training camp when others had been given too much of the drug. Some of them seized until their bodies went perfectly rigid and they stopped breathing. Some vomited blood. While she'd been out with Fyodor today he had acted like he was going down that path. He'd had nosebleeds and coughing fits—real fits where it seemed like he would never be able to inhale again. She'd thought he was going to die alone in the woods with her.

"It's to be expected," Dr. Safin said, addressing the general more than Zasha. "His body is under stress and he's reacting as we would anticipate."

"But for how long?" Zasha asked. "How much longer will he be able to handle this high of a dose?"

She looked at the general, who stared back at her stoically.

Zasha began speaking again, her words coming out short and apologetic. "We have to break through the American lines. I know that. But Fyodor can't handle much more. He'll be used up before we achieve our goals. Should we, I don't know, ration him?"

They weren't the words she wanted to say—she wanted to plead for his life, and instead she found herself merely pleading to prolong his suffering. But it felt like the only recourse she had.

She looked back and forth from the doctor to the general, waiting for someone to answer her. The two men were looking at each other, not at her or at Fyodor.

Finally the general spoke. His voice was rough and stern. "We will use the asset until the situation is resolved or until the asset is no longer viable. We cannot afford to spare his life and lose thousands of others."

THIRTY

AUBREY WAS UP BEFORE THE sun, out on the training field, practicing the obstacle course. She was wearing her exercise clothes—a gray army T-shirt and a pair of shorts—despite the cold, and despite the threat of attack. If anyone could see her, the bright white gauze bandage over her leg would have stood out in the predawn light, but she was invisible. She was pressing herself hard, knowing she needed to increase her endurance.

She really was getting better. Back when she was home in Mount Pleasant, spying on her high-school peers, she could barely handle twenty or thirty minutes of invisibility before being overcome with exhaustion and losing her sight. Now she could do three times that.

Peers. She'd never seen them as peers. Nicole was too

far above her to be a peer, even though they'd outwardly been best friends. It had been a partnership, not a friendship. Even Jack wasn't a peer. Maybe he used to be, before Aubrey had gone off the deep end and entered a world of spying and shoplifting, but he was always better than her. Always straight as an arrow. Always true to her even when she wasn't true to him.

Aubrey was dripping with sweat by the time she got to the cargo-net climb, but she grabbed on to the loose nylon and began fighting her way up. This was probably the opposite of what her doctors would have recommended for her healing leg, but she didn't care. She was determined to be a good soldier.

She wondered what the day would hold for her. There would be more combat, she was sure. At least now they knew what to look for, even though the flying lambda would be hard to track down. But Jack could probably smell the flyer long before she would ever hear them, and she couldn't call for backup—her electronics were down, too.

Every part of Aubrey stung when she reached the top of the cargo net. She knew she should call it a day. She'd need energy for the fight, and she wanted to be on top of her game. She climbed down the well-worn thirty-foot ladder, and looked toward the next obstacle.

The rope climb.

At least it hadn't started snowing yet, Aubrey thought as she took a firm grip on the rope. That was something. They could be having this entire battle in two feet of snow.

She pulled herself up, feeling the burn in her biceps and triceps, and then wrapped her feet, locking them in place and putting her weight on them. She pulled up again, locked her feet, and then once more, and in one more movement she was at the top of the rope.

Aubrey paused there, resting and looking out across the active camp. No one seemed to sleep much here. Fighter jets were constantly patrolling, and Aubrey had even heard the roar of rockets.

She slowly let herself down the rope, careful not to get rope burn on her legs or rip off her bandage. She hit the sand at the bottom and started jogging back toward the barracks.

Sweat was running into her eyes, so she didn't recognize Tabitha and Krezi until she was almost on top of them, standing a few tents down from theirs. Both were fully dressed, as they should be—as Aubrey should be—in ACUs with helmets and vests.

"I don't know how it works," Tabitha said, "or who's in charge. But there has to be a way we can find out."

Krezi looked uncomfortable. "I don't know if I want to be a part of it. All I know is that this is bullcrap."

Tabitha nodded. "Look at Aubrey. I don't know what's going on with her, but she's screwed up. Did you see her at the roadblock? After, I mean? It was like she wasn't even there."

Aubrey stopped a few feet away from them. She didn't like being talked about behind her back, but this didn't seem like gossip. It seemed like Tabitha actually cared.

"And last night?" Tabitha continued. "I don't know what Aubrey did. But she had that same look on her face. Forced to kill. It's not right, Krez. It's just not right."

"What about me?" Krezi said. "I have one job, and that's to shoot stuff. I killed people yesterday. And the day before, at the roadblock. And you know what the worst part was? Nick congratulated me. He seemed thrilled because my blasts went through their body armor. 'Hooray for Krezi! She's really good at killing people!'"

Aubrey's heart hurt. She faded in, reappearing beside them.

"Hey, guys," she said, her breath still rapid from jogging. "What's up?" She didn't want them to think she'd been listening in, but maybe she could help.

Tabitha looked stunned to see her, the confusion of Aubrey's reappearance plain on her face. Krezi stammered for a minute.

"Aren't you freezing?"

"Pretty much," Aubrey said, folding her arms and rubbing them.

"You'll get in trouble if someone sees you out here without your gear," Krezi said.

"I know. I'll go take a shower and get dressed. Are you

guys okay? It sounded like you were talking about bad stuff."

"What do you mean?" Tabitha said, sounding defensive.

"Nothing," Aubrey said. "You looked worried."

"Were you listening in?" Tabitha asked.

"No," Aubrey lied. "I just got here. I was wondering if I could help with something. You sounded so serious."

"Everything here is serious," Krezi said with a grimace. "We're in the middle of a war."

"We were talking about having to kill people," Tabitha said. "About how it's not right."

Aubrey nodded. She really wished she could talk to Krezi without Tabitha right there. She knew what Krezi was going through.

"It's not right," Aubrey agreed. "That's why I'm trying to be the best soldier I can be."

Tabitha rolled her eyes.

Aubrey laughed, to try to ease the tension. "I'm serious. I don't mean being a supersoldier. I just mean a soldier who follows orders and does what's right."

"But isn't *I was just following orders* the excuse that war criminals always use?" Tabitha asked.

That made Aubrey's face darken. "It's also the difference between being a soldier in a war and a murderer."

"I don't know if that distinction is as clear as some people seem to think it is," Tabitha said.

"It's not perfect," Aubrey said, taking a breath and

thinking of her discussion with Jack. "But it's helpful. War is never good. We do the best we can."

"If you can live with that."

"I don't know what else to do." Aubrey was starting to get angry. What exactly was Tabitha implying? Did she think that Aubrey was a murderer?

"We're trying to figure that out," Krezi said.

Before Aubrey could ask what that meant, Tabitha took Krezi by the arm. "We're going to get breakfast. Want to come?"

Tabitha knew Aubrey couldn't come—not dressed like she was.

"Next time," Aubrey said, plastering on a smile.

"Next time," Tabitha said with an equally fake smile.

Aubrey turned, feeling the cold more deeply now, and headed for the tent. She wanted to follow Tabitha and Krezi, but it would only make her mad. Or confused.

When she got into her tent, Josi was at the mirror pinning up her hair.

"I swear," she said. "I'm ready to cut this all off. Guys have it easy."

"Do you know what Tabitha and Krezi were talking about?" Aubrey asked, flopping onto her cot.

"Do you want a word-for-word transcript?" Josi asked, tucking in another bobby pin. "And how far back?"

Aubrey thought for a minute. "No. I've heard enough."

Josi eyed her through the mirror. "Did you want to hear that Krezi has a crush on Rich?"

Aubrey pulled her towel out of her bag. "They'd be cute together."

"Well, she doesn't," Josi said with a grin. "She has a crush on Jack."

"Great."

"I thought you'd like that," she said, inspecting her hair.

"What did you tell her?"

"What do you think? That Jack was taken."

"And that, even if he wasn't, she's fifteen and he's almost eighteen?"

"She didn't seem to think that was a big deal. Her exact words were, 'Age is just a number.'"

Aubrey laughed. "I'm surprised she doesn't go after Captain Gillett."

"Tabitha likes Nick."

"I guess that just leaves you," Aubrey said, swinging the towel over her shoulder and standing up. "All alone."

Josi smiled. "I think I'll manage, somehow."

Aubrey readjusted one of Josi's bobby pins in the back. "There."

"Thanks."

"You okay? Your brain, I mean?"

Josi turned to face her. "You know that feeling after Thanksgiving dinner, where you're so full you could burst and you feel like throwing up? That's how my brain feels. I wish I could puke out half its thoughts."

"Does anything make it feel better?"

"Ironically, thinking helps. If I consciously try to organize my thoughts, it feels like there's a little more room in there. I've started making lists of things."

"Lists?"

"Like *conversations with Aubrey* or *loud sounds* or *thoughts about home*. If I can put something in a list, then it seems like it all fits a little better."

Aubrey moved toward the door. "Some neuroscientist is going to fall in love with you."

Josi pumped her fist. "Ka-ching."

THIRTY-ONE

BREAKFAST IN THE MESS HALL was cold cereal and powdered milk. Jack had overheard the cooks talking, and there were huge food shortages across the country—all of the roads were out, bridges and overpasses down everywhere.

For once, Jack was glad that his parents lived in a poor little town. No one had much, but what they had, they shared. His parents wouldn't go hungry. If the turkey farmers couldn't ship their turkeys, then there was probably plenty of food to go around. Especially right now, days before Thanksgiving. They probably had turkeys stuffed in every freezer and oven. They were probably getting sick to death of turkey.

He missed home. He missed his parents' quirky little thrift shop, and the small house he'd grown up in. He even missed his old job, janitor at the high school. He'd hated what it meant—that he couldn't really enjoy any activities because he had to stay after the games and dances to clean up—but right now he'd give anything to be walking the halls of North Sanpete High. To be home again.

Captain Gillett appeared at the door of the mess tent, and once he caught sight of Jack and Rich, he came striding over.

"Anything good?" he asked, looking at the meager food.

"Depends on your definition of good," Jack said. "But no, probably not."

Gillett walked over to the coffee machine and made himself a cup.

"I hate powdered milk," Rich said.

"Try it when you have hypersensitivity," Jack said, making a face. "It isn't just my eyes and ears—I can taste really well, too. And this is horrific."

"I don't know how you do it."

"I've lost twenty pounds since my powers manifested," Jack said. "And that's after going through basic training and gaining all that muscle."

"I think I'm the lucky one," Rich said. "I don't have a lot of side effects. Not any, really. One day I'm going to just keel over and die of a tumor or something."

Gillett came back and sat across from them. "We're going out again," he said. "Today. We have to find that flyer."

"I don't know how we're going to do that in the daylight," Jack said. "I was only able to find the center of that circle because I could see the lights in the distance."

"Now that you've seen her, can you track her? I don't mean to be rude here, but like a bloodhound or something?"

Jack smiled. "I didn't get her scent. Plus she flies, so she won't leave a trail on the ground."

"What's the status of the battle?" Rich asked. "I haven't heard artillery since the middle of the night."

"No one is attacking yet. It's quiet. They're regrouping and we're regrouping and everyone's waiting for orders."

Rich took a bite of his cereal. "Has anyone thought about using the computers inside the Bradleys? Or the Abramses?"

"Using them for what?" Gillett asked, sipping his coffee. He grimaced.

Rich glanced at Jack and then back at Gillett. "When I was in there yesterday, I noticed how many computers are running inside the Bradley—you've got your targeting computer, and the driver's computer, and the computers that run the TOW launchers—there's a whole mess of computers for that. And the IVIS system especially."

"What's IVIS?" Jack asked.

"Inter-Vehicular Information System," Rich said.

"So they have computers," Gillett said. "So what?"

"So they all record the time when they shut down," Rich said. "And when they reboot, they record the time they come back on."

"How do you know that?"

Rich laughed. "It's what I do. I know how machines work. And I know that a lot of them talk to your computers back here—probably in your logistics offices."

Gillett set the coffee down and stared at Rich.

"Here's what I'm thinking," Rich said. "We find out when all of those computers came back on, and we compare that to the GPS in the vehicles, and we'll be able to make a perfect map of where the lambda was last night."

Gillett looked at Jack. "Will that work?"

"Don't ask me."

"Of course it'll work," Rich said.

"Well," Gillett said, a spark in his eyes, "that helps us find where the lambda was yesterday, but will it help us find where she is today?"

"Sure," Rich said. "If we're tracking all the vehicles, and they're all spread out, we'll be able to record what time their computers stop transmitting, and we'll compare that to the GPS. Then, assuming it's a bubble, we fit a circle against the data of the vehicles that have gone offline. The lambda will be in the center of that circle."

Gillett stared at Rich for a minute. "Why didn't you say something about this before?"

"I just thought of it," Rich said.

"You need to think more often." Gillett stood up. "Let's get you to a computer."

$$\lambda$$

Within fifteen minutes, Gillett had explained to whoever was in charge what they wanted to do, and a crowd had collected in the tent around Rich and his computer terminal.

His fingers flew across the keys, faster than any typist Jack had ever seen. It was like the computer was an extension of his body.

"See," Rich said, scrolling down a list of time signatures on the screen. "These are all the computers' last recorded times before the lambda shut them down. If we link them to GPS, and plot them on a map of the battlefield, then we should get this."

He actually had to wait for the computer to catch up with *him*. Little red triangles began appearing on the screen. He tapped a dozen more lines of code and blue triangles lit up.

"Red are the vehicles that were disabled," Rich said as he typed. "Blue are the ones that were outside of the bubble."

There was a clear swath of red down the center of the battlefield.

"Now the hard part," Rich said, and he began typing even faster. Jack looked over at Gillett and the faces of the techs in the room. There was even a lieutenant colonel watching. They all seemed entranced.

A moment later a circle appeared, and then another and then half a dozen more. It was like the images Jack had seen on The Weather Channel showing the path of a hurricane— eight circles starting at the front lines and moving back across the battlefield. A line was drawn connecting each of the circles by their center points.

"That line," Rich said, "is the lambda's flight path. And that circle is the bubble. It looks like it has a radius of just over eight miles."

"Can you do it in reverse?" the colonel asked. "Show where the return flight path is?"

"Sure," Rich said, biting his lip. "That's the same thing, just using the data of when the computers turned back on." He typed for a solid minute before anything appeared on the screen, but eventually the new circles appeared, tracking the lambda's course back. It matched what Jack had thought last night—the lambda flew back in little spurts, a jump of five hundred yards, and then a jump a little longer, and so on until finally taking off and disappearing.

This was the first time that Jack saw the damage from above—how many of those red triangles never turned back on again. They'd been devastated.

"How accurate is this?" Gillett asked.

Rich pointed to a number in the corner. "Plus or minus a hundred yards."

Gillett turned to the colonel. "This should change our entire strategy. We need to keep our units spread out so that we can get reliable data to pinpoint the location of the lambda."

"This looks good on a computer, but what if they hit us a different way today?"

"They've been using that lambda to sink our fleet, to land, to get through the pass—I think they'll use it again," Gillett responded.

"So we know where the lambda is," the colonel said. "But we can't radio to anyone to tell them where to go."

"My team will track her down," Gillett said.

"Eight miles without power? By the time you get there, the battle will be over."

"Not if we go on bikes," Gillett said.

"You're kidding."

"You have a better idea? If we're at the edge of the circle, we can get to the center on bikes in what? Half an hour? And I've got the best powerless recon team." He reached out a hand and put it on Jack's shoulder.

"I'll take it upstairs," the colonel said. "Son, can you do this when the battle starts?"

Rich looked up. "I don't have to. I just wrote a program that will track them in real time."

THIRTY-TWO

TABITHA SAT IN THE BACK of the truck, her hand resting on the frame of a black-and-silver mountain bike. They were going to come under artillery fire, just like they did yesterday, and this time they were going to be on bicycles. It sounded ridiculous.

She'd been on the detail to pick up the bikes from a store in Yakima. The town was evacuated, and Josi had smashed the glass of the building with a rock. They'd gone in through the window and collected a dozen.

It would have been thirteen if Lytle were still alive. Tabitha had said that, but Josi didn't want to hear it. Josi never wanted to listen to Tabitha.

Tabitha had actually thought about leaving while she was at the bike store—it was just her and Josi and VanderHorst.

But Tabitha had promised Krezi she'd take her. And Krezi was useful. Tabitha didn't need a gun if she had Krezi. Plus, if they disappeared from the battlefield rather than the bike store, they might not be listed as AWOL. Just MIA.

"You see this?" Tabitha said telepathically to Krezi. "This is why we have to get out of here. They're so hell-bent on finding this lambda that they're willing to get us all killed in the process. They keep talking about how the lambda is at the center of a bubble, but you know what else is at the center of the bubble? All of the fighting. That's the whole point of the lambda—to be in the middle of all the action so that no one inside can do anything. And we're going to drive—ride—right into it."

They were traveling north of the battlefield, north of where they expected the lambda to go. They couldn't get too close and get swallowed up in the bubble themselves, or else no one could radio them with the proper coordinates.

The fact that this was Rich's plan made it even worse. Who was Rich? A fifteen-year-old computer nerd. He hadn't even graduated from basic training. He hadn't done anything except write some computer code.

He should have been back at the base instead of out here with them. She wondered if he could even keep up on a bike.

The truck came to a stop on a pine-lined dirt road.

Josi was studying a stack of USGS maps—maps they'd also taken from the bike shop. They showed every contour line, trail, and unused road. Josi had taken enough of the maps to get them all the way to Snowqualmie Pass, and now she was storing them all in her memory.

Josi would have been useful to escape with Tabitha and Krezi, but she'd made it clear a dozen times that she did not like Tabitha in her head.

Jack would be useful, too. And maybe he could convince Aubrey to come with them. Aubrey had no love of rules. She'd proven that over and over. The problem with Aubrey was . . . Tabitha couldn't put her finger on it. Maybe it was an overly active conscience. Or maybe it was that she was living with a constant sense of guilt. Either way, Aubrey was always questioning whether she was doing the right thing, and she always needed Jack to reassure her that she was.

If Tabitha wanted to get Jack on her side, then she would need to get Aubrey, too. They were a package deal. But if she got Jack, then Aubrey was sure to come, wasn't she?

"Jack," Tabitha said with her mind. "Can I talk to you for a minute?"

He met her eyes. He looked tired. Or was he annoyed? He was a self-righteous little bastard, wasn't he?

"I don't want to talk about this in front of everyone," Tabitha said. "But I'm scared."

The look on his face changed slightly. She wished she could read minds as well as talk to them.

"I don't know if this plan is a good idea or if it's suicide," she said. "Think of the artillery that opened on us last night.

Think of the shrapnel. That's all going to come raining down again. They've probably got more guns today—more that they brought through the pass during the night. They wouldn't attack us if they didn't have guns, right?"

The look on his face was one of concern but not much else. He looked like he was trying to be nice, not like he actually cared.

"We need a code," she said, "so you can respond. If you want to say yes, touch your chin. If you want to say no, don't do anything. Okay?"

He rubbed his chin.

"I'm not trying to do anything secret. I just can't talk about this kind of thing in front of people, and you seem like a good listener. You always listen to Aubrey. She tells us about it. You really care about her, don't you?"

Jack furrowed his brow, like he was trying to figure something out. But he touched his chin.

"Do you mind that I talk to you?"

He didn't make any movement. No, he didn't mind.

"That's the thing that I don't get about the two of you," Tabitha said. "You obviously care about each other. Maybe you love each other—I don't know. Maybe it's more complicated than that. But she's always going into harm's way. That's, like, her job description. I don't know how you handle it."

His lips were pursed, and he kept looking at her, but she couldn't read his expression.

"I don't like this war, Jack. I think you know that. I'm not exactly quiet about it."

He touched his chin.

She smiled. "Yeah, I know. It's the thing that I constantly harp on." She looked out the back of the truck at the frost-nipped pine trees. "It's almost Thanksgiving. I don't know what your family was like, but mine always had a big party with lots of relatives." She looked back at him. "I miss it. I don't want to be here."

Jack touched his chin.

Yes.

She gave a tiny nod. "Did I ever tell you about one of my first missions, back when I was first assigned to the Green Berets?"

He didn't move. He seemed to be listening more intently.

"I had been in a quarantine center at Fort Sill, but there was another quarantine center, just across the Texas border at the Red River Army Depot. I was in an ODA with two other lambdas. I didn't really have much of a job—they kept me around in case the radios didn't work, or something like that.

"Don't get me wrong. That was fine with me. I only joined up because it was that or stay in quarantine, in those tiny little cells. And I thought—I really thought—that we were going to be doing good, fighting the bad guys. But that wasn't what we were doing."

Jack was watching her closely. He looked like he wanted to say something. Instead, he rubbed his chin.

Did that mean to go on? She assumed it did.

"We weren't fighting terrorists," she said. "In fact, I never fought terrorists. While you and Aubrey were out being heroes, do you know what I was doing? I was fighting against American kids. The rebellion."

He sat upright. He acted like he was stretching his back, but she could tell she'd surprised him.

"The Green Berets were killing them," Tabitha said. "I know you don't want to hear about it. No one does. But the rebellion was trying to free lambdas from quarantine, and I was in the group of Green Berets that shot them down."

Jack looked annoyed now.

"We murdered them."

He shook his head, just a slight shake.

"You can say that," Tabitha said. "But I was there. All they were doing was trying to open the gate. They weren't attacking anyone. They weren't a threat. They were just trying to tear down the gate. That's all. And we shot them."

Jack stared back at her.

"You don't believe me."

She waited for his finger to touch his chin, but she was surprised to see that it didn't.

"You do believe me?"

He rubbed his chin.

Captain Gillett pressed the radio in his ear and announced, "I think this is it, people."

"You ready?" Aubrey asked Jack, a fake eagerness on her face. "I can outride you any day."

"It's not a race," he said with a smile. He met Tabitha's eyes for just a moment.

Tabitha spoke to his mind again. "I don't understand you, Jack. If you believe me, then why do you always change the topic when the rebellion comes up?"

He shot her a look, a stern, fixed stare. But he wouldn't talk out loud.

"Good news," Gillett said. "About ten miles. Let's get on the road."

They could hear the thunder of artillery in the distance. Gillett helped Josi out of the truck and then gave her the coordinates—coordinates from Rich's computer program. "You can find it?"

She closed her eyes. "Easy. She's in the woods, by some cabins. There's a road."

"Well, that's something," Gillett said. "Heads up—they're saying this is a major offensive. Reports of a lot of infantry. We may run into more than her up there. But let's try to make it there faster. They're closer, but we're on bikes."

Jack helped Aubrey down, and as she got onto her bike, he turned and helped Tabitha. "I believe you," he breathed. "But that doesn't mean I agree with the rebellion."

THIRTY-THREE

JACK CLIMBED ONTO A BIKE, his muscles already sore. His rifle was slung across his back, like everyone else's, and he thought they all looked ridiculous. Full combat ACUs, fully armed, riding mountain bikes. He wondered how Aubrey would do with her injured leg.

Josi led the way, the map stuck in her brain. She was followed closely by Gillett. The rest of the group was strung out behind, with Chase-Dunn and Uhrey taking up the rear.

Tabitha's voice was in Jack's head. "I wasn't trying to get you to join the rebellion, silly. I'm not part of it, so how could I even be recruiting?"

Jack pedaled a little faster, pulling his bike alongside Aubrey's.

"I just want people to understand what I've been through,"

Tabitha continued. "That's all. I don't think it was right what happened. When this war is over, someone is going to have to tell the parents of those teenagers how their kids really died, and they'll have to know that it was the army."

Jack wished he could respond. The army attacked the rebels because the rebels were attacking an army base. Maybe the rebels were right—maybe the quarantines were a horrible suspension of civil liberties. Jack could agree with that. He'd been taken from his hometown by force, in handcuffs. He'd had a bomb strapped to his ankle, for crying out loud, and that was even after he'd agreed to help the army. So, yes, there were some very bad things going on.

But right now they were riding their bikes into a war zone. He didn't need his exceptional senses to hear the bombardment of artillery—it shook the entire area and echoed from hill to hill. American soldiers were being killed this very minute. Protests about the treatment of the kids in quarantine could wait.

Whenever their bikes reached a high point in the road, Jack could see smoke in the distance, and he knew that the Americans were once again sitting ducks. Powerless and unable to return fire. There were a lot more American infantry on the ground this time, he saw, prepared for a war without vehicles. And more airpower would be brought in—hopefully with the knowledge of how the lambda's bubble worked and where it was situated. Jack didn't know if the higher echelons of power fully believed Rich's computer model and had passed it along to the air force. Jack hoped so.

But that made Jack think about Tabitha's words. Did the army or air force really trust the lambdas? Sure, they'd assigned Captain Gillett's ODA to follow up on Rich's prediction, but if the commanding generals actually thought this lambda could be found with Rich's computer model, wouldn't they throw more resources at it than a single team of Green Berets?

So, in a way, Tabitha was right. Not in the sense that they needed to rebel, but in the sense that lambdas were undervalued.

Something exploded high in the sky, and Jack looked up to see the white smoke trail of a missile. It didn't look like it had hit anything—it looked like it crossed into the bubble and exploded harmlessly. He could see the fighter that had fired it far in the distance, over Snowqualmie Pass, in a dogfight with an American Hornet.

"How's your leg?" Jack asked Aubrey as they pedaled hard along the trail.

"I'm okay," she said. "This is more what I trained for."

"Biking?"

"No," she said with a smile. "Sneaking up on the bad guys."

"Well, it's a good thing you'll be invisible. I don't know about you, but I'm going to be panting like a dog." He felt so heavy with all this gear and body armor that he was amazed he hadn't fallen off the bike already.

"I'm a little worried about that," she said. "I get tired so quickly when I disappear. I'll already be tired by the time I start. That won't be good."

"Hopefully we'll get in and out fast," Jack breathed.

"There's no sign that this flyer has any backup, is there?"

"Just the lambda that she carries with her, and that's the one who can disrupt electronics. We assume."

"Good," Aubrey said. "If I can sneak up on them, I'll be okay."

Josi directed them off the road and onto a forest path. Jack had to fall behind Aubrey because the trail was too narrow to ride side-by-side.

He tried to focus on listening to the battle. He could hear shouts and calls in both English and Russian. The Russians sounded closer than Jack expected. Their infantry was moving quickly. Maybe they'd started their advance before the lambda had flown over the battlefield.

Even so, Jack's team was still going to be okay. They were moving fast on the bikes, and they'd get to the flyer soon. Assuming the flyer didn't move. But in the last battle the flyer hadn't moved until late in the battle—when planes began hitting the Russian front lines near Cle Elum.

The artillery bombardment was heavy, but still in the distance. Jack kept waiting for the American bombers to come in and silence the Russian guns like they had last night, but so far it hadn't happened. Other than a handful of Hornets, Jack hadn't seen much of an air presence.

The trail headed uphill, and Jack had to pedal harder to keep up. He was amazed at how quickly everyone was moving. He focused on Josi at the head of the line, and heard her panting heavily and her heart thrumming in her chest.

Jack moved down the line and found everyone to be much the same. A few of the Green Berets were doing better—they had to be in great shape and a few of the lambdas were doing worse. Krezi was really struggling.

The trail turned again, onto an old road with two grassy wheel ruts. Jack pumped the pedals until he could catch back up with Aubrey.

"Hey," she said.

"Hey."

"This is going to be a waste if we get there and I can't do anything."

"That's what I'm worried about."

He focused on the battlefield again, listening for the sound of Russian voices. They were close, maybe a few miles off.

"We've got to be getting close," he told Aubrey.

Tabitha's voice appeared in his head. It sounded so out of place—there was no panting or heavy breathing, just a calm, soothing tone. "Jack, I know you don't care about what I say, but I know you care about Aubrey. We need to call this off.

You and I have both trained with her. We know how tired she gets when she's invisible."

He shook his head, but halfheartedly. They couldn't call it off, could they? Not when they were so close.

"She's going to struggle up here. She's going to struggle and she's going to make a mistake. It won't be her fault, but things happen when you're tired."

Jack looked at Aubrey. Her face was splotchy, and her cheeks and nose glistened with sweat. She pushed her glasses back up, and glanced over at him.

"You worry about you," she said, with a huff of breath and the faintest smile.

Tabitha's voice continued. "It's not just her, Jack. It's all of us. If this doesn't work, we're all on the front line."

But it was too late for whatever Tabitha was going to say next, because up ahead Josi slowed to a stop. She laid her bike on the side of the road, and then turned to Gillett, her hands on her hips as she gulped in air.

"We're five hundred yards northeast," she said, and pointed into the woods. "That way."

Everyone climbed off their bikes and stashed them against the side of the road. Gillett came down the line to where Jack was standing next to Aubrey.

"Are you ready for this?"

She let out a deep breath of air, her tongue on her lower lip, and nodded.

Tabitha spoke up. "Captain, are we sure about this?"

"What do you mean?"

"Well, after what happened yesterday . . ."

He turned and looked in the direction Josi had pointed. "There's no artillery falling here. They're probably avoiding this area because they're protecting the lambda. This is the safest place on the battlefield. Now be quiet so the fish doesn't swim away."

Jack said, "Russian infantry's coming, though. I can hear them. They're not as close as the lambda, but they're headed this way."

"Then let's get moving. Jack, find me the lambda."

He nodded and stepped forward, closing his eyes to focus on sounds. Behind him eleven people wheezed heavily, and their clothing rubbed as they stretched.

The forest in front of him was quiet, all the animals gone to ground. In the far distance—maybe a mile or more away—he could hear the chatter of automatic-weapons fire, the voices of troops. He tried to focus on something closer.

There was water burbling, not much more than a trickle. It was probably an irrigation ditch, he thought. He knew there was farmland up ahead.

Something metal was swinging on a squeaking hinge. A gate, maybe, or a barn door, or possibly a weathervane.

He heard breathing, and he zeroed in on it. It was rapid, and the heart was pounding, and it didn't seem right. Not for a human. Was it a deer? It had to be something like that.

He searched again, scanning the woods for any sound. A

squirrel chattered. Branches rubbed together.

Something ticked.

He focused on that. Something ticking. A watch. And there was breathing nearby. Two separate bodies.

"Found them," Jack said, and opened his eyes, pointing into the forest. "Two people. They're probably a lot closer than five hundred yards. Maybe three hundred."

Gillett turned to face Aubrey. "Your job is to stop that flyer from flying. We could all march in there and she'd be gone in an instant. You sneak in, and you do what you have to."

She took a breath and nodded. "Yes, sir."

THIRTY-FOUR

AUBREY WAITED UNTIL SHE WAS fifty yards ahead of them before she first spoke to Jack. The plan was to let her get a hundred and fifty yards in front—to where they could all see her—and then to track down the flyer.

"I'm sore, Jack," she said, more to keep herself calm than because she really needed to say it. "It's been too long since I rode a bike. You probably did fine. You always rode your bike back home."

They used to ride together—she rode even more than he did, because she lived out on the edge of town—but she'd given that up when she started getting rides to school in Nicole's Audi convertible.

She stopped walking for a minute, slung her rifle, and pulled the bottle of Flowerbomb perfume from her pants pocket. She sprayed herself with it, the scent of the forest disappearing in a burst of floral fragrance. As much as this stuff reminded her of every dangerous, bloody event in her life, she loved the smell.

"Remember I'm relying on you, Jack," Aubrey said. "You tell me if I'm crossing a line."

Aubrey looked back. She judged the distance between them now as being close to one hundred yards. That meant she was only two hundred from the flyer.

"I'm going invisible," she said. "I'll see you in a minute."

She disappeared and immediately felt her strength drain. She was too tired. Hopefully she wouldn't have to do much more on this mission than get in and get out.

An old farmhouse with a shingle roof and white plank siding came into sight. Aubrey couldn't see the lambda, but she had to be there. That was where Jack had pointed.

For a moment Aubrey worried that the lambda might be on the roof, or somewhere Aubrey couldn't reach, but as she moved through the pines and the building became more visible she saw the steep pitch of the gables and knew no one could be on top.

"Jack says he can smell you," Tabitha's voice said.

"Hey, Jack," Aubrey said. "We're at it again. Just like old times."

The house wasn't a square—far from it. It looked like it had once been a rectangle, but had been added on to several times. Rooms jutted off in random directions, and on the far side it connected with a barn.

"There's a house," Aubrey said. "I'm trying to find the lambda. I'm assuming she's not inside, because she wouldn't be able to fly away."

There was a pause. A long pause.

"Aubrey?" Tabitha said. "Make sure you report in before you take a shot."

"Got it."

She moved in a semicircle around the house, staying about fifty yards from it, giving it a wide berth. Even though she was invisible she didn't want to come up on the lambda unexpectedly. Most of all she didn't want to take the shot.

"This lambda could be like us, Jack," Aubrey said. "Recruited into the army, taken from her home. She could be doing this against her will. Granted, she could always fly away and escape, but fly away where? Maybe she wants to defect and doesn't know English?"

Aubrey continued to prowl around the building. She could see past a corner and into an alcove where a short evergreen grew. She peered at it closely—someone could fit behind it. But after adjusting her glasses again, she decided no one was back there.

She kept walking, her rifle held up to her shoulder as she sighted down the scope at every new edge of the building, expecting to see the girl standing there.

"Take your time," Tabitha said. "Check everywhere."

Artillery was rumbling in the distance, and Aubrey wondered how many lives were being lost while she was looking for the lambda.

"I am checking everywhere, Jack," Aubrey said. "You can hear them. Am I getting close?"

She suddenly thought to check above her, and she pointed the gun up—was the lambda hovering? Could she do that?

"Jack says you've got a little farther to go. Hold where you are for a minute."

Aubrey stopped, aiming the gun up and all around into the trees, half expecting to see the girl clinging to a limb above her. But wouldn't Jack be able to tell if she was up in the air?

"Jack? What about up in the trees? Or floating up in the air? Somewhere I can't see?"

She hadn't checked the whole house yet, but she didn't dare leave the shelter of the pines in case the lambda was more than a hundred and forty yards up—flying where she could see Aubrey.

Tabitha spoke. "Jack's not sure. Check every tree."

THIRTY-FIVE

"DAMN IT, JACK," GILLETT SAID. "What's taking her so long?"

"I don't know," Jack answered, frustrated and afraid. "Tabitha, does she know how close the infantry is getting?"

"She knows," Tabitha said. "Unless she can't hear me."

"She's so close," Jack said, listening to Aubrey's breathing and the breaths of the other two lambdas. They had to be just around another corner, just behind a tree. He couldn't pinpoint them with the breeze in the air, but they were so close. And the Russian infantry was only a few hundred yards on the other side of the house. "I don't know why she's standing in one place."

There was a pause.

"I'm checking everywhere," Aubrey said, still not moving.

She couldn't be doing this, Jack thought. Not going

against orders. Not again. Not after their talk last night. She said she was going to be the best soldier that there was. And here she was, disobeying every word Tabitha was telling her. Every order from Gillett.

"Tabitha," the captain said, his voice terse and deliberate. "Tell her to circle that whole damn house. Tell her to search the barn. Tell her to do anything, but quit standing there."

"I'm telling her," Tabitha said.

"Tell her again," the captain snapped.

Aubrey still wasn't moving, and Jack wished he could see her. She hadn't taken a footstep in more than a minute.

"Ask if she can hear you," Jack said.

Aubrey moved a foot but only one. It was like she was standing in one spot, rotating in a circle.

"I can hear her, Jack," Aubrey said. "Every word, loud and clear. I swear, I'm checking everything."

Jack could hear the Russians coming. They weren't fighting anyone. They were advancing toward the house. Toward Aubrey.

"Does she know the Russians are going to be there in a minute?" Jack said.

The captain turned to Jack. "You know her. What's she doing?"

"I—I don't know," Jack said. "She's reluctant to shoot. Maybe she's freaking out about that. But usually she'll talk to me when she's scared."

"I'm going to have to send my guys in," Captain Gillett said.

"Give me one second to reason with her," Jack said. "I can get her to do this."

He looked at Tabitha, who stared back at him. "Repeat every word I say."

THIRTY-SIX

"YES, TABITHA, I CAN HEAR you," Aubrey said, getting annoyed. She had almost gone in a full circle, searching every tree. Her gun was getting heavy in her arms and she wondered how long she could stay invisible. The bike ride had drained so much out of her.

"The captain wants you to make sure you leave no stone unturned," Tabitha said. "Every tree. She could be up any one of them."

"What do you think I'm doing?" Aubrey said. "Jack, I'm trying. I'm really trying, but I wish Tabitha would shut up."

She turned past the last tree and was facing the farmhouse again.

She took another step, hearing the crunch of dry pine needles and brush under her feet. She aimed her gun at the edge of the house, continuing in her original path around it. Five more steps. She stopped and looked at the trees again, hoping she was getting a different view, maybe seeing the lambdas in the trees.

It was a painfully long search, but these trees all seemed clean. She focused back on the house, took five more steps, and another alcove appeared. She thought she saw movement.

"Wait, Jack, I think this is them. I can see—hang on—I can see, okay, there's a girl. She's wearing a harness with some kind of latch in the center, and there's a boy on the ground, wrapped up in a tarp. It's like the carrying harnesses they use to lift cattle into trucks, like the one we saw the Fredricksons use that one time. They aren't latched together right now, but they could be in a second."

Aubrey took a breath, watching the girl through her scope. The girl wasn't wearing body armor, just some kind of black bodysuit under her harness. She didn't even look to be armed. Aubrey aimed at the girl's chest.

"Should I take the shot?"

"Hold on a minute," Tabitha's voice said. "They're thinking of taking her alive."

Aubrey almost yelled. This was already so hard for her—she was staring down her sight at this girl, this blond, pretty, normal-looking girl. And now they wanted to talk it over.

Aubrey took a step toward the lambdas, and then another. Her shooting arm was aching, and she lowered the gun for a minute to rest her arm, to get rid of the shakes.

That's when she saw them.

"Jack," she said, raising her M16 and taking a few stumbling steps backward. "There are Russians here. Soldiers. They're coming through the trees. I think—I think they're too close to see me, but Jack, that means they're close. What do I do?"

There was no answer. Tabitha was completely silent.

"Jack, what do I do? I don't think these lambdas are going to stick around. As soon as the flyer hears noise, she could take off. All she has to do is connect that latch. You told me to report in."

Tabitha spoke. "Engage with the Russian soldiers."

"What?" Aubrey said, swinging her gun around to the approaching infantry. "Check that: You said the soldiers, not the lambdas? This doesn't make any sense. Is that an order from Captain Gillett?"

The Russians were getting close. There had to be an entire company—over a hundred men. They were strung out in a loose line crossing the fields on the far side of the barn. Aubrey dropped to one knee to get better aim, and then thought better of it and ran to a tree she could lean against. She was getting so tired.

"Engage with the Russians," Tabitha said again.

"Jack, this is stupid," she said. "As soon as I do this the flyer's going to take off."

She centered her scope on one of the men who seemed to be in charge. She couldn't see insignia, but he seemed to have people clustered around him. Maybe he was just popular.

"Okay, Jack," Aubrey said. "But mark me down as objecting to this order. 'Ours is not to reason why.'" She breathed out.

She heard something just before she pulled the trigger, but it was too late. She'd squeezed, and the man dropped, her shot just above his Kevlar vest, right in the neck.

"Take the shot!" a voice called, somewhere behind her. "Take the shot!"

Chaos erupted on the Russian line, and Aubrey turned to see the flyer scrambling with the latch. She turned farther to see Captain Gillett in a full sprint.

"Take the shot!" he yelled. "Shoot the lambda!"

Aubrey set her scope on the girl, whose latch was now locked. She lifted off the ground.

Aubrey fired.

THIRTY-SEVEN

JACK WAS RUNNING FORWARD, FOLLOWING the Green Berets. He left Tabitha in his dust.

What could she have been thinking? Feeding Aubrey the wrong orders? What good would that do for anyone? Even for the rebellion, what good would that do?

There were strange noises coming from all around him, and it took Jack a moment to recognize what they were. He was too close to Aubrey to hear her, so he wouldn't hear her rifle either. But he would hear the echoes of that rifle as the sound bounced off of trees and hills and the side of the barn. Aubrey was firing, still invisible.

A second rifle joined in, and he recognized the sound as an M4—Captain Gillett's gun.

Jack could see Russians now, and he dropped to his knee,

aimed at a soldier, and fired. The man dropped.

Bullets began to fly from the Russian line—muzzles flashing with bursts of flame as the soldiers shot into the forest. They probably couldn't even see what they were aiming at—they just knew that they were under attack.

Jack lined up another man in his sights. He could hear all of the Green Berets firing now, the chatter of six M4s. And Jack recognized one M16. Josi. Krezi should have been using her power, though Jack hadn't seen her blasts of energy. Gillett had snatched away Tabitha's rifle and handed it to Rich, so she wouldn't be firing unless she took it back.

Jack shot at another Russian, hitting him squarely in the chest. His armor probably held the bullet, but the man dropped anyway. It likely cracked his ribs.

The returning fire was incredible now. Jack dropped to his stomach. He tried to listen, tried to focus on the lambdas, to see if Aubrey had hit her target, but he couldn't hear anyone's breathing through the cacophony of gunshots.

The air over his head began to screech with flying lead, and the trees were erupting into matchsticks.

There was one explosion, and then another. Fragmentation grenades. And then there was the fizzing sound of a smoke grenade being thrown back, obscuring everyone's view. It didn't stop the guns from firing, though. Fully automatic bursts from Russian AK-74s and 105s. And then there was the loud, buzzing fire of a machine gun—a PKP or a

Kord. Jack had only seen pictures, and he didn't know them by their sounds yet.

Someone threw another grenade, which detonated close enough that Jack felt the blast wave.

He pulled a grenade from his own vest, but didn't dare throw it. He had no idea where Aubrey was hiding, and he didn't trust his aim to get it in between all the trees and over to the Russians.

"Fall back!" Jack heard the order, though he was certain he was the only one who had. It was Captain Gillett's voice, barely audible over the noise of the battle.

Jack hoped that Aubrey was down and safe. The only way she could retreat safely was to crawl back—that was the only thing Jack could do, too.

"Fall back!" he heard again. Jack took a deep breath and began to push himself backward across the pine needles, wriggling on his belly under a hail of bullets. It was only as he was moving that he heard footsteps nearby and saw Josi running. He thought she was crazy, but if she was running, then he should, too. He said a silent prayer, then darted after her.

THIRTY-EIGHT

AUBREY WATCHED CAPTAIN GILLETT DIE.

He was crouched behind a tree, trying to get orders to his team, when someone spotted him. The tree exploded as bullets shattered the wood into splinters. At first she thought he was dropping down to get out of sight, but his rifle fell from his hand and he didn't move again.

Aubrey returned the Russians' fire until she ran out of bullets. By the time that she fired her last round, her eyes were so bad that even through the telescopic sight the men just looked like blobs of camouflage green. If she was honest, she wasn't even sure all of them were soldiers—she might have been shooting at bushes and trees.

But she stayed invisible.

When they came closer, when there were no more shots being fired from her side of the forest, she drew her sidearm—an M9 Beretta—and shot at the blurry shapes until she ran out of that ammo, too. The Russians continued to fire past her, into the forest, thinking they were being hit by snipers. Eventually, they all moved forward, passing her invisible body as she lay in the pine needles.

Aubrey had killed the flyer, and as the blurry Russians discovered the body, they all started speaking rapidly and loudly, calling for their superiors and gathering around the body.

And helping up the other lambda.

Aubrey's stomach fell. They had been so focused on the flyer that they hadn't—she hadn't—saved any bullets for the lambda she'd been carrying. The real threat. Aubrey had always assumed that she'd kill the flyer and that the captain would deal with the electronic-interference lambda.

She struggled to put a foot underneath her, but she was so exhausted that it wouldn't stay. They were lifting the boy out of his harness, trying to get him to stand, but the boy couldn't walk any better than Aubrey could. She pulled herself along the ground, trying to get to Captain Gillett's body, to take one of his guns and finish this job. This job that she'd bungled so completely.

What had happened? Why had Gillett told her to engage the Russians, and then come charging after her, yelling at her to shoot the flyer instead? Had he changed his mind at the last minute?

Aubrey had only made it halfway to the captain's body before the Russians carried the boy into the barn and out of sight. Aubrey had failed.

She had tried to do everything right this time. Tried to follow orders. Tried to be the kind of soldier that she'd promised Jack she was going to be. And she'd failed utterly.

She called to Jack, but her words came out as a slurred grunt. She'd never been this exhausted before. Her body was screaming for sleep, but she knew that if she slept she'd reappear.

Hand over hand, she pulled herself toward the captain's body. It was excruciatingly slow, with Russians walking all around her, looking for the rest of her team. One man tripped over her, falling into the dirt and cursing. She got to the captain's body just as a Russian did. Aubrey snatched the Beretta from its holster while the Russian picked up the M4 and began to drag Gillett's body away.

Aubrey had to go somewhere. She had to reappear or she would fall asleep.

She was only seeing shapes now—white rectangles, brown rectangles, green splotches.

White is the house, she told herself, and remembered the little alcove with the evergreen tree. She could make it there. She had to make it there.

What would Jack think? That she was dead? She was getting close.

Using only her arms—her legs were dead weight—she crawled toward the alcove. It reminded her of the crawls in basic training, scrambling under barbed wire, only now she felt like she was dragging someone else behind her, and her fingers were useless, though she managed to keep a grip on the pistol.

There was a sudden flash off to the right and gunshots sounded for a moment. Then everything seemed to go quiet. She felt like her head was in a bubble, wrapped in cloth to muffle all sound.

Her eyes started to droop. She shoved herself forward, willing her body to stay awake.

The evergreen was close.

THIRTY-NINE

TABITHA AND KREZI RAN THROUGH the forest. Tabitha was getting out of this war, and back to her life. Krezi jogged beside her, a look of fear and excitement on her face.

"We're going to be in so much trouble," Krezi said.

"No one is going to find us," Tabitha said. "We talked about this."

They were in a battle, and they'd been overrun by the enemy. So they'd run. So what? They shouldn't have been in the war to begin with. They should have been at home with their families. Sure, Tabitha was a private, but she was a lambda private, and when this war was over and the government sorted everything out, a lambda going AWOL would never get court-martialed. Once the ACLU or any other civil-rights group got ahold of this case, the situation with the lambdas would go to the Supreme Court, and the military would be found to be in the wrong.

That was obvious. Tabitha wasn't afraid of any army court. All she had to do was get out of this war zone and lie low until the war was over.

It was unfortunate that she had to get Aubrey involved in the middle of her escape attempt, but Aubrey could turn invisible. She'd be fine.

Rich knew that they had run. Tabitha had invited him to come along. But instead he checked her rifle and headed toward the fight, not away from it. He wasn't smart like Krezi. He didn't know a good thing when it landed in his lap.

Now they just had to find a house and steal some clothes. There were plenty of civilian refugees right now. Tabitha and Krezi would join their migration. Maybe they'd head south to Krezi's family—they sounded nice, and Las Vegas was far from any battle—or maybe they'd head all the way to Oklahoma to Tabitha's parents. They certainly wouldn't turn her in. Never.

Tabitha would lead the crusade. She'd be at the front of the fight, on the news, on the steps of the courthouse.

She would even join the rebellion. She didn't know how to find them, but there had to be a way. They were fighting the military, weren't they? So they'd be on the news, or at least they'd be on the outskirts of the military bases. They might still be focused on quarantine centers or lambda training camps. Tabitha could find them. She had to find them.

Maybe she could get Krezi to go with her. The two of them could be a good team. Tabitha could direct Krezi, mold her. Krezi was still so young and irrational. She needed Tabitha to help steer her right.

Would that make it harder to defend themselves against a court case? No. They weren't terrorists. They weren't enemies of the state. They were kids who were fighting to free other kids. What law empowered the government to turn fifteen-year-old Krezi Torreon into a killer? Even if there was a draft, this wouldn't hold up in court.

"This way," Krezi said, and scrambled up a short rise. The road was in sight.

"I told you it was easy," Tabitha said. "I told you we'd be fine."

They darted the last dozen yards through the forest and out onto the road where their bikes lay.

Tabitha raised her arms in triumph, and Krezi jumped to high-five her.

Then Krezi's face froze and Tabitha turned.

For just a moment they stared at one another—Tabitha and Krezi and the patrol of Russians. Everything seemed to stop as Tabitha's world silently fell apart.

The Russians went for their rifles and Tabitha went for her Beretta.

But it was Krezi who fired first, a blast of white-hot light slashing through the air. It hit the lead Russian in the chest and he flew backward.

Then bullets filled the roadway.

Tabitha squeezed off every round in her pistol, even while feeling the whisper of bullets flying past her body. Krezi fired again, her energy blasts completely melting through the soldiers' armor.

The gunfire ended as quickly as it began. Tabitha's slide was locked back, empty.

"Zakroitye ogon," one of the soldiers said down the street.

Tabitha was on her knees, but she didn't remember dropping down. She felt all over for wetness, knowing that adrenaline could be masking the pain of a hit.

She felt fine.

She moved to Krezi, who was lying on her back, staring at the sky.

"Are you still with me?" Tabitha inspected Krezi for blood.

"I can't breathe." She barely got the words out.

Her vest was a shredded mess, but it had saved her life. There were dozens of bullet impacts in the Kevlar. The problem with Kevlar, as they'd learned in basic training, was that it stopped a bullet from entering the body, but it didn't stop those foot-pounds of pressure from smashing you to pieces. Every bullet—and there were dozens—was a potential broken rib, or, worse, a broken sternum.

There'd be no way to ride their bikes out of this one.

Again the fourth and final Russian cried out, and Tabitha walked over to him and shot him in the head.

FORTY

JACK HAD CHASED AFTER JOSI as they fell back. Instead of finding Tabitha, Krezi, and Rich, they only came upon Rich, kneeling in the pine needles firing shot after shot from Tabitha's M16. He moved so quickly with it, just like he'd moved on the computer, like the gun was a part of his body.

Together the three of them had formed a firing line, aiming through the trees, shooting at the few Russians who came into view.

The Green Berets did not fall back with them. Jack could still hear the chatter of their M4s, a sound wholly different from that of the Russian Kalashnikovs. But there were so many more of the Russians, and so few of the Green Berets.

In the end, Jack never knew whether they couldn't hear the order, or they had simply dug in and refused to surrender.

Either way, the sounds of the M4s eventually stopped, and Jack motioned Rich and Josi to stop firing.

The rest of their team was dead, or captured. Tabitha and Krezi were gone. Jack prayed that Aubrey was still invisible. That she was hiding somewhere. But they had to get out of there.

"Where do we go?" Rich asked, eying the forest that stood between them and the enemy.

"We have to wait for Aubrey," Jack said. "She's going to come back."

"Agreed," Josi said.

"Then where?" Rich asked again, his voice more urgent. "The bikes?"

Jack paused before he could form the words. "There was gunfire back by the bikes. Not our guns—Kalashnikovs." Jack knew more—he'd heard the electric crackle of Krezi's lightning blast. But it had stopped as the Russian guns continued.

He didn't want to think about it. He didn't want to be here, in the middle of any of this. He didn't want to be a soldier. But he needed to stay strong.

Jack turned to Josi. "You studied the maps. There's a culvert somewhere. I could hear the water earlier." He strained to hear it now, but his ears had been deadened to such delicate sounds by the constant gunfire.

Josi nodded. "There's a ditch."

"Can you get us to it?"

"Can you make sure we're not going to run into a bunch of Russians?"

"I'll try."

She bit her lip. "Then so will I."

Josi turned south and began to jog in a low crouch, holding her rifle in front of her. Rich followed, swapping out a magazine while he ran, tucking the empty into his vest ammo pouch. Jack checked his own gun. He still had half a mag left in place, and a full one in his vest.

Josi left the road at no discernible trail and headed west, on a diagonal course past the soldiers at the farmhouse. Jack listened for them, hearing dozens of voices, but they were all on their right, not in front.

Aubrey was somewhere by the farmhouse, in the middle of it all. He could still smell her perfume, carried on the wind. But she was being perfectly silent, perfectly motionless.

He didn't dare to wonder what that meant.

Josi reached a short, steep hill, and she stumbled as she skidded down it, trying to keep her feet on the dry grass. Rich didn't make it all the way without landing on his butt. Jack ran, letting the forward momentum keep him upright.

"It's just up here," Josi said, and she led them over a low rise to a deep ditch. The water was shallow—maybe a foot deep at the bottom. It was late November, not prime farming season, and the valve to this row of ditches was probably closed.

The culvert was a broad pipe, probably five feet in diameter, that carried the irrigation water under a dirt road.

"This is a death trap," Rich said.

"Only if someone looks inside," Jack said, trying to be optimistic. "And who's going to want to get their boots wet in this weather?"

"Certainly not me," Josi said, but she was already sliding down the side of the ditch and into the muddy bottom. She held her rifle out, like she might find someone else hiding in the culvert already, but Jack could tell that it was empty. There was no breathing. He watched Rich slide down the side, struggle for balance, but stay upright. Jack came down last.

"We're going to get hypothermia," Josi said as she climbed inside. "There's six inches of water down here." She walked about twenty feet in, and Jack and Rich followed her. Because the pipe was round, they could sit on one side and prop themselves up with their feet on the other side to stay out of the water.

"Thank God for small blessings," Jack said.

"I don't know how long we can wait like this," Josi said.

"We've been overrun," Jack said, and felt his throat begin to close up. "And our whole team is dead. What choice do we have?"

Rich spoke. "I do not want to turn myself in."

"Neither do I," Josi said quietly.

Jack stood up and moved toward the far end of the culvert.

"What are you doing?" Josi asked.

"I'll hear anyone before they see me," he said. "And I have to be able to hear Aubrey when she comes back."

"If she comes back," Rich said.

Jack had always suspected that Rich liked Krezi. Now Krezi was gone. Not everything has a happy ending. Not for everyone. But Jack wasn't about to let the Russians get away with this.

FORTY-ONE

IT HAD TAKEN ALL OF Alec's effort to not get killed, and the best that he could do was wind up with an American infantry company in the invasion—trying to ram the same memories down the throats of everyone he met, trying to remind them of all the good times they'd had back at base, about that time when he'd thrown a perfect game of darts, about the hot girl that he'd bombed with at the bar, about anything else he could think of. It didn't help that the name Waterslaw was stitched into the uniform he'd taken. And, wait a minute—there was another Waterslaw in the company, and he didn't come back from the last mission. Alec literally spent every waking minute trying to dig himself out of his grave.

But it had finally worked, and now Alec was in the compartment of a Bradley, heading into battle.

It was because Alec was the very best at what he did. The thought made him smile.

Above them, sooner than Alec expected, he heard the chatter of big chain gun on the roof. It was intensely loud, like being in the center of a thunderstorm.

He held his rifle between his legs, pointing up. He'd never fired an American gun before, but he'd studied it back at the camp.

"You look nervous," another man said. His name badge read Tayler. "Nothing to be afraid of."

Another man leaned over, and though he had to shout to be heard above the noise, Alec heard every word. "His whole unit was killed."

"I know that," Tayler said. "I was just saying that we're the best company the army's got."

Alec wanted to laugh at this man's tactlessness, but he held it in and tried to look somber.

"Okay, team," the sergeant said. "Most of the fighting is settling down, but there are pockets of resistance, and we're here to put them six feet under. They've got Ellensburg, and we want it back. We're going to—"

And the power went out.

"That's it," the sergeant said. He stood and threw the latches for the giant back door to drop. "Spread out. Advance down this street."

Ellensburg looked like any small farming community

Alec had ever seen. They were in the city center, where there were dozens of houses on pretty little streets. It was almost hard to tell a war had been taking place here, except for the odd blast crater in the asphalt, and the occasional charred tree or building.

The small unit moved quickly, leapfrogging one another— one person would hide behind a brick wall, and then his partner would run forward and put his shoulder against a thick oak, ready so the first man could find cover behind a parked car.

It all worked smoothly, until Alec saw Russian soldiers up ahead. He didn't want to lead these Americans right to them—the Russians weren't acting like they expected a squad of infantry to arrive.

Tayler saw them, too, and motioned at Alec to call for the rest of the squad. Instead, Alec took aim toward the Russians.

"Don't," Tayler whispered. "You'll just attract their attention."

At the last second, Alec dropped his gun to the space between Tayler's helmet and his body armor. He fired twice, and it was the second shot that did it.

The Russians were suddenly on full alert, and Alec twisted around the side of the tree, the Russians to his back. One American peeked around the corner of the fence and Alec shot him in the face.

There was a sound like the world's largest zipper and Alec

could see the gunner on the Bradley was using the machine gun. He couldn't use the chain gun without power but he could use the big 7.62mm. He was pummeling the Russians, and they were scattering for cover.

Alec ran into the closest yard, but as he ran up the stairs he fell. He tried to get up, but his legs weren't responding. He looked down and saw blood oozing from at least four holes. At first there wasn't any pain—it just felt funny; his legs didn't work. He didn't know who had shot him. Was it the Americans, realizing he was a traitor, or was it the Russians, shooting anyone in American clothes?

Alec clawed at the doorknob, felt it slipping in his bloody, wet grip.

The door opened, and a girl stood there. She wore American gear, but not the bulky body armor or helmet.

"It's okay," she said, with a grim smile.

She pulled him by the shoulders, like a soldier would, he thought, but she was too young to be a soldier. Inside, another girl lay on the couch, obviously in pain.

He wanted to play with her mind—but he was in too much agony himself.

For now he had to be content to be a soldier together with two other soldiers, all of them injured.

FORTY-TWO

IT WAS EVENING WHEN AUBREY woke—still light, but gray.

She was crammed in the alcove behind the evergreen tree and the wall, and everything around her was silent.

She flexed a hand to see if the feeling had returned to her fingers. It had, and her sight was back, too. She was surprised to find she was still wearing her glasses—she'd thought they'd gotten lost.

She felt at her vest for a PowerBar, suddenly ravenous. There was one tucked into a pocket—a thick, dense protein bar that the doctors told her would help her with her recovery.

Like they really knew what would help. Aubrey was the first and only invisible lambda they'd ever seen. Still, she ate the bar—she was starving, and it was food. She felt for her canteen, but it was missing—probably came off while she was crawling.

There were noises from inside the wall. The house was occupied.

But there were noises everywhere, as though this little farm had become a forward base.

Or was it? Her team had been overrun by the Russians. Maybe the front was well past them, and Aubrey was deep behind enemy lines. Had the Russians captured the town of Ellensburg? Had they made it down to Yakima, to the army base?

Their electronic-interference tactic wouldn't work as well without the flyer. Aubrey could still see that shot burned into her eyes. Captain Gillett running, yelling at Aubrey to fire, Aubrey sighting the flyer just as she was lifting off the ground, just as the latch on the harness holding the lambda was pulling taut. Aubrey aimed for the center of the chest from only forty yards away, and fired. The flyer had dropped from the air immediately, collapsing on top of the other lambda. Instantly killed. A bloody stain on the white, wooden wall behind her.

Was that why Aubrey hadn't thought to shoot the other lambda? Because they were lying in a bloody heap together? Because she still expected Captain Gillett to come in and take the lambda? Because she was just a weapon to be pointed and fired, like Tabitha always said?

Aubrey flexed her legs, testing the strength in them. She seemed to be back to her old self. Her old, stupid self, who botched this mission.

She stood up, disappeared, and slid out from behind the tree. She checked her Beretta. The magazine was full. She chambered a round and held the gun in a two-handed grip as she snuck out of the alcove.

She might be able to solve all of this at once. Before she'd fallen asleep—hours ago—the lambda had been taken down to the barn. If he was still down there, she could fulfill the mission right now.

There were lights coming from the open barn door, which wasn't a good sign. She didn't know how the lambda worked, but unless he could turn his power off and on, he'd have to be eight miles away for the lights to be on. Granted, almost every other lambda could turn their powers on and off, but this boy hadn't even seemed fully conscious. Could he control himself at all?

She walked to the barn door, past two soldiers who stood as sentries, and stepped inside. Long tables had been set up, each with rows of computer terminals. But there was no body, and no one was saying anything in a language that she could understand.

"Jack," Aubrey said. "I don't know if you can hear me. I don't know if you're anywhere nearby. Probably not. I think I'm stranded. Way behind enemy lines. They must have rolled right over this area. I'm at the barn—at the farmhouse—and they've set up some kind of base here. They wouldn't do that if this were the front lines. I think I'm screwed."

She left the barn and headed into the house. It was a similar hive of activity, but there seemed to be more officers inside. It was a place for them to eat and talk, rather than a place for the soldiers to do their work.

"I'm checking all the rooms," Aubrey said. "I'm going upstairs right now. But I don't think the lambda is here. I failed, Jack. I got the flyer, but I didn't get the important one."

She paused at the top of the stairs, feeling her hand shaking on the banister. "And I don't know where you are, Jack. Or if you're anywhere. I saw Captain Gillett die. I don't know what happened to the others, but it was bad. I was right in the middle of it, and we were horribly outnumbered. Like, a hundred of them to our twelve."

Aubrey checked the first bedroom and found a sleeping man. He was still in his uniform, and definitely not the boy she'd seen. She moved to the next room. "I don't think the lambda is here. We had him and we missed him—I missed him—and now the Russians are free to keep tromping all over the Americans, and the Americans can't do a damn thing about it. They're going to win this war, Jack."

She'd cleared all the rooms on the top floor, and unless there was a basement she couldn't see, there was no lambda in this building. She moved into the dining room, to where papers were splayed out on the table. She flipped through them, but not only did she not understand the language, she couldn't even read the alphabet. There were a few maps, and she inspected them, all while men were moving around her. The satellite maps showed a town surrounded by the circular plots of farmland she knew so well from home. Was this a map of where they were?

She flipped through another scattering of maps. The city center, the bridges, the airfield. But nothing with a big, red circle that blinked *Lambda Here*.

"Okay, Jack," she said. "I'm going to leave. If you guys are anywhere nearby—if you can hear me—I'm going to go south out of the farmhouse. I'm going to head where there aren't any Russians around. Find me if you can. If no one is listening to me jabber, then I'm just going to—well, if no one is listening, then I don't think it matters."

She stepped out the front door of the farmhouse and into the evening air. It was chilly, and she was glad she was walking. She unclasped her helmet—the straps had been digging into her neck all day. She holstered the pistol, too. She wasn't going to shoot anyone. She didn't want to bring the weight of the Russian army down on her head.

Once she got far enough away from the farmhouse and was walking along a wooded fence line, she reappeared. She needed to save her energy.

She paused once, remembering the bottle in her pocket. She sprayed on some Flowerbomb perfume, hoping that it might help Jack to find her. Still hoping against hope that he was even out there.

"Jack, do you know what I want right now?" she said as she walked. "A mushroom burger from the Dairy Freez. I can't even remember the last time I went there with you. It's been a year? Before everything with Nicole. Wow, even a year seems short, though. It feels like a year since the homecoming dance. But it's only been, what? Two and a half months? Something like that. The world changes so fast.

"We need to plan something special for when we get out of here. When this war is over and we're done being lab rats in whatever experiments they have planned for us. We'll go back to town, and we'll—I don't know. Something great. I'd say we could go hunting, but I don't know if I ever want to carry a gun again. Let's go fishing. We can go to Nicole's cabin. I know what you're going to say, but Nicole's got to have normalized a little bit. She's in the middle of this, too. Besides, I can blackmail her. So we go to Nicole's cabin, and we'll invite the whole team, and I mean everyone. Even Tabitha, as much as she drives me crazy. We can even invite the Green Berets. Invite Nick Sharps, and all the others.

"It'll be nice. Everyone together again."

FORTY-THREE

JACK WAS FREEZING, HIS FEET wet and his ACUs muddy, as he, Rich, and Josi stalked along the ditch bank. It was breezy, and he couldn't hear Aubrey—he hadn't been able to zero in on her voice—but a gust of wind had brought a strong, sweet scent of her perfume, and it had made him run to the edge of the culvert and breathe it all in.

"Power's out again," Rich announced, looking at his wristwatch.

"You're kidding," Josi said.

"That or my watch got wet."

"Mine's out, too," Jack said.

"So we did all of this for nothing?" Josi stopped walking, hands on her hips. "Seriously?"

"You know what happened," Jack said. "Tabitha was

giving Aubrey the wrong orders."

"If the lambda wasn't dead, then why would Gillett give us the order to fall back? Wasn't that more important?"

"Maybe he thought it was dead."

"Or maybe he was trying to save his team," Rich said.

"No way," Josi said. "Green Berets don't run if they can complete their mission."

Jack turned and kept walking. "We're the only ones who fell back. Maybe they had a different signal for the rest of them. Maybe he was trying to save us." He could smell Aubrey off to their left, and pointed. "We need to cross this field."

"You're the recon guy," Josi said. "Are we clear to run?"

He could see everything as though it were noon, even under the shadows of trees. It looked clear, and it sounded clear.

"—never would. And that dress I was wearing? It cost six hundred dollars. Six hundred dollars. Who would pay that much for a homecoming dress? I'll tell you who: Nicole Samuelson. But I stole mine. I hope you're listening to this, Jack, because I'm running out of things to talk about."

"Found her," Jack said, turning to the others with a broad smile. "She's safe."

Josi breathed out a sigh of relief, and Rich raised his hand to give Jack five.

"Follow me." Jack held his rifle in front of him and ran

across the field. He was sure there was no one in the field, or along the bank of the ditch, and he hadn't seen anyone on the far side.

They reached the fence, and stopped.

"My watch is working again," Rich said. "It started up while we were running."

"What does that mean?"

"The lambda is on the move. Probably flying. Going fast."

From his place on the field, Jack didn't have a good view of any buildings. He couldn't tell which lights were out and which weren't. He focused on Aubrey.

She was coming along this fence line, maybe three hundred yards away. Jack ran up and down the fence with his mind, listening for anything. He heard the chatter of a squirrel, the swaying of branches.

The zip of a lighter catching flame.

"Damn it," he breathed. "There's a sentry. Maybe a hundred yards up."

"She's invisible, right?" Josi said. "She can slip right past him."

"If she's invisible," he said. "I doubt she is. She doesn't sound strained or tired."

"What do we do?" Rich asked, already bringing up his rifle.

"You can't see him," Jack said. "That's the problem. I can't see him either. He's in the trees. Maybe she'll catch scent of

271

the tobacco smoke, but the wind is blowing toward us, not toward her."

Aubrey spoke. "I'm beginning to think there's no one out here, Jack. That I'm talking to myself. Which is really too bad, because I've been spilling my guts about a lot of stuff."

"If we fire on him, everyone will come running," Jack said, putting a hand on Rich's barrel and lowering it.

"But if we don't," Josi said, "he might fire on her. And everyone will come running."

Jack reached to his belt and drew his knife. It was a bayonet knife, twelve inches long with a seven-inch blade. He'd always thought it felt clumsy in his hand.

"You're going?" Rich asked, surprise and worry in his voice.

"At least I can see in the dark," Jack said. He handed his M16 to Josi. "I'll be back."

Aubrey's voice was dry. "Jack, I'm going to keep talking a while longer, and then I'm going to shut up. If you haven't heard me by now, then you're probably not here anymore. I don't want to think about what that means."

Jack was jogging forward, smelling the cigarette now, listening to the sentry's breathing, short inhalations of smoke and then slow, relaxed exhalations. Aubrey was getting closer to him, and she was plodding through the dry November grasses sounding about as quiet as a truck.

No, he told himself, trying to calm down. Only he

could hear her like that. The sentry probably couldn't hear her at all.

Short inhalation. Slow, relaxed exhalation.

Jack was picking his trail as lightly as possible, moving across the dampest grasses on the bank, stepping on tree roots and rocks.

"If you can hear me," Aubrey said, "I miss you. I really don't know what I would do if you were dead, so you can't be dead, you hear that? If you were dead, I don't think I could keep going. I don't think I could keep up the fight. Even if the other guys were still around, which I don't think they are. I think a lot of people died in that firefight. More than just Captain Gillett. You'd better not be one of them. I'm doing this for you."

She was talking too loud, and she was getting too close.

Short inhalation, short exhalation.

The sentry moved. There was a rattle that could only have come from the strap on his rifle.

Jack heard the hiss of hot ash as the cigarette was tossed into the ditch.

"Jack, I'm going to give this up. When I reach the end of this field, I'm going to stop talking. I don't think there's anyone out here to hear me."

Very slowly, the sentry chambered a round into his Kalashnikov. Aubrey probably never heard it, but it sounded like a freight train to Jack.

He could see the man now, and Aubrey forty yards down the fence line. She was walking normally. The Russian was setting himself into shooting position against the tree.

Jack was nearly on top of him. If Jack couldn't see Aubrey, he didn't know if he'd have had the will to kill the man, but he *did* see her, and he *did* have the will. He ran the last dozen yards in a heartbeat.

The Russian turned just as Jack reached him, and Jack plunged the knife into the side of the man's chest, in the gap between the front and back of the Kevlar vest. There was resistance on the knife as it hit ribs, but Jack shoved it hard, twisting it flat, and it slid hilt-deep into the man's body.

His face was a stunned, quiet grimace, and Jack pulled the rifle from the man's hands, wrenching his finger from the trigger. A moment later the Russian slumped to his knees, coughing blood. It was Jack's first kill up close and personal, but the trained warrior in him came out. He yanked the knife free, smelling the coppery scent of pouring blood, and he slashed the knife into the man's neck, severing the jugular.

Jack stood over the body, staring down at it—at what he'd done, at the death he'd caused—when Aubrey suddenly appeared beside him. Jack felt the familiar confusion of her invisibility, and he dropped the knife into the dirt and turned to face her.

"Jack," she said, her face a stunned, uncertain smile.

"Aubrey."

He grabbed her, and they collided into each other, body armor to body armor, and their helmets clunked as they hugged closer.

She pulled back, her fingers entwined in his. "He was going to kill me." It wasn't a question, just an amazed statement.

"Yes," Jack said simply, staring into her eyes.

"And you killed him."

"Yes."

She threw her arms around him again, and this time they were both weeping, crying for the lives they'd both taken, for the innocence they'd lost, and for the miracle of being together again.

FORTY-FOUR

TABITHA WAS ROOTING THROUGH THE bathroom cabinet, looking for something clean and sterile to staunch the bleeding. She finally grabbed a tube of Neosporin and a box of Band-Aids. They were worthless against a bullet wound, but she took them back into the living room anyway, where Alec had his foot up on the ottoman.

Gingerly she began cutting away his ACUs just above the knee.

"This is good," Tabitha said, trying to stop her own gag reflex at all the blood. "It's not four bullets—it's two that went in and out."

Krezi strained to look from her place on the couch.

Tabitha prodded a little more firmly, feeling bone and watching Alec wince. "I don't know who's worse off. Your shots went through and through, just muscle. Krezi, I think, has broken most or all of her ribs."

"Tabs, did you know that Alec and I went to the same elementary school? He's older than me, but he had brothers who went there."

"Really?" Tabitha said. She used the scissors to start a nick in a bath towel, and then tore it lengthwise with her teeth.

"Yeah," Krezi said, out of breath over the few words she'd uttered. "He had a brother named John. I remember him—I used to go to his house."

A voice appeared in Tabitha's head. "I went to your middle school. What was it called?"

Tabitha froze. Was he talking to her telepathically? He wasn't looking at her—he was still grimacing at the pain in his leg.

Something was wrong. If Alec worked with lambdas, why didn't he come right out and say it? If his job was to track down AWOL lambdas, then why weren't they already arrested?

But she had an overwhelming desire to trust and confide in him. Tabitha wondered if this might be something like that friend of Aubrey's, Nicole, who could control pheromones.

"I went to East Hill," Tabitha lied. "Go Tigers." There was no East Hill school in her hometown. There was an East Hill deli. And there were tigers at the zoo.

Alec laughed and clapped his hands. "You're kidding me. One of you from Las Vegas and one of you from my old hometown in . . ."

"South Dakota," Tabitha said with a plastic grin.

"Liar," Krezi said. She looked at Alec. "She's from Oklahoma."

"I just got shot," Alec said, his smile never fading. "And she's already playing games with me."

Tabitha was suddenly aware of her guns—the M4 and the M9 sitting on the kitchen table, along with an assortment of grenades and knives. Krezi's pistol was there, too.

Tabitha could slam her finger into one of his wounds, and while Alec was screaming in pain, she could go for the guns. But Alec still had a gun on his hip.

"Krezi," Tabitha said with her telepathy. "This guy is no good. I don't know what's going on, but he can make us trust him, or he can make us remember things that never happened. I think I'm immune, since my power is putting thoughts in people's minds."

Krezi shot Tabitha a look that was half disbelief and half annoyance.

"I'm serious, Krezi. This guy is bad."

She finished one of the bandages—a mass of Band-Aids laid in place over the entry and exit wounds, wrapped in a long strip of towel—and then she moved to the second set of bullet holes, just below the knee.

"I think this one went through the bone," she told Alec. "We need to find a splint."

FORTY-FIVE

THE FOUR OF THEM CROSSED two more fields without seeing any other sentries or hearing any alarms before they paused for a breath. When they did, Aubrey hugged Josi and Rich, so glad to see them alive.

"Where are the others?"

"I don't know how much you figured out on your own," Jack said, watching the open field behind them. "But Tabitha was relaying false orders to you. We think she was trying to stall you so that the infantry would reach you."

Rage flared in her chest. "What? Why would she do that?"

"To run away," Rich said. "After the firefight started, Tabitha and Krezi ran for the bikes."

Aubrey was too stunned to answer. Tabitha had told her to

go slow. To check every tree. Had told her she couldn't kill the lambda until she got confirmation—confirmation that Tabitha never passed along. That was why Captain Gillett had come running.

"She got Gillett killed," Aubrey said, staring at Jack's shadowed eyes.

"They were all killed," Josi said, her voice breaking. "They died protecting us."

"But I heard the order to fall back."

"They didn't do it," Josi said. "We don't know why."

"I don't think they heard it," Jack said. "I could barely hear over that noise. Or maybe they got a different order than we did."

"I couldn't fall back," Aubrey said. "I couldn't move or I'd get hit."

Josi took a deep breath. "Maybe it was the same for them."

"What about Tabitha and Krezi?"

"We don't know," Rich answered.

"There were Russians behind us," Jack said. "We couldn't go back that way."

"And we weren't going to abandon you," Josi said, a tear rolling down her cheek.

Aubrey let the words wash over her. Everyone had gotten killed because of the bad orders, but then the team had come together, fighting to save everyone.

And only Aubrey, Jack, Josi, and Rich remained. Tabitha

and Krezi were AWOL. The rest of their team was dead.

Rich looked at his watch, and then at Aubrey. "You didn't shoot the lambda, did you?"

Her stomach fell. "No. I got the flyer, but I didn't get the lambda, not the important one."

"You got the flyer?" Rich asked, sounding surprised.

"Yes." She was certain of that one.

"It's flying again," Rich said, and held up his watch. "Power's off."

"That was quick," Jack said, looking up into the sky.

Aubrey didn't understand. "Has it been going on and off?"

"Just for the last twenty minutes or so," Rich said. "Off, then on, now off again. I figured it was the flyer because it's moving so much."

"Then they must have another flyer," Aubrey said. "Because I hit her in the chest, and she wasn't wearing armor. Maybe she survived. *Maybe*. But no way she's flying again."

"This is all Tabitha's fault," Josi said, her fists clenched. "We knew she was unstable. Why didn't we say something?"

"I had no idea she'd do this," Rich said.

"Neither did I." Aubrey was seething with anger. She had trusted Tabitha. She had let Tabitha into her head, let her guide her every movement, even when the orders didn't make any sense. And now the lambda was back at work, and the Russian killing spree could start again.

"I did," Jack said, still looking at the sky. "I mean, I didn't think that she'd sabotage everyone, but I'm not surprised she ran. She tried really hard to get me to go with her—to join her rebellion."

Aubrey didn't know that, and it made her angrier. That Tabitha thought she could get Jack to betray everyone. Jack, of all people. Aubrey had never met anyone so loyal.

"She made some good points," Jack said, more quietly. "She was very persuasive. I mean, obviously, I didn't go with her. But she made some good points."

"Well, she's going to get court-martialed," Josi said, without a hint of remorse. "She screwed us all."

"There," Jack said, stabbing a finger toward the sky. "Can you see it?"

"What?" Aubrey said.

He grabbed her arm, pulled her to him, and then pointed at something moving in the sky. Aubrey leaned her face against his sleeve, trying to follow the path. All she saw was the darkening sky.

"I don't see anything."

"You're not supposed to," Jack said, finally smiling. "It's not a flyer, guys. It's a glider."

"A glider?"

Aubrey strained to see it in the darkness and wished her eyes were better.

"A plane," Jack said. "It's got a dark, navy-blue, really narrow body with thin wings. And it's circling over the battlefield. They need a towplane to get it up in the air, and then it can circle for hours, probably for however long the lambda can use his powers."

"You should have seen that lambda," Aubrey said. "He was thin—like, anorexia thin. And sickly. He looked like he couldn't even walk on his own."

Josi spoke. "Maybe they're using him all up. Aubrey, think of your power if you were on meth or something like that. You could stay invisible a lot longer, and you'd be a lot stronger. But you'd also be crazy and get sick. If the Russians' entire strategy revolves around this lambda, maybe they don't care about his long-term health. Maybe they're just going to use him until they can't use him anymore."

"We need to report this," Rich said. "We could get some anti-aircraft guns on the glider."

"All our anti-aircraft stuff is electronic," Jack said.

"We still need to report this."

"Wait," Aubrey said. She looked at Josi. "Not to get all Dora the Explorer on you, but you're the map. Do you know of any place this thing could land?"

"Sure," Josi said with a nod. "If we're assuming that this entire area is overrun, then the Russians have taken Ellensburg. There's an airport there. It's small, but it sounds like this glider wouldn't need much. There's also a landing strip in Cle Elum, farther away."

"They'd use the close one, probably," Jack said. "Because

they keep putting this lambda as near to the front lines as possible."

Josi held out her hands. "Just so we're all clear: you're talking about going in there instead of heading back for help."

"I am," Aubrey said.

"What?" Rich said—he almost shouted.

"We haven't completed our mission," Aubrey said. "And we still have the best chance of getting eyes on that target. Plus, how close is the airfield to here, and how close is our army base?"

Josi didn't even have to pause to do the math. "About six miles to the airfield. About thirty-three miles to the army base."

Jack put his hand on Rich's shoulder. "At the rate they're going, the Russians will have overrun the base before we can walk there. Plus, we'd have to go through their front lines. We're already behind the enemy lines, so we should be able to avoid the bulk of their forces."

"Besides," Josi said, with a wink, "Aubrey's in command. She outranks all of us."

Aubrey laughed in spite of herself. "I didn't want to say anything."

Rich wasn't laughing. "You're talking about a full assault on their most protected asset. And we're three lambdas and a lambda private."

"You're forgetting that lambdas are pretty powerful,"

Aubrey said. "And I don't know how protected this one will be. The airfield will probably be covered with anti-air defenses, so that no American bombers hit it. But they won't be expecting a ground assault."

"You assume," Rich said.

"I assume. And that's where I think we should be going. It's where I'm going to go. But I'm not going to make you salute and follow orders." Aubrey had to finish this. She'd failed enough.

"I'm going to make you salute and follow orders," Josi said, surprising Aubrey. "We're still in the army. We saw what happens when orders don't get followed. And we need you, Rich." Josi looked up at Aubrey. "Turns out the kid is a whiz with guns, too."

"They're machines," he said, with a reluctant nod of his head.

"We can use a sniper," Aubrey said.

Finally, Rich looked into her face. "Yes, sir."

FORTY-SIX

FYODOR'S BODY WOULDN'T STOP TWITCHING. It felt like electricity was running through his veins—both sharp and dull pain at the same time. Every arm, leg, finger, and toe danced to a different deadly beat. Right now his fingers were flying, like he was playing the piano again—something he hadn't done in years.

He could barely see anything, his eyes rolling back in his head involuntarily. He wondered if they even knew he was conscious. He wondered if he was, or if this was just a dream. He didn't dream much anymore. He didn't do much of anything anymore. He was a corpse, a hollow boy.

Something wet touched his useless right arm. He tried to bat at the sensation with his other arm, and though it felt like he was using all the energy and strength he possessed, he couldn't make either limb obey him.

Pain pierced him, the all-too-familiar stab of a hypodermic needle. His neck turned sharply to one side, and then his teeth began to chatter.

He strained to see where he was, and he managed to get one eye open—just long enough for a mental snapshot of the room. But it wasn't a room; it was the interior of the glider. He must have been too out of it to know he'd been flying.

He tried to speak, to ask where Zasha was, but the words came out as a garbled groan. For all he knew, Zasha was nearby, getting some much-needed sleep. That must be why they were using the glider—to give Zasha a chance to rest. It was probably too much to ask that she be there to meet him when the glider landed. He knew they had no future together. He knew he would be permanently damaged by the constant stream of drugs in his system. And Fyodor knew what General Gromyko had said. The army would use Fyodor until the war ended or Fyodor died.

Fyodor didn't think he had much life left in him. And from the few snippets he heard, the Russians hadn't broken through the American lines yet.

He tried to ask about her again. "Za . . . Za . . . sha."

A deep voice spoke to him, but the words meant nothing. He felt like he was locked inside a dark, padded box, unable to move, speak, or hear.

Zasha, he thought. *I will stay alive for Zasha.*

FORTY-SEVEN

JACK LED THE GROUP, WALKING slowly in the low ditch beside a dirt road. He scanned everything ahead of them, his gun at the ready.

This entire area had seen artillery fire. It looked like some apocalyptic landscape: an abandoned grocery store with a plywood sign warning looters that someone was waiting inside with a shotgun. A gas station on the other side of the road that had exploded. A burned-down feedstore. They passed an Abrams tank on the road, its turret askew and acrid smoke pouring from the gap. Beyond it was an abandoned Stryker. Jack wondered if they would come across any other groups of soldiers on this road—crews or infantry teams.

With every step, Jack thought about how lucky he was to have Aubrey back. And with every step he thought of the man he had killed to get her. It had been so fast. So *easy*. That was the part that scared Jack the most—not that he was upset by the kill, but that he wasn't. He had stabbed a soldier who couldn't have been much older than himself, and it had been so simple, and so completely justified. It wasn't supposed to be easy, was it?

He knew it hadn't been easy on Aubrey. She fought on—she was a soldier, a warrior—but it ate her up inside. No matter how Jack looked at what he'd done, he couldn't muster those same feelings.

"There," he said, stopping and pointing. "The glider is coming in to land."

He watched the dark shape descend right to the place where Josi had suggested. It wasn't more than four miles away—maybe only three. Josi could tell them for certain, but he'd let Aubrey worry about that. He had to focus on the road.

"I think I can see it," Josi said.

Rich and Aubrey just watched the darkness without saying anything.

"It might not be down very long," Josi said. "Maybe it was losing altitude and needs to be towed back up."

Rich spoke. "They have to give him a chance to sleep at some point, don't they?"

"I don't know," Aubrey said. "But I agree with Josi. We ought to act like it won't be down very long. Jack, can we go faster?"

He started walking again, and called back, "We can go

faster. But I don't know if we can go faster and stay safe."

Suddenly, lights popped on all around them—the nearby house, a street corner, the lights on the abandoned Stryker. Jack ducked into the shadow of the ditch. Everyone was silent.

"Hold on, Jack," Aubrey whispered, and he couldn't hear her breathing anymore. She'd disappeared.

Jack scanned the horizon, over the lip of the road. There were lights on everywhere. The power was back on.

Aubrey was next to him. "Sorry. I thought we were getting ambushed."

"So did I," he admitted. "Power's back on. I guess the lambda does take breaks. We're not going to be able to stay on the road."

"Agreed," she said. "So where to?"

"You're the boss, but that tree line looks good. It's going in our general direction."

The trees seemed to follow another irrigation canal, off in the fields away from the road.

"Okay," she said. "Lead the way."

He raised his head up again, looking across the empty field to the house that stood beside it. He listened to the house, smelled the house, searched for any reason he shouldn't use it as cover. But it was silent. He turned back, stood into a crouch, and motioned for the team to follow.

He ran as fast as his low posture would allow, darting to the side of the house and pausing there. It was a midpoint for them to regroup before the longer run to the tree line.

He heard a rumble.

"Everyone down," he said, and he closed his eyes to listen. It was something big—a diesel engine coming toward them.

Then another engine joined it, the same size, though maybe a little older. And then another and another.

Aubrey popped her head up. "Even I can hear that," she whispered. "We can't stay here."

"They're all moving," Rich said. "The Russians who were stuck because of the power outage. They're all moving toward the front lines."

Jack could hear engines everywhere now. There was a tremendous crash, and a burst of light flickered across the farmland.

"What was that?" Aubrey asked, a hand on her helmet.

"A tank shot at something. Maybe it was one of our guys, sitting and waiting for the power to come back on. Or maybe it was target practice on one of the empty vehicles."

"Tanks will be coming down the road," Aubrey said. "And probably through the field. Let's get into this house. The infantry probably already checked this place and made sure it was empty."

The front door of the house faced the road, and the back door faced the field. Josi stood up and smashed the glass out of a side window with the butt of her rifle. She reached inside and unlatched it.

"That works," Aubrey said, and stood as Josi hoisted the

window frame up and then used the drapes to brush the broken glass away from the sill.

The four of them climbed through. There were no lights on inside—just a porch light out the front. Jack crossed the room to the big sofa and knelt on it, looking through the white, lacy drapes at the road. The others joined him. Soon there was a parade of Russian vehicles moving in front of the house and even in the ditch where they'd been walking. Armored personnel carriers, tanks, support vehicles, trucks carrying more infantry. Jack recognized most of them from training. BMPs, BTRs, T-90s, and T-80s.

There was a distant screech, barely audible to Jack above the noise of the military convoy. But it was growing louder.

"Crap." He jumped to his feet. "Is there a basement?"

Everyone looked at him with surprise, but no one moved.

The screech was getting closer.

Too late. "Everybody down!"

He grabbed Josi and Aubrey by the straps of their vests and yanked them off the couch. Rich followed, ducking down and holding his hands over his head.

Jack was on his knees when the first bomb struck, and he was thrown forward, over a coffee table and across the room. The plate-glass window shattered into a thousand shards and filled the room with shrapnel.

The noise stung his ears, and he clamped his hands over them.

Another bomb hit the road. The house creaked and swayed, as though it was getting pushed off its foundation, and the dust blew into the room through the open window, covering everything in a cloud of dirt.

There was another bomb, but it was farther down the road. It still shook the house, and the ceiling fan broke, collapsing to the floor. Josi let out a tiny shriek as it smacked into her helmet.

A fourth bomb exploded, farther still. And then the air raid appeared to be over for a moment.

"Everyone okay?" Aubrey asked, her voice wavering.

"I'm good," Josi said.

"I'm okay," Jack said, though his ears burned fiercely and he worried he might have some hearing loss.

Rich looked through the cloud of smoke and examined his hands. "I'm bleeding. But I don't think it's bad."

Aubrey sat up beside him and looked at his hands. They were peppered with a dozen shards of glass.

"Jack," Aubrey whispered, as she opened the first-aid kit on Rich's waist. "Make sure no one is coming to the house. Everyone be quiet. I don't want a tank crew to find us."

Jack definitely had some hearing loss. He could understand everything Aubrey had said, but it sounded muffled, like she was speaking through a blanket.

The drapes were in tatters, but the porch light had been blown away as well, so Jack got a little closer to the window and watched. He tried to listen to the Russians on the road, but his ears ached and the voices were muddy. Some men were screaming, others were shouting orders. No vehicles were directly in front of the house, but the remains of a tank sat at the edge of a crater a hundred yards to the east. There was another crater in the field on the far side of the road. He couldn't see where the other bombs had fallen.

Rich was swearing as Aubrey cleaned the glass out of his hands. None of the cuts seemed deep, but there were a lot of little ones.

"Can you still hold a gun?" Jack asked.

"Yes," he said with a wince. "I'd swear vengeance on somebody right now, but those were our bombs, weren't they?"

"Yeah."

"Damn it."

"At least we managed to do something," Josi said. She sounded dazed. "Finally."

Aubrey turned to Jack and gave him a look, her eyes flickering to Josi.

Jack moved from his place on the couch to where Josi sat on the floor.

"Is it the old brain again?" he asked with a smile in his voice. He put his hand on her back, and noticed a three-inch shard of glass hanging from the cloth of her Kevlar vest.

She rolled her eyes at him. "Isn't it always?"

He pulled the shard loose with two fingers, and then held it out in his palm. It was dark, but the glass still reflected light from the windows. "At least you don't have this in your spine."

Josi looked at it, and then closed her eyes. "I need a sensory-deprivation chamber."

"Why don't you lie down?" Aubrey said. "We can't move out until this road clears."

"You sure you don't need me?"

"Positive. We'll wake you up if something happens."

"Hang on," Jack said, and stood up. "I'm going to see if this place has a basement. I hear more planes."

FORTY-EIGHT

THE BOMBING CONTINUED FOR OVER an hour—long enough that Aubrey thought the Americans surely had to be winning. The house shook and shuddered, and something collapsed. The garage, maybe, or the porch.

The four of them waited in the dark of a basement family room, Josi lying on the couch and the three others sitting in overstuffed chairs. Aubrey had finished bandaging Rich's hands by the glow of her flashlight—the door was closed, and there were no windows. By the time she was done, the backs of his hands and fingers were covered in bandages and he looked like *The Mummy*, but the palms were clean—he'd had his hands balled into fists when the window exploded. He could still hold a gun, and his trigger finger only had a nick.

Aubrey was keenly aware that everyone was looking to her for leadership. Even though they'd all gone through the same training except for a week or two, she was somehow in charge. She'd been so annoyed when Tabitha was made second-in-command on their first mission, but now she wanted nothing to do with leadership.

She'd seen real leadership. She'd seen Captain Gillett sacrifice his life for the sake of the mission, running toward battle, screaming orders at her. He was a true hero. Aubrey was just a seventeen-year-old girl with two months of basic training and a couple weeks of real-world experience. She wasn't ready to make decisions. She wasn't even ready to decide when it was safe to go upstairs.

"What do you hear?" she asked Jack.

"Not as much as I want to," he answered. "My ears are still numb from that first bomb. But the traffic on the road sounds pretty light. It's been a while since a tank came by. There might be some trucks, but nothing big."

"They've cleaned up the damaged stuff?"

"I don't think they're cleaning anything up," he said. "Just moving forward. There were some injured people, but they're gone now, or . . . well, they're quiet. No more screaming. Maybe a field ambulance came."

"Anyone know what time it is?"

Rich spoke. "My watch is running, but it's turned off and on so often that I have no idea what time it is."

"There's a grandfather clock upstairs," Josi said. "It was still ticking. It probably isn't electric."

"What time did it say when we were up there?" Aubrey asked.

"Twelve thirty-five."

"Any guess how long we've been down here?"

"An hour?" Jack said.

"I was going to say two," Josi answered.

Aubrey gripped the arms of the chair tightly, and then forced herself to stand. "I'm going to check."

"I can see in the dark," Jack protested. "I'll go."

"No," Aubrey said. "I'm going."

She crossed the room, feeling her way along the wall until she reached the door. As she opened it she smelled dirt and smoke.

"Jack," she said. "Are we on fire?"

"No," he said. "The smoke is coming from somewhere outside."

"Okay." She was trembling, and she headed up the stairs rather than let Jack see.

Moonlight filled the stairwell, and even with her bad eyes she could see that something above her wasn't right.

One entire wall of the house had collapsed outward, and Aubrey found herself on the top step looking at the field beyond the house. To her left, she could see the road, lit by a burning BMP. Across the field another house had been pounded into oblivion, and a wide crater lay beside it—something was in that crater, but she couldn't tell what it was, other than something shiny and metal.

She looked up at the ceiling. It was drooping at a sharp angle. She quickly made her way into the living room and found the grandfather clock. All of the glass had been knocked out of the case, but it was still ticking. The face was in shadow, and she felt for the hands with her fingers. They were right on top of each other, pointing toward the two position. 2:10 a.m.

Good, she thought. That still gave them plenty of darkness to get to the airfield.

A shiver ran down her back. She had no idea what they'd do when they got to the glider. Would the lambda even be there? Would the glider have taken off before they could do anything? Would they have to wait until it landed again?

All she knew was that the power was on right now, which meant he wasn't using his powers.

Aubrey hurried back downstairs. "Josi, how far are we from the airstrip?"

"About three and a half miles."

"It's two ten," Aubrey said. "Let's get moving while we can. You feeling better, Jos?"

"I'll live."

Aubrey led the way up the stairs, but didn't step outside onto the collapsed wall. "Jack, you take point again."

"Which way are we going?" he asked.

"Wherever we can stay out of the light. House to house, maybe?" She chastised herself for that. Real leaders didn't end their orders with *maybe*. "House to house. If we can find better cover, then let's take that."

Jack nodded and took her hand to give it a squeeze. "Yes, sir."

She squeezed back, and then he climbed out through the broken wall, rifle at the ready, and began jogging toward the next cover—the ruined house she'd seen across the field. Aubrey ran after him, Rich and Josi falling in line behind.

The dirt was hard, the frozen earth of winter. Aubrey was grateful that no snow had started falling yet. That would have made this entire operation miserable. She'd thought the same thing back at the base. Winter had to come soon. Their luck couldn't last much longer.

It made her even more surprised that the Russians had chosen now to attack. Granted, Seattle and Portland didn't get a lot of snow, but the mountain passes certainly did. They'd been lucky to get through—even if they were being held back at Cle Elum and Ellensburg.

It made her wonder if they had a lambda who could control the weather. Wouldn't that be something. Already, this lambda they were chasing was the most powerful lambda Aubrey had ever heard of, though she wondered now if Josi was right—if it was because of drugs. The US Army hadn't been exactly fair with their treatment of the lambdas, but at least they weren't trying to turn any of the teens into super soldiers.

Then again, the Russians had had a lot more time to plan this all out. These lambdas had probably been trained for years; Aubrey had heard enough about the terrorists to know that they had been in sleeper cells for at least a decade, if not longer. This plan was a long time in the making. Maybe the Russians even had more powerful strains of the virus, and had created stronger lambdas who were more powerful and had fewer side effects.

Jack slowed as they approached the ruined house. The object Aubrey had seen in the crater was fully visible now— the wreckage of a plane. She couldn't identify it from the twisted and shredded steel, but she saw the American insignia—a white star in a blue circle with red-and-white stripes—beneath the cockpit.

No one was in the cockpit. The chairs weren't there—the pilots must have ejected.

Aubrey felt a sudden pang of fear. If pilots had parachuted down, would the Russians be searching the ground for them?

"Jack," she said, "are any people around?"

He was quiet for a long time. Aubrey rubbed at her face— her nose and cheeks were freezing.

"There's someone up ahead. Two men on the road."

"Our guys or theirs?"

"Not sure. They're not talking."

"Get us closer," she said.

He nodded and pointed at a wooden fence that ran the length of the next field, parallel to the road. "Let's go on the far side of that fence."

She agreed, and he jogged off. She followed, watching him run, wondering what she would do if the men were American. They wouldn't be armed with more than a sidearm, and they'd be trying to get back to the American lines, not wanting to go on a mission to kill the enemy lambda.

They were likely air force. How did rank work between different branches of the military? She had no idea, and that made her almost want to laugh. Here she was, leading a mission behind enemy lines to take out one of the most wanted targets in this war, and she didn't know something as basic as how rank worked.

Jack stopped at the end of the fence and turned. A paved road ran in front of them. "They're Russians."

"You're sure?"

"Yeah."

"Can we move around them?"

He lifted his head above the fence just enough to see them. "They're watching the intersection. They don't look like they have night vision, but one of them is staring this way."

She peered up and over the fence. She could barely see the men. They were probably a hundred yards away. But if she could see them with her bad eyes, she had to be sure they could see her team.

Aubrey took a deep breath. "I'll distract them. You watch. When they're distracted, you guys cross the road and get to the next cover—that barn over there. I'll meet you there."

Josi grabbed her arm. "Be careful."

"I will."

Aubrey disappeared. She paused to kiss Jack on the cheek, even though she knew he wouldn't feel it, and then she climbed the fence and started toward the Russians.

FORTY-NINE

AUBREY DIDN'T BOTHER TO CROUCH or hide. She didn't have a rifle—she'd left hers at the farmhouse when she'd run out of ammunition. But she carried Captain Gillett's Beretta on her hip.

She didn't want to kill these men—there had to be an easier way to create a diversion—but she felt good knowing she had the option.

They looked young—her age, or maybe a little older. Aubrey wondered if the Russians had a draft or if these guys had enlisted voluntarily. She glanced around for something to distract them with, but the intersection was empty. All of the wreckage was off the road, or farther away—not that she knew what she'd do with it if it were closer.

Both men had radios with headsets, so they could talk

immediately to their superiors and report whatever Aubrey was about to do.

She could kill them. Fast and easy. She was so close that it wouldn't be a challenge, not even with her tired hands.

She'd started a fire the last time she was supposed to create a distraction. But neither of these men was smoking, and she didn't have any matches.

They had grenades attached to their vests. She could pull the pin on a smoke grenade. She stepped closer to one of them—a baby-faced boy with a gap between his teeth—and inspected his grenades. The two fragmentation grenades were easy to identify—they were round, a little like the American M67 that she'd trained with. But the other grenades were cylinders. That was what smoke grenades looked like, but it was also what incendiary grenades looked like. She could be pulling the pin to send off a lot of smoke, or she could pull it and light this man on fire with phosphorus. The grenades had writing on them, but it was in Cyrillic.

And time was ticking.

She knew what she should do. She'd known it since she started walking up here. She just didn't want to do it. But it would work, and there wasn't anything else jumping out at her.

The baby-faced soldier's rifle hung around his neck, and he rested his arm on it.

"Forgive me," Aubrey breathed. "This is for you, Nick."

She put her hand on the trigger and gently pointed the gun at the other man's leg. She set the selector switch to automatic and pulled the trigger.

FIFTY

JACK HEARD THREE DISTINCT SHOTS, not from Aubrey's Beretta but from a Kalashnikov.

"Come on," he said, and the three of them ran from the fence and across the street.

"*Ti menyah ubil!*"

"*Ya, nyet. Ya eto ne zdyelal!*"

Jack kept running, making sure Josi and Rich were with him, pounding across the field at a full sprint until he reached the barn. He slid to a stop in the shadow of the building, his heart pounding. He hadn't thought that Aubrey was going to shoot, but he should have known.

He peeked his head out around the corner and focused in on the men. One was down, holding his leg, shrieking at the other.

"Schto ti zdyelal?"

"Mnye nuzhen vrach k peresechenyu dvesti trinadtset. Propuska. Propuska, ya skazal!"

Jack pulled back, looking at Josi. "How's the head?"

"I'll be fine," she said. "If everyone would stop shooting."

"That's probably what that Russian is thinking," Jack said with a tired smile.

"That's a little morbid."

"It's been a long day."

A moment later Aubrey appeared, out of breath and leaning forward, hands on her knees.

"Nick's plan?" Jack asked.

"Shot him in the calf," she said.

"How's your leg?"

"Fine. I probably need to change the bandage. I think I may have pulled some stitches earlier."

"We should have checked it back at the house."

Rich jumped in. "You just want to look at her legs."

Josi and Aubrey stared at him.

"What?" he said. "Jack just joked about a Russian getting shot and I can't joke about Aubrey's legs?"

Jack started to laugh.

Aubrey's face broke into a smile. "That's *Private Aubrey's legs* to you, lambda."

"Yes, sir."

Josi snorted.

Aubrey sighed through her smile. "We need to get moving. Jack?"

"Let's do it." He turned and began running toward the next cover—a cluster of trees at the edge of the next field.

They ran for what felt like hours. It was the same routine the whole way—darting from cover to cover, watching for Russian patrols and sentries. They were able to avoid everyone else that they came across. Security seemed to be getting looser, not tighter, as they got deeper into enemy territory and closer to the airfield. There were more houses, which made running and hiding easier, and the airport was on the north end of town; they didn't have to go through the city center, or even go past many buildings to get there.

But for all the ease they were having, and the jokes they were telling, Jack was growing more and more uneasy. The airport was going to be hard to access. And the lambda was going to be guarded.

They ran past a group of three ponds to a large house.

"Okay," Josi said. "It's right over there." She pointed to a street, and to the field beyond it.

"It's dark," Rich said. "Is the power out again?"

Aubrey shook her head and pointed at a house to the south that still had a porch light on. "It's probably—"

Jack held up his hand for her to be quiet. He was listening. The airfield lit up as two dozen rockets shot into the air, just in time to meet four very low-flying American planes.

The whole house seemed to shake as the planes flew over. Two of the planes—they were Super Hornets—were hit by the rockets and burst into flame. But all four of them managed to drop their bombs, which hit the airfield like an earthquake.

The house they were huddled beside shuddered violently, its windows warping and shattering.

"I am getting so sick of glass," Rich started to say, but another wave of American planes came right over them louder than a freight train, louder than anything Jack could compare it to. A second set of explosions rocked the airfield and Jack was knocked to the ground by the force of the blast. He watched the sleek black jets—F-35 Lightnings—veer up in a sudden climb.

Instead of climbing and disappearing, they slowed, stopped, and then began to fall.

Jack glanced back at the porch light, but Rich was ahead of him.

"Power's out."

All four of the aircraft tumbled helplessly back to Earth, exploding in the fields beyond the airstrip.

"Jack," Aubrey said. "Find me the glider."

So much of the airport was burning that it was easy to see across it.

"There are two runways," Josi said. "And they only hit one of them."

"Where's the glider?"

"I'm looking," Jack said. "It might be burning rubble. I can see the remains of six Russian jets."

"The airport is laid out in a triangle," Josi said. "Two runways, and then a road connecting them. There's a row of hangars and buildings on the south side—I think that's what just got bombed."

Aubrey was on her feet. "We need the glider. Where the glider is, the lambda will be."

"There it is," Jack said, and pointed. "Over by the far buildings—the ones that didn't get smashed."

"Let's get closer," Aubrey said. "Quick."

Jack stood up, hating to move when there was so much light, and ran through the yard of the house and past two more. He stopped at a row of trees. They were at one point of the triangle, where the two runways came together. A tank was sitting quietly at the point, its crew watching the fires off to the west.

"Damn it," Jack said, and pointed. "The glider is being hooked up to a towplane."

"Then the lambda's going to be on it. What guards are there?"

Jack pointed. "There's that tank. And we can probably bet there are enough soldiers to fire all of those surface-to-air missiles we saw."

"Those weren't coming from a vehicle?" Rich asked.

Josi answered. "They were coming from all over. I'd guess Grinches or Gimlets."

Jack looked at her. "What kind of names are those?"

"It doesn't matter," Aubrey said urgently. "Is the lambda in the glider?"

Jack closed his eyes and tried to focus in on it. "It's too close to the fires," he said. "I can't make out something like breathing."

"Where will it take off?"

"Straight ahead," Josi said. "Past the tank. The other runway is too bombed out."

"Rich," Aubrey said. "You're good with that rifle?"

"Yeah."

"You're our sniper. Josi, you stay with him and keep him safe."

"What am I supposed to shoot at?" he asked.

"Don't let that glider get off the ground," she said. "Take out the towplane or the glider once they get over to the runway. They'll be driving down the runway coming toward you here. Shoot the pilot or the tires or something. But not until they're on the runway. We have to make sure the lambda is inside."

"Should I stay here?"

"Wherever you have a clean shot."

Jack looked at Aubrey. "What about me?"

"You come with me. We're going to find that lambda, and kill him."

FIFTY-ONE

THE AIRPORT WAS ONCE SURROUNDED by a chain-link fence topped with barbed wire, but the bombs had blown it to steel ribbons. Aubrey and Jack could have easily run onto the small airfield; there wasn't much to it—just two landing strips and a handful of buildings. But if they did, they would be bathed in firelight and clearly visible. Russian soldiers were trying to extinguish the flames and soon they'd patch the runway. Aubrey could see a bulldozer standing by.

"They're going to have to turn the power back on," Aubrey said to Jack. "To get that towplane up in the air, and get the bulldozer working."

"Can we use that to our advantage?"

"I'm not sure," she said.

She ran, her Beretta out and in a two-hand grip, to a cluster of trees—the last trees before the open airport road.

"Tell me what you see," she said, breathing heavily. They'd spent the night jogging and hiding, and she was already feeling tired. She couldn't do this whole operation invisible.

He pointed west, close to the building with the glider. "There's a sniper on top of that water tower, or grain silo. I'm not sure what it is. I can see five or six Russian fighters still intact after the bombing. Pilots are getting in them."

"What about ground troops?"

"There're about thirty around the fires. None of them are paying attention to anything else. The glider is hooked up to the towplane now, and there are pilots inside both."

"I've got to get over there," Aubrey said, and watched the sniper. "How close do you think he is?"

"Not close enough," Jack said. "He'll see you even if you're invisible."

"Can you hit him from here?"

"You're a better shot than me."

"When my eyes are good," she said, adjusting her glasses and trying to get a clear look at the man. "And I don't have a rifle, and yours doesn't have a scope."

Jack paused before he answered. "I think I can hit him. But if I don't, we're going to have hell rain down on us."

"How far away is he?"

"I'd say two hundred yards."

"So I've just got to get sixty yards before he can't see me." She thought of how fast she could run, about their timed trials in basic training, when she was carrying all her gear. Right now her armor felt like she had rocks piled over each shoulder.

"He's pointed this way," Jack said.

"Then you'll have to take the shot," Aubrey said.

"We should get Rich. He's way better than me."

Aubrey shook her head, glancing at the men putting out the fires. They were spraying foam from a fire truck. It looked like it had been trying to drive close to the burning airplanes when the power went out.

"The noise of those fire hoses will cover your shot," she said. "You've got to do it now."

"But—"

"Just do it," she said, "and I'll use it as covering fire, and I'll run. So even if you miss, I'll get close to him." She was trembling as she said it, but she tried not to let him see. Hopefully he wasn't listening to her racing heartbeat.

Jack was quiet as he knelt beside a tree and aimed his M16. "Aubrey."

"What?"

"This is the real deal."

"I know," she said, trying to calm herself with long, slow breaths.

"I want you to know—"

She cut him off. "Stop. Just stop. I know where you're going, and we can't do this right now."

"I don't care," he said. "I love you."

Aubrey felt a tear in her eye, but she didn't want to acknowledge it. "Just take the shot."

"Okay."

"I love you, too."

All was silent, except for the pop and crackle of the fires off to their right.

The lights came back on.

"Damn it," Jack said. "Okay. On the count of three."

Aubrey watched the tower, not sure she could even see the sniper up there. Her heart seemed to beat a hundred times in the three seconds Jack counted down.

He fired, a sharp crack splitting the air.

Aubrey jumped from the trees, sprinting toward the tower. As she ran she disappeared, knowing she had to get sixty yards before the sniper—who might have been alive or dead—fired back.

There was another gunshot, and then another. They weren't sniper shots. They were coming from Jack. He must have missed, and was now just trying to keep the sniper's head down. She heard one ping off the giant steel tower.

And then she was close enough to him, out of the sniper's vision, invisible. She kept running, slowing only slightly as she approached the base of the tower. She nearly collided with a fence that she hadn't seen. It was surrounding the tower on three sides.

She breathed a sigh of relief, though she heard the sniper returning fire on Jack.

She stumbled around the edge of the fence, ready to climb the ladder and take out the sniper with her Beretta, but the power was on and that meant the glider could be moving.

A blaring, metallic voice burst above all the noise.

"Amerikanskiye voiska priyehali. Amerikanskiye voiska priyehali."

She searched the darkness for the glider. She saw dozens of troops scrambling around the broken fence, apparently not sure whether they should be putting out the fires or defending against an unseen enemy.

The glider was beyond them, its black body lit orange by the gleam of the flames. It was attached to a small single-propeller plane, like a large Cessna, and it was parked in front of the largest of the buildings at the airport.

No one was shooting anymore. Not Jack or the sniper. Aubrey didn't know what that meant, and she had to force herself not to think about it.

He's okay, she told herself as she started to run toward the glider. *He's okay.*

The men in front of her were abandoning the fire, forming a loose battle line where the airfield's fence used to be. Two men were shouting at them to get them organized. Aubrey thought about how easy it would be to shoot one of those officers, but she didn't need to. She could slip through the ranks easily enough.

Then Aubrey fell to the ground, landing on her butt and sprawling onto her back. She heard the report of the rifle a moment later, but she was too dazed to realize what it meant.

FIFTY-TWO

JACK SAW AUBREY FALL. AND he rose to his feet. *No.*

There had to be a second sniper somewhere. Jack had finally hit the one on the tower after six shots, but there had to be another one. And that second sniper had shot Aubrey. And she'd fallen. And she wasn't getting up.

There was nowhere for Jack to run. If he moved from the trees, the string of soldiers—a full platoon—would open fire on him.

She has to be alive, he told himself.

Jack took aim at one of the officers, let out a slow breath, and squeezed the trigger.

The man dropped like a bag of wet sand.

No, she really *had* to be alive. If she were dead, she'd reappear, and she was only twenty feet in front of the line of soldiers. She was alive.

But that didn't mean she wasn't hurt. She still wasn't moving.

Jack took aim at the second man, who'd been herding the men into line—the man who had to be their commander. Jack squeezed the trigger and watched that man fall, clutching his hip.

Jack's rifle must be like a beacon in the darkness—a bright muzzle flash in a dark cluster of trees in a dark night. A moment later, bullets began to whiz past his head. Jack dropped prone and started returning fire.

Talk to me, Aubrey.

He could hear the breathing of dozens of people, but he couldn't pick out hers. Worse, he had no idea where the sniper was who had hit her. He had no way to help other than to engage an entire platoon.

An entire platoon that was advancing.

Crap.

FIFTY-THREE

AUBREY LAY STUNNED IN THE dirt, pain digging into her shoulder like a dozen daggers.

She was having trouble getting enough air—she wasn't sure if she was getting any at all.

She tested her right hand. It seemed like it was working, though as she tried to curl her bicep bolts of electricity shot all the way from her elbow to her neck. She felt for the wound with her left hand, and found a bloody spot torn into her shoulder. She didn't prod—it hurt far too much for that—but she guessed that the bullet had gone through her collarbone.

Above her, the row of soldiers was moving and firing, which meant they'd seen a target. Jack was under fire.

She had to be bleeding badly, but she didn't know what

she was supposed to do for a shoulder wound. She couldn't put a tourniquet on it. And there wasn't time.

That glider was still out there. And so was a sniper.

She didn't dare lift her head. If the sniper had shot when she was standing, but hadn't shot her while she was moving her arms just now, then he couldn't see her on the ground. She assumed that meant he was standing—maybe somewhere in the center of the airfield?—and wasn't perched on the roof of a building. Someone on a roof would see she was still moving.

"Jack," she said, with a wheeze. "I'm okay, I guess. If you could find that sniper for me, I'd kiss you senseless."

With a grunt, Aubrey rolled onto her stomach, and began to pull herself forward through the dirt with her left arm— her hand that held the Beretta. Her right felt absolutely useless. She wondered how she'd be able to aim her gun if she ever got close enough to that lambda.

"And you've got super senses, Jack," she wheezed as she moved, "so kissing you senseless would be some serious kissing."

There wasn't any nearby cover—ahead of her were the burning remains of several planes, and to the west were the six Russian fighters, just starting to taxi away from the fires. Much farther to her west was the large building where the glider sat. Since there was nowhere else to go, she began to scramble over there.

It was slow going—slow and horribly painful. But she forced herself to go on. She held her right arm to her side, trying not to bump it while she dragged herself with her good arm. The glider still hadn't moved. Maybe it was waiting for the tarmac to clear of the fighter jets, or maybe it was waiting for the lambda to be somehow prepared.

She had one smoke grenade. She could throw it and use it to obscure herself from the sniper, but she didn't know where he was. She might as well be throwing it blind.

Still, it might slow the fighters, which might slow the glider.

Or it might make them go faster, if they knew they were under close attack.

She heard a pair of loud bangs behind her, much louder than the chatter of automatic weapons, and for a moment, all the shooting stopped.

She didn't wait to find out what it was. She kept crawling toward the building.

FIFTY-FOUR

JACK WAS UP AND RUNNING as soon as the flashbang grenades exploded. He crashed through the trees and bushes, forcing his way out of the cluster of greenery that the platoon of soldiers had been swarming around. Jack threw a fragmentation grenade as he ran, then a smoke one for good measure, and then he was sprinting west toward Aubrey and the sniper's tower.

He wished he could turn invisible, and wished it even more as soon as the bullets started to fly around him. A few were coming from the platoon—the platoon that had lost at least eight men in their advance toward him, and surely men from the frag grenade. Pops of new shots were coming from a different angle—from the center of the airfield.

He could see Aubrey as he ran, saw her holding one arm

tight to her chest as she dragged herself with the other.

It was only now that he realized he had no idea where he was going. He'd had to get away from the advancing platoon, and it only made sense that he run after Aubrey, but he was in the open, completely visible to everyone, and only armed with his rifle.

If he could just sit down somewhere, he probably would be able to see the sniper in the dark. But the sniper was already taking shots at him. As soon as Jack stopped running he'd be dead.

He turned slightly, darting around the fence and stopping behind the tower.

He was backed into a corner. There was nowhere else to run. Even as he began to climb the ladder to the top of the three-story tower, he knew it was a dead end. He couldn't shoot everyone from there—not an entire Russian platoon. And while he could hide up there for a little while, eventually someone would get a shot at him—maybe from the roof of another building, or maybe with a rocket-propelled grenade.

This wasn't a hiding spot—it was a suicide mission.

But he'd get that sniper. He'd clear the way for Aubrey.

He reached the top of the tower a moment later, bullets pinging off the steel around him, and he found the Russian sniper—the one he had killed.

Jack lay flat, a bullet winging past his head, and searched

the airfield. There. The other sniper was on his stomach in the grass in the center of the large triangle-shaped airfield.

Jack saw the sniper's muzzle flash and an instant later felt a bullet graze his helmet.

Jack took aim, not letting the sniper get off a second shot, and he fired.

FIFTY-FIVE

AUBREY SAW THE GLIDER DOOR open ahead of her. Three soldiers emerged from the building, carrying the lambda, still lying flat in his harness.

Aubrey rolled onto her stomach, pain flaring through her right arm as she put pressure on it. She was aiming using her left hand instead of her right, but her arm was steadied against the ground.

She fired, and the bullet went wide, punching a hole in the fiberglass body of the glider.

The men didn't seem to even notice the shot, and they continued to carry the boy to the plane, no change of pace, no ducking.

Aubrey lined up the shot again, thought about trying it with her right arm, but knew it would be just as jumpy as her left. Or worse.

She centered the sights on the lambda's body, on the middle of the big canvas harness, and squeezed the trigger.

The gun didn't fire.

"No," she breathed, and pulled the trigger again.

Nothing.

"Come on."

She clicked the trigger four more times, and each time the gun did nothing. She ejected the magazine and a tablespoon of dirt came pouring out with it.

"Damn it," she whispered, ejecting the current round and working the slide back and forth. She slapped the magazine into place. She aimed at the lambda just as he was disappearing into the body of the glider, and pulled the trigger.

Nothing.

"Damn it, damn it, damn it," she said, dropping the gun and rolling onto her side to take the pressure off her bad arm.

She'd come all this way, and her gun was jammed. She'd failed.

From somewhere above her, she heard Jack's voice.

"Aubrey, you're clear! You're clear! Sniper down!"

Too late, she thought, but she forced herself to her feet. *Too late.*

She was woozy from loss of blood, and exhausted from being invisible and from a night-long jog, but she made herself move toward the glider. The three men were dashing away from it, back into the building.

Aubrey was running out of clandestine maneuvers. She ran toward the closest man, tried to trip him, and body-checked him instead. They both went sprawling.

He wasn't armed like an infantryman, but he had a pistol. It was blockier than her Beretta, but it was clean. She snatched it out of his holster, fumbled with the safety, and fired ten rounds into the body of the glider.

She could see the holes—light glowed out of each—and they were a scattered mess. She was too shaky, too tired. Too not-left-handed.

The towplane was moving, pulling the glider toward the runway.

She ran after it. There was nothing else she could do. She had to chase it down. She didn't know how many shots were left in the gun—didn't know if this kind of pistol held thirteen or fifteen or seventeen or however many rounds. The gun still felt heavy—still felt like there was something inside it.

She wasn't going to keep up with the taxiing towplane. It was going too fast, and she was too tired. She left the tarmac and cut across the dirt center of the airfield. It had to go the long way following the triangle, but she could head it off with a hundred-yard run.

As she sprinted, Aubrey wondered what had happened to Jack. He had yelled at her, told her that he'd killed the sniper, and that must have brought down a rain of fire from the

Russians. His voice had come from above her—had he gotten up on the tower? That was crazy. They could surround him. Granted, he could hide up there and stay out of their line of fire, but for how long? Soon someone would get up on a building. He was trapped by what was left of a platoon.

She turned to look, but by now the tower was just a blur. She couldn't tell how many men were surrounding it.

When this was over, when she stopped the glider—somehow—she'd go back. An invisible girl could clear out a platoon of soldiers standing around a tower. Even if all she had was her left hand, she'd go back and save him. She could do it. She had to do it.

She wasn't walking in a straight line. She was weaving and nearly tripping over the uneven ground.

But the glider was coming in her direction. It had reached the runway, and was taxiing into takeoff position. She needed to be in place.

And if she failed, there was still Rich at the end by the tank, ready to take a last-ditch shot at the towplane's pilot as it took off.

The propeller was roaring like a buzz saw as it approached her. She stood just off the runway. Rich had to see her by now. He was more than a hundred and forty yards away. She almost wanted to wave at him—a sad, good-bye wave. She didn't think she was going to make it out of here anymore. She was bleeding too much. It was over.

Rich would take his shot once the plane had turned.

She watched it rotate in place, turning in a very sharp circle that brought the glider to a stop in front of her.

"Take the shot, Rich," she said, holding out her pistol toward the towplane's cockpit window. Her arm was shaking so bad she thought she might miss the plane entirely. But Rich could shoot.

Why wasn't he shooting?

"Come on, Rich," she said. "Take the shot."

There was nothing. Had the platoon of Russians found Josi and Rich? Had Josi and Rich tried to help Jack?

"Now!" she screamed, tears starting to stream down her cheeks. Her words were caught up in the wind of the propeller and were blown away.

Aubrey pulled the trigger, walking toward the cockpit, buffeted by the winds with every shot she took.

Seven rounds. That was what was left in the gun. Seven rounds, and she put them all into the cockpit.

And the plane didn't move. The pilot didn't punch the throttle and try to get away. Aubrey couldn't see a thing inside the dark cabin of the cockpit.

She turned toward the glider. She had to walk back around the wing of the towplane, and toward the door. As she did, she caught sight of the glider pilot, a confused look on his face as the towplane didn't move.

Aubrey stepped to the glider door, halfway back on the

skinny little plane. She yanked it open, and looked inside just long enough to see the lambda, a boy who couldn't have been more than fifteen, shriveled and emaciated. He had an IV in his arm that was hanging from the inside wall.

The pilot turned in his seat. He would have seen the door open and empty.

"Schto eto takoi?"

"I'm sorry," Aubrey said, her eyes still wet with tears. "I'm sorry they did this to you. I'm sorry for what I have to do."

The boy writhed in his canvas harness.

Aubrey pulled a grenade from her vest. She glanced back toward the edge of the runway, toward the short grade down to the dirt.

"I'm sorry."

She pulled the pin and threw the grenade, and then ran.

FIFTY-SIX

THE FUSELAGE OF THE PLANE ripped in two. Aubrey waited and listened, but there was nothing— —no movement or noise.

Aubrey began to sob. She knew she had to get up, she knew she had to run, but she sat on the side of the road and cried. She cried for the boy, and for Jack, and for all the Green Berets, and for whatever had happened to Josi and Rich and even for Tabitha and Krezi. She cried for those nine men she'd killed at the roadblock and all the men she'd killed since then. Enough for a lifetime. More.

FIFTY-SEVEN

"I GUESS YOU'RE GOING TO be holed up with us here," Tabitha said. "Until the medics come."

She was trying to make something in the kitchen out of canned goods. Alec kept speaking to Krezi, kept trying to make her say things. Tabitha didn't know who he was, but he wasn't on their side.

At one point, Tabitha moved to the table and, as surreptitiously as possible given its size and weight, holstered her M9.

Still Alec's mind continued to assault her. She should trust him. They knew each other, back at that birthday party—at the dance—hanging out, getting ice cream. It was like he was feeding her memories so generic that her mind would fill in the details. He never said what kind of party it was, or what ice-cream shop. He'd probably done this very thing to a dozen—maybe dozens—of people. But for whatever reason, her telepathy turned his psychic promptings into plain English and she could understand simply what he wanted her to believe.

Tabitha took the plates of food—mostly crackers and a little Spam—into the front room. She scooted a small stool between Alec and Krezi. Alec bent forward to get a cracker, and as he did so, Tabitha grabbed at his pistol. He wheeled away, faster than any movement she'd seen from him yet, and drew the pistol himself. Tabitha was on her feet, her M9 in a two-hand grip.

"Who are you?" Tabitha demanded. "Why can I hear your thoughts?"

He looked completely in control, even with a gun aimed right at his heart—he'd taken off his body armor, too.

"You can hear my thoughts?" he said, sounding genuinely surprised. "No one can hear my thoughts. You must be special. Lambdas? I got quarantined with all the lambdas, but I was able to talk my way out of it. It's a shame you didn't. Now you're on the losing side of a very nasty war."

"We're joining the rebellion," Tabitha said. "And . . . and . . . it's none of your damn business. You come in here and play with our minds like you can do whatever you want."

He held the gun steady on Tabitha but glanced over at Krezi.

"I—I can't do anything."

"Liar," he said with a grin. "I do so much enjoying getting secrets out of people. It's where I really shine." He focused back on Tabitha. "Of course, it's easier without a gun pointed at you. Do you know what the problem with a standoff is?"

Tabitha just stared back at him.

He fired his pistol, three quick shots.

As she lay dying on the floor, staring at the peeling paint of the ceiling, she heard him say, "You always think you're fast enough to beat the other guy to the trigger pull."

There was a brilliant blaze of light and a cry of rage.

FIFTY-EIGHT

THE EXPLOSION AT THE GLIDER had attracted attention, and the tank that had been sitting at the front of the runway came rolling toward Aubrey. She dropped the pistol, and gingerly stood up. She needed to get back to Jack. She needed another gun.

She slowly walked around the wing of the plane and past the sputtering propeller. She could barely see. That didn't matter. She needed to get back to Jack. He and the platoon were a hundred yards away.

"Aubrey?" a voice called out.

She stopped and looked around. It sounded like Josi. She hoped the tank crew hadn't heard.

"Aubrey?"

The tank stopped.

"Aubrey? Where are you?"

The voice was coming from on top of the tank. Aubrey squinted in the darkness, trying to make out the face of the person in the tank commander's seat.

She turned visible. It felt like a huge weight was suddenly lifted off her back, like she could suddenly breathe again.

"Josi?" she asked, exhausted.

"Aubrey! You did it!"

The driver's hatch opened, and a face popped out. "Aubrey! You stopped them! What happened to your arm?"

"I got shot," Aubrey said, an exhausted smile covering her face. "How did you get the tank?"

"The crew got out to pee," Rich said. "Josi killed them."

"And Rich can understand any machine, including tanks," Josi said proudly. "We were waiting down there for the plane to come. I have the mounted heavy machine gun." She slapped the giant gun mounted on top of the tank.

Aubrey stepped toward them. "I'm going to need some help up," she said. "I've only got one arm."

"We watched you from the end of the runway," Rich said, clambering out of his seat. Josi was climbing down from her perch as well. "You were awesome."

"Yeah," Aubrey said, pain in her voice. "The plan worked."

"Where's Jack?" Josi asked.

The two of them pulled Aubrey up by her armpits. She wanted to scream, but she held it back.

"He's in a place where a tank would really come in handy."

The tank rolled across the airfield, passing the wreckage of the earlier bombing run and ignoring the calls from annoyed soldiers. Aubrey sat in the commander's seat, and Josi in the gunner's, both of them sticking their heads out of the turret. A dozen soldiers still stood around the tower.

"Josi," Aubrey said. "Clear us a path. That tower's full of fuel, I think, so try not to blow us all up."

Rich had given Josi all the basics in how to operate the machine gun, and she pointed it at the soldiers sieging the tower. She only had to fire a dozen rounds—dropping five men and sending the rest of the infantry running. Their own tank was firing on them.

Jack was ready. Aubrey had been talking to him the entire drive over from the glider. Rich pulled the tank in next to the tower, smashing the fence as he did so. Aubrey ducked inside the tank, watching as Jack scrambled down the ladder and climbed in to her commander's seat. These tanks technically were only made to hold a crew of three, but Aubrey was tucked tight in the center.

Rich revved the engine and in a minute the tank was going fifty miles an hour away from the airfield and into the residential streets of Ellensburg.

"Hey," Jack said, peeking down inside the body of the tank.

"Hey."

"I killed that sniper."

"I noticed."

"Senseless. That was the word."

"Senseless. Agreed."

"Are you okay?"

"Not really. Let's go home."

FIFTY-NINE

AUBREY'S ACU JACKET WAS SOAKED in blood, from her collar to the middle of her chest. Jack and Josi began to help her take off her Kevlar vest. Together they opened Aubrey's jacket to reveal an even-more-soaked T-shirt.

"I promise I'm not being forward," Jack said, "but we have to get you out of that shirt."

Aubrey stuck out her tongue. "You say that to all the girls who get shot."

Josi used her knife to slit Aubrey's shirt from collar to sleeve while Jack opened Aubrey's first-aid kit.

The wound was gruesome—a jagged hole that punched straight through the collarbone. Josi exchanged a glance with Jack.

"What does that look mean?" Aubrey asked.

"I don't know," Josi said. "The bleeding has mostly

stopped, so that's good. This is going to hurt a little bit." She reached to Aubrey's back and felt for the exit wound. Aubrey gritted her teeth in pain.

Josi pulled her hand back, wiping the blood—new and old—onto her pants. "It might have hit your scapula. I'm not sure. It'll be a while before you play baseball again."

Jack wiped the wounds with alcohol pads, as gingerly as he could, which wasn't very gingerly at all. Aubrey managed to keep from crying out, but he could tell it was taking all she had. She bit her lip until he was worried that she'd bite it clean through, and her fingers were wrapped around the strap of his vest, squeezing like a vise.

Finally, he was able to apply gauze to the oozing bullet hole and secure it with tape. Josi held up a piece of cotton cloth tied into a loop.

"It's not perfect," she said. "But you need a sling." They closed her jacket and helped her lean forward enough to get the sling over her head and shoulder.

"Thanks," she said.

"You guys done?" Rich called.

"Yes," Aubrey said.

"Do you want to know how to work the radio?"

"We can call our base from here?" Aubrey asked.

"We can. Normally the Russians would hear us, but I'll walk you through the procedure of how to get a secure line."

Jack was sitting in the commander's chair, so he pushed

the buttons on the radio in the order that Rich dictated—the red button, the yellow one in the bottom corner, a series of numbers, the red one again, then the other yellow.

Jack handed the headset down to Aubrey. He had to help her slip it over her ears.

"FOB, this is Lambda Private Parsons from ODA nine-one-one-nine. Come in."

There was a long pause, and then Aubrey repeated her name. "Serial number eight-oh-one-six-nine-one-nine-one-one-five. Yes, I'm calling from a Russian radio. We're in a Russian tank, actually."

There was another long pause, and Jack began to wonder whether they'd disregard this as some kind of hoax or disinformation campaign.

"I understand," Aubrey said. "I understand. We need to report: the Russian lambda who could disrupt electronics is KIA. Repeat, the Russian lambda who could disrupt electronics is KIA."

It seemed to take whoever was listening a long time to process that information. Aubrey was waiting, not answering more questions.

"Yes," she finally said. "Yes, sir. This is Lambda Private Parsons, ODA nine-one-one-nine."

She tried to turn to look at Rich, and winced.

Jack was quicker to ask the question. "Rich, where are we?"

"Forty-six degrees, fifty-nine minutes, thirty point zero-zero-eight seconds latitude, negative one hundred twenty degrees, thirty-one minutes, twenty-three point six-five-six-eight seconds longitude."

Aubrey repeated the coordinates to Major Brookes on the radio. "We're in a Russian tank—"

"A T-eighty," Josi said.

"A T-eighty," Aubrey repeated. "We're trying to get back across the lines. Preferably before you bomb this place again."

They made Aubrey relate the entire story of how they found the lambda and how they killed him. Jack offered to take the headphones from her and let her rest, but she seemed to act like it was her duty.

"Yes, sir," she said. "All the Green Berets in our ODA are either KIA or MIA. And two of the lambdas are AWOL." She paused. "Yes, sir, we're very lucky. Thank you, sir. We'll be waiting."

She looked up at Jack and moved the mouthpiece away from her mouth.

"They're not sure they believe us," she said. "They're going to try to find some way to confirm our story."

"Some way to confirm it?" Josi said. "Can't they just fly some planes in and watch them not crash?"

"That's just it," Jack said, having listened to the entire conversation. "They think this might be a trap to get us into another one-sided fight."

"So what do we do?" Rich asked.

"We find somewhere to wait," Aubrey said. "And hope we don't get caught. We're supposed to check back with them in forty-five minutes."

SIXTY

TABITHA WAS DEAD. IT WAS too hard to handle the thought.
Tabitha was dead.

Whatever Tabitha had known about Alec, she'd been
right. Alec was bad. Krezi still didn't know how, but he had
fired his gun, and he had smiled while he'd done it. Krezi
had let loose when she saw Tabitha fall, blasting an arc of
energy that even she didn't know she had within her. Alec
had been thrown like a rag doll across the room. He didn't
bleed; he was far too charred to do that.

Krezi didn't know what to do now. Tabitha could be bossy
at times, but she always had a plan.

No plan prepared her for this.

And her chest hurt. Her fever was back. It felt so good to
release all of her energy and to have her fever drop, but it
came back soon enough.

She had to move before she got much sicker—she couldn't stay in this house. She stumbled into the cold night air of Ellensburg, keeping to the shadows. She could feel the breath-stealing, sharp grind of her ribs rubbing against one another. It started mostly as a sensation of pressure, a feeling that something was moving that shouldn't be, but soon the stinging jolts began.

She didn't dare stop.

Why had she listened to Tabitha? It wasn't because Tabitha had made any great sense; it was because Krezi was scared, and Tabitha treated her with respect.

No. Tabitha's arguments *had* made sense. Every time she talked to Krezi about being too young to be in a war, about being used by the government as a weapon, about being taken away from her family—that made sense.

But it was all too scary now. Krezi wished she had never heard of the rebellion. She wished that she'd stayed with her team, wished that she had someone watching out for her. She didn't know what had happened to Aubrey and Josi and Captain Gillett and all the others, but they were probably sleeping in their tents now. They were powerful lambdas with a whole team of Green Berets. They would have made it. They would be fine. It was Krezi who was alone and sick and freezing.

There was no way she could get to the American lines, not in her condition. She needed to find shoes and painkillers and a coat.

And a bed. She couldn't keep walking like this. Her entire chest was shattered.

When she reached a corner she turned off the sidewalk and onto a short driveway. There was a house with yellow siding and a pillared porch. The concrete felt like ice under her numbing feet as she put her hand on the knob and set off a tiny explosion from her palm, blasting the lock inward and shattering the edge of the wooden door. It still wouldn't give, so she did the same thing to the deadbolt, looking over her shoulder to make sure no one was watching.

She pushed the door open, stepped gingerly inside, and then closed it behind her.

The house was dark and abandoned, but the carpet felt good under her feet and it seemed at least twenty degrees warmer than outside. She thought about starting a fire in the fireplace, but didn't want the smoke to attract attention. Instead, she pulled a blanket off the couch and wrapped it around her shoulders.

She searched the house for the bathroom, and when she found it she raided the medicine cabinet. There weren't any prescription drugs—but there was ibuprofen. She took four tablets, swallowed them with a handful of water from the tap, and then found a bedroom. She'd worry about escaping later. Right now she just needed to lie down.

Sleep came easily.

SIXTY-ONE

AUBREY KEYED IN THE PROPER buttons on the radio, in the order that Rich indicated.

"FOB, this is Lambda Private Parsons."

"Private Parsons, this is the FOB. We think we've got a way you can verify your identity. We've got Lambda Private Matt Ganza here."

Aubrey covered the receiver on the headset and told Jack. The three of them used to be close friends. Jack nodded—he could hear both sides of the conversation.

"Copy that," Aubrey said. "Go ahead."

"If you are speaking of your own free will," the radio officer said, "then answer the following question truthfully. If you're compromised, do not."

"Copy that."

"Give us the name of the boy that you went to the home-coming dance with."

Aubrey closed her eyes. The events of that night came flooding back to her. That was when this had all started—when the military had come to the Gunderson Barn and rounded everyone up for quarantine. Aubrey's date had been the star linebacker on the football team, and, as it turned out, a lambda. The army had killed him after he panicked and attacked them.

"Nate Butler," Aubrey said. "His name was Nate Butler. He's dead."

"Copy Nate Butler," the radioman said. "Can you confirm for us the information that you delivered earlier?"

"The lambda that was causing the electronic interference has been killed," Aubrey said. "It's now clear to attack."

"You're certain?"

"Roger that," she said, and there was a hitch in her voice. "I did it myself."

"Okay. You said you're in a Russian tank?"

"A T-eighty," Aubrey said.

"You're going to want to get out of that. Find somewhere safe. Get underground if you can."

"Roger," she said. "How much time?"

"This is a party line, Private Parsons. Get underground."

"Roger."

"And Parsons," the radioman said. "Good work."

"Thank you, sir."

She used her good hand to pull off the headset, and then looked around the tank at the dimly lit faces. "We've got to get out of here. I think they're going to start bombing, or maybe another armored assault. Either way, we don't want to look like a target."

Above her, Jack opened the hatch and looked outside.

"All's quiet on the western front," he said, and he began to climb out of the tank. Josi helped Aubrey stand, and Jack reached down to help pull her up. She grimaced, especially when she had to narrow her shoulders to squeeze through the hatch, and yelped as Jack took her by the arm and helped her down off of the big metal machine.

Josi followed her out, carrying her Kevlar vest. Aubrey's heart fell, but she knew that one gunshot was enough. She stretched her arms the best she could so Jack and Josi could strap it into place. The weight on her shoulder was tremendous and nauseating.

"Let's find a place with a basement," she said to Jack. "Fast."

As much as she wanted to be out of that vest, she didn't want to be close to the tank if a missile was coming in to hit it. They crossed the street, Jack leading the way, and moved in the shadows of tall trees until they reached an alley. It was lined with the back fences of a dozen houses, and Jack moved from one to the next before stopping at the fifth and gesturing.

"Basement window," he said as she reached him.

"Let's do it."

They entered the small backyard and crossed the grass to the door.

"Anyone know how to pick locks?" Aubrey asked, looking at Rich.

"A lock is mechanical. Anyone have a bobby pin?"

Both Aubrey and Josi reached up to their hair.

It didn't take Rich more than a minute to open the door, and they slipped inside. The house was old, and smelled of rotten food—there were dishes on the counter that had obviously been left in a hurry when the homeowners evacuated. Jack was moving ahead of them. A moment later, he called out.

"Here's the door."

He held it open as Rich, Josi, and Aubrey all made their way downstairs. As Aubrey walked by, he grabbed her good hand and she interlaced her fingers with his.

The basement was broad and open, with three beat-up couches and a pool table. Jack helped Aubrey to one of the couches, but when he tried to leave she didn't let him go. She clutched on to his hand tight, and made him sit next to her.

"Think of it as an order from your commanding officer," she said with a smile.

"I think that could constitute harassment."

"Are you going to report me?"

Josi plopped down on the next couch over. "You guys know I can't forget anything, right? So no more lovey-dovey stuff, okay?"

Aubrey laughed, and let go of Jack's hand long enough to toss a pillow at Josi.

Rich lay down on the third couch, unstrapping his helmet and pulling it off.

"I don't think that's a good idea," Aubrey said.

"What?"

"Taking off your helmet. I'll bet you we're hiding under the pool table before long."

Rich sighed and pulled it back on, though he left the straps undone. "War is really uncomfortable."

Jack put one foot up on the edge of the pool table. "So what do we do now? Are we just waiting out the Russians?"

Josi answered. "The Russian military isn't a match for the American military if they're in a head-to-head battle. The only reason they've been winning is because of the lambda."

"Airpower," Rich said with a nod. "It's all about airpower."

"Haven't we been running out of planes?" Jack asked.

"Not by my count," Josi said. "So far I've seen twenty-eight aircraft destroyed."

"That sounds like a lot," Jack said.

"It's a lot for the Russians. You saw their airfield. It had six fighters left. And they only have one aircraft carrier. Granted, they probably have a lot more spread out over the whole battlefront—and I bet there's a ton guarding Snowqualmie Pass—but the Americans have hundreds of fighters. Almost a thousand F-sixteens. Four hundred F-fifteens. Three hundred A-tens. I bet you anything that they just haven't been fighting because they've been afraid of the bubble."

Aubrey interjected, "And I bet you anything they are going to pour down hell on the Russians now that the air is clear."

"And we're sitting right in the middle of it," Jack said.

She squeezed his hand. "That's why we have a pool table to hide under."

He looked at her in the darkness—one of those probing looks. "How did you get so optimistic?"

"I got shot," she said. "And it hurts like crazy. But I survived, didn't I? A little lost blood, and a torn shirt, and a couple broken bones. But I survived. I don't plan to die now."

SIXTY-TWO

KREZI WOKE TO THE SOUND of thunder, and had to try hard to remember where she was. She felt like she was sleeping with a huge weight on her chest, and when she moved pain exploded from her sternum, radiating out in all directions.

She could use more ibuprofen, but she'd left the bottle in the bathroom, and she didn't feel like getting up.

It was morning outside, and it looked sunny enough—too sunny for a thunderstorm.

As the fog of sleep cleared from her mind, she had to remind herself: this isn't thunder; this is war.

She groaned, and forced herself to swing one leg over the edge of the bed. She needed medicine. She needed to be asleep again.

There was a crash and the house rattled. And then another.

The windows shook in their frames.

She needed to get somewhere safe.

Krezi slipped out of bed and onto her feet. She swore as she stood, and her bones all seemed to rearrange themselves in her chest. She had to stop for a moment, clutching the bedframe, trying to regain her balance.

There were more crashes outside, but farther away.

Krezi took an unsteady step away from the bed, leaned on the wall, and then staggered across the rug toward the bathroom. She felt like a zombie, like she was already dead. With every step new jolts of pain stabbed her torso. She tried to go as fast as she could without moving anything—her arms or her shoulders or her waist.

The ibuprofen bottle had fallen into the sink, and she pulled it out, trying to twist the cap off while tears burst from her eyes. The pressure from squeezing the bottle was too much for her to take.

And then the world seemed to explode. The small bathroom window blew in, followed by a burst of flame. The mirror split down the center and shattered, and water started spraying from a faucet. Krezi flew into the wall, lost all her breath, and the ibuprofen fell from her hand, spilling little red pills across the floor.

There was another crash, and she tumbled into the shower curtain, trying to grab on to hold herself up but falling into the tub.

She let out a shriek of horrific pain that was drowned out by another explosion. She heard glass break, heard wood creak and split. The bathtub faucet began to trickle and then to pour cold water.

Another boom sounded and plaster fell from the ceiling. The porcelain tub cracked and the water began to leak onto the bathroom floor.

Krezi hugged the torn shower curtain to her chest and sobbed as the bombs continued to fall, one after another after another.

SIXTY-THREE

JACK, AUBREY, JOSI, AND RICH spent three days in the basement. The first day was sheer terror. When the bombing started, Jack, Josi, and Rich slid the backs of the couches up against the sides of the pool table, calling it the safest pillow fort ever. Rich even thought to turn off the gas line and so, as the bombs began to crash around them, he had run outside with a wrench, found the gas, and switched it off. Josi had kissed him, turning his dark cheeks rosy.

The bombing was unbelievable, and Jack had to wrap a blanket around his head to block out the noise. Josi couldn't handle it either, storing up every incredible sound until she left the safety of the pool table and threw up. When she came back, she still looked green, but she was able to handle it better.

The house didn't take a direct hit, but something landed nearby, and everything shifted. From their view in the basement they couldn't see any structural damage except that the Sheetrock ceiling was cracked in a half dozen long, jagged lines. No one dared go upstairs to investigate further.

The bombing continued until dark. Jack had been able to smell fires all day, but it wasn't until night that he saw the orange glow flickering out through the small basement windows. He had crawled out of the fort, peeked around at the world above them, and seen that the entire block across the street was either flattened or burning, or both. The pavement was plowed up in a crater.

He got back under the table.

The next morning more explosions rattled the house. Nothing as big as the day before—though he couldn't be sure, Jack thought these sounded more like rockets than bombs. And nothing came too close to the house—these seemed to be focused attacks. Even so, they all stayed under cover all day, leaving the table only to use the toilet, which, amazingly, still worked. Kind of.

Aubrey seemed to be getting worse, and even though Jack was feeding her amoxicillin that he'd found in the basement bathroom, he was worried about infection. She was going to need surgery—they all knew that—but there had to be something more they could do for her.

She kept bleeding—that was one problem. They'd gone

through all the bandages in her first-aid pouch and had moved on to Jack's.

On the third morning, after a long, sleepless night, Aubrey looked up into Jack's eyes and spoke.

"Do you know what today is?"

He shook his head.

"Thursday," Josi said.

"I thought you didn't forget things," Aubrey said with a small, pained laugh.

"Oh," Josi said. "Oh yeah. It's Thanksgiving."

"Seriously?" Rich asked.

"Yep," Aubrey said.

Jack stretched as much as he could in the tiny space, and poked his head out of the fort. Everything was quiet.

"If it's Thanksgiving," he said, "then I'm going to find us something to eat. We need a feast."

"Is the house safe?" Aubrey asked.

"We'll find out," he said. He pulled the straps of his Kevlar vest tight and adjusted his helmet.

"Be careful," Aubrey said.

Rich climbed out of the fort after him. "I'll come with you."

Rich picked up his rifle off the couch, and Jack drew his pistol. They cautiously made their way to the stairs and then slowly began the climb up and out of the basement.

Already Jack could see that things were wrong. The

basement door led out into a hallway, and pictures had crashed down from the wall, the glass shattering out of the frames. More importantly, the ceiling was sagging, which made Jack nervous. Still, he couldn't hear any creaking. The house was motionless, for now.

"If I say run," Jack told Rich, "you run. Don't wait."

"Run where?"

"Downstairs or outside. Whichever is closer."

As they got to the top of the stairs, the damage was more apparent. The wall that the pictures had been on was leaning toward them, about ten degrees off of vertical. The Sheetrock was buckled and broken, revealing the two-by-fours and wiring underneath.

Jack held his Beretta as he moved through the hall. He should have been able to easily hear breathing or heartbeats, but he still was nervous and his own pulse sounded like a bass drum. At the end of the hall was the kitchen. All of the windows were blown in, glass sprayed across every surface. The French doors that led out onto a small back deck were off their hinges, and cold air slipped through the gaps. Turning to look at the cabinets, Jack could see that the walls were also leaning ominously toward him. Most of the dishes had fallen to the floor and shattered.

Rich slung his rifle over his shoulder at the sight of food. He picked up a box of Ritz crackers and a package of Oreos. He looked ecstatic, like he had found a roast turkey. Jack forced open a tall cupboard full of cans—as he got the door open, the contents all came tumbling out, making a tremendous clatter on the glass-covered floor.

"See if you can find a can opener," Jack said, as he began sorting through the food. For two days, none of them had eaten more than the PowerBars they carried with them in their gear. "Canned chicken," Jack said. "That's like turkey, isn't it?"

"I've never had canned chicken," Rich said as he rooted through messy drawers of utensils.

"It's like canned tuna. Better with mayo. We could make chicken salad. Speaking of . . ." Jack reached to the back of the cabinet and found two unopened jars of mayonnaise. He checked the expiration dates. They were both still good. "We're going to eat like kings. Or pilgrims."

A few minutes later Jack had two plastic bowls filled with food—chicken and mayo, strawberry jam, black olives, baby corn, and a half dozen other cans. Together with the crackers and cookies, they'd be a perfect Thanksgiving feast. He handed the bowls to Rich, who took them downstairs, and then Jack left the kitchen to explore the rest of the house.

The front door was blown out completely, and Jack very cautiously—and very slowly—crept outside.

It was light, though overcast and chilly. The opposite side of the block was destroyed—houses knocked to the ground and most of them burned. Smoke rose from a few, and there were small fires still smoldering among the piles of rubble. Jack listened for other soldiers, but didn't hear so much as a footstep or an engine. It was like the town was dead.

He stepped into the front yard, standing amid the chunks of asphalt that had been flung onto the lawn by the craters in the street, and he turned around to look at their house.

It looked as if it had been pushed a few inches off its foundation, and was tilting backward and to the left. But as much as it was leaning, Jack felt confident that it wouldn't collapse. Nothing was creaking; nothing was moving. It was only a one-story, too, which made him think that even if the roof did collapse, the basement would be safe.

He went back inside and down to their fort. One of the couches had been pushed away to create a little more room for their feast. Josi must have sent Rich upstairs again, because there were a few more dishes—she was mixing up the chicken salad in a bowl, and Rich was arranging olives, baby corn, pickles, and sweet peppers onto a plate. Aubrey was propped up on a couch cushion, her lips tinged with black from eating an Oreo. They all agreed they hadn't had a Thanksgiving dinner that good ever.

SIXTY-FOUR

KREZI WAS SURE SHE WAS going to die. The bedroom had collapsed, and the hallway was a cave. She had spent the last three days lying on a couch, smothered in blankets, too sick to eat and too tired to try to escape. The ceiling in the living room bowed in, like an ominous bubble ready to pop and shower down debris from the roof.

First she thought she would die from the bombing. Then she thought she would die from hypothermia—she'd spent nearly that whole first day in that bathtub, cringing to avoid the cold water spewing from the tap. Now she knew she was going to die of starvation, or of complications from her broken ribs. She couldn't go anywhere. Couldn't escape to find help.

On the second day she had taken some debris and started a fire in the fireplace, lighting it with her hands. But now, the third day in, even that seemed too hard. She would fight off the cold with her blanket, and that would have to do.

She reached out a hand and slowly blasted a piece of wood in the fireplace. It had mostly burned, but there was still a fresh corner of a two-by-four. It burst into flame, briefly igniting the charcoal beside it, before it mellowed into a slow smolder.

It was so little wood and so far away that she could barely feel its heat. For a moment she began to push herself up to get more wood, but the pain in her chest exploded and she fell back into the couch. She pulled the blankets over her face and screamed.

And then she heard it.

She yanked the blanket down, cocking her head toward the broken and collapsed front wall.

Voices.

She tried to make out what they were saying, but they were muffled, whispering. She didn't care. American, Russian, it would be someone who would take her away and give her morphine and make the hurting stop.

"Help!" she called. "Help me!"

There was noise outside, close.

"Help!"

Suddenly the door flew toward her, and men poured into the room. Krezi tried to raise her hands but pain stopped her from fully extending.

Guns were in her face, but she recognized the uniforms,

recognized the muzzles of the rifles.

"I'm American," she said, tears streaming down her face. "I'm American."

Someone yanked away the blankets from her, revealing her ACU pants and olive T-shirt.

"I'm a lambda," Krezi said. "I'm hurt bad."

The guns were still on her, but someone reached to her neck and pulled at the chain to expose her dog tags.

"Lambda Lucretia Torreon," she said. "Please help me."

"Where are you hurt?" the man said, dropping her dog tags back.

"Broken ribs, broken sternum," she said. "I think. I was shot in the chest and my vest took the bullets. I escaped."

Two of the men exchanged a look, and then one of them stepped to the door and called for a medic.

"You're very lucky," the man said soberly. "Just down the road we ran into two lambdas who killed each other."

SIXTY-FIVE

JACK HEARD THE AMERICAN INFANTRY first, and Aubrey had to wait in the basement while Jack, Josi, and Rich all ran upstairs to greet their rescuers. As Aubrey sat alone, she stared at the bottom of the pool table and wondered what would happen now.

Combat was over for her—she knew that. The shoulder injury was going to put her out of commission for months. Granted, she wasn't certain that the war would be over before then, but if this bombing raid was any indication, then things had turned around.

There were sounds on the stairs, and then the jabber of five voices all talking at once.

Jack appeared, grinning from ear to ear. "The cavalry has arrived."

"The infantry," a man said, and knelt down. He wore a medic's badge. "I hear you're gunning for a Purple Heart."

"Two," Josi said. "She got shrapnel in her leg six days ago."

"That was already stitched up," Aubrey said.

"Well," the medic said, pulling down the flap of shirt and inspecting the bandage. "We can't guarantee anything, but you have earned yourself a nasty scar."

"No more strapless gowns," she said with a tired smile.

"I wouldn't say that," the medic said, pulling a new package of gauze from his pack. "This is a badge of honor. I don't know exactly what happened, but these guys tell me you saved everybody's asses."

"Is that what happened?" she asked. "All the bombing?"

"They're heading for the hills," the medic said. "They still have Seattle and Alaska, but we'll get you fixed up and you can kick them out of there, too."

The medic redressed her wound, and then another man brought down a stretcher and laid it next to the pool table. Gingerly, they shifted her onto it and maneuvered it up the stairs and out of the house.

Aubrey's eyes widened as she saw the devastation. "I didn't know it was so bad, Jack," she breathed.

"This is one of the good streets," the medic said. "There's not much left of Ellensburg. I expect we'll find Cle Elum is worse."

They placed her in an army ambulance that had been waiting on the lawn, and another medic started her on an IV. Aubrey couldn't help but notice that the man in the stretcher across from her was Russian.

"We'll see you back at base," Jack said from the end of the ambulance.

"I'll be waiting."

EPILOGUE

JACK STOOD ON THE CORNER of State and Main, in front of Mount Pleasant's Memorial Hall. It was January, and a gentle snow was falling as he watched the workmen smooth the newly poured concrete. Aubrey held his hand, her fingers warm against his.

The governor had poured the first shovelful of cement. The mayor had poured the next, and the principal of North Sanpete High had poured another. Jack and Aubrey had shaken a hundred hands—probably many more than that—and the interviews seemed endless. The reporters all asked the same questions, most of them dumb. Aubrey had smiled her way through them, her confidence overwhelming.

They were both in their dress uniforms. Both had their Northwestern War medal and their lambda medal. Aubrey had the purple bar of the Purple Heart, a small oak-leaf pin in the center to denote both of her awards. And, of course, she wore her Medal of Honor. It had been given to her two weeks before at a ceremony at the White House. She, Jack, Josi, and Rich all attended, and while Jack and the others got Distinguished Service awards, the Medal of Honor was reserved for her.

As it should be, Jack thought.

She'd had two surgeries on her shoulder and was scheduled for another. It likely would never be the same, and she'd always get pinged at the metal detector at the airport, but a few plates and pins in her clavicle were a lot better than the alternatives. Several of the muscles had come close to being severed, but none of them were. And the scapula only received minor damage from bullet fragments.

Krezi wasn't invited to the White House, though no one made a big deal about it. Jack had heard that she spent several weeks in the hospital and then got sent home to her family in Las Vegas—honorably discharged and swept under the rug.

The media had found out about Tabitha, and they made a stink about it, and about the rebellion. There was no getting around it. Tabitha's betrayal was part of the story that led to the Green Berets getting posthumous Distinguished Service medals. Jack didn't like it, didn't like the way she'd been treated. She was just a kid, just like any one of them, and she'd made a bad choice. Any one of them could have. Jack had come close.

The war wasn't over, technically. There were still Russian

troops dug in to northern Alaska—the citizens as far south as Fairbanks still weren't allowed to return to their homes. But everyone agreed that this was a seasonal problem. Once the seas freed up from the ice and the skies calmed from their storms, the Russians would probably turn tail and run.

"It doesn't even look like me," Aubrey said, squeezing Jack's hand and staring at the bronze monument.

"Sure it does," he said. "Kind of."

The statue had been done by one of the premier artists in the state, and would stand in front of Memorial Hall, next to the memorial honoring those who fought in World War I. Aubrey was the subject, but the monument was for all those in the state who fought in the war. There was going to be an identical one, with the names of all the lambdas, everywhere, placed at the capitol building.

"You could come with me, you know," she said.

He smiled. They'd been over this a dozen times. A hundred times. "No. I'll see you more often this way. Besides, I have work to do."

Jack had become a figurehead for the rebuilding efforts in Utah—a kind of spokesman. But he was determined to finish school and go to college—with a full-ride scholarship. Eventually he would settle back into his old life.

Aubrey put her arms around his shoulders. Most of the reporters were gone, but the few who remained started to take pictures. Jack ignored them.

"If I came with you, this wouldn't be allowed," he said, smiling and brushing her lips with his.

"Since when have I followed the rules?"

He wrapped his arms around her waist and pulled her toward him. "You won the Medal of Honor. I think they're going to pay attention. Besides, I bet people are a little more strict at West Point."

"People are taking our picture right now," she said, and kissed him. "They're paying attention. I don't care."

And then her hands moved from his shoulders to his head, and she pulled him in for a kiss, deep and lingering. He loved this girl, and though he couldn't bear to think of being away from her, he knew she needed to go. They'd be together again soon.

He cupped her face in his hands, wishing her hair wasn't pinned up so he could run his fingers through it. He loved the very touch of her, the feel of her skin under his fingers. Her breath hot against his face. The scent of her perfume— she still wore the Flowerbomb, a constant reminder of all they'd been through together.

"We never got to go to a dance," Jack said.

"We will. We have all the time in the world."

And they kissed.

ACKNOWLEDGMENTS

THIS BOOK WOULD NOT EXIST without my dad, Robert Wells, who filled my childhood with superheroes and military trivia. So much of this book and the earlier book *Blackout* is based on places he took us on family trips, from the Coronado Naval Base in San Diego, to the Bremerton Naval Base near Seattle. He made his passions my passions.

Many thanks to my fact checkers. The military descriptions were checked by my dad and double-checked by Sergeant First Class Ethan Skarstedt of BSC 1/19th SFG(A). However, if there are errors in the details of vehicles, weapons, tactics, or strategies, I take full responsibility.

I'd also like to thank my Russian translators: Marion Jensen, Aaron Larson, and Nathan Wright.

And, as always, many thanks to my alpha and beta readers:

Patty Wells, Krista Jensen, Jenny Moore, Annette Lyon, Sarah Eden, J. Scott Savage, Heather Moore, LuAnn Staheli, and Michele Holmes.

And, of course, my wife, Erin. The most supportive, long-suffering, inspiring, best person I know. My entire writing career would be nonexistent without her.

Many thanks to Erica Sussman, my editor at Harper, and to her amazing team: Stephanie Stein, Christina Colangelo, and Alison Lisnow. And a thousand thanks to Erin Fitzsimmons for the amazingly beautiful covers in this series.